✓ **W9-BVO-378**

THE VIOLENT LAND

Large Print Ove
Overholser, Wayne D., 1906-
The violent land

WESTERN

THE VIOLENT LAND

Wayne D. Overholser

Chivers Press • G.K. Hall & Co.
Bath, Avon, England • Thorndike, Maine USA

This Large Print edition is published by Chivers Press, England, and by G.K. Hall & Co., USA.

Published in 1996 in the U.K. by arrangement with the author.

Published in 1995 in the U.S. by arrangement with the Golden West Literary Agency.

U.K. Hardcover ISBN 0–7451–2884–X (Chivers Large Print)
U.S. Softcover   ISBN 0–7838–1385–6 (Nightingale Collection Edition

The text of this Large Print edition is unabridged.
Other aspects of the book may vary from the original edition.

Set in 16 pt. New Times Roman.

Printed in Great Britain on acid-free paper.

British Library Cataloguing in Publication Data available

Library of Congress Cataloging-in-Publication Data

Overholser, Wayne D., 1906–
   The violent land / Wayne D. Overholser.
   p. cm.
   ISBN 0–7838–1385–6 (lg. print : lsc)
   1. Large type books.   I. Title.
[PS3529.V33V56   1995]
813'.54—dc20   95–11097

To my sisters
Violet and Glady

CHAPTER ONE

I did not like my father, Bartram Nathan. I had never disliked him more than I did the day we first saw Howard Valley. We had been wanderers, my father and mother and my little brother Ben and I, Daniel Nathan, eighteen then, six feet of bone and hide with a hunger that had been satisfied only a few times as long as I could remember.

I can't recall how many states we had crossed, how many jobs I had worked at to make a little money for food that was never enough, how many times we had stopped for my mother to have a baby and how many we had buried beside our camping places and then gone on.

There were many reasons for me feeling about my father as I did, but forcing himself upon my mother was one. I was the first born, coming when my mother was young and strong and still in love with my father. She had milk for me, but not for any of the others.

The rest were born dead, or at most lived only a few hours, all but Ben who was five when we came to the valley. It would have been better if he had died too, for he wasn't right and he never would be.

She had no more babies after Ben. That's something else I remember well. We were

1

camped among some aspens on Colorado's western slope, just below a small spring. I was sleeping under the wagon, the Winchester beside me, for my father had thought a deer might come to the spring about dawn.

I don't know when it happened. After midnight, I think. I remember Ben had kept us awake for several hours with his crying. He had finally gone to sleep, and I must have dropped off. Then I heard my father and mother arguing in low voices so that they wouldn't wake Ben. My father was begging, and my mother was saying, 'No, no,' and crying a little, and then I heard her say: 'I won't have another baby, Bartram. I just won't!'

'You have an obligation as a wife, Martha,' he said. 'Have you forgotten I'm your husband?'

'You're not my husband,' she said. 'You're a monster. You're a liar to God and man.'

I wasn't very wise about things like that, but I knew what I had to do, and I knew what she meant by calling him a liar to God and man. He was a preacher of sorts: he could quote the Bible or Shakespeare for hours at a time and never repeat himself; he could marry a couple; he could preach a funeral sermon at the grave of the worst renegade in the country; and while he was talking you'd think St Peter was shaking hands with the dead bastard and welcoming him into Heaven. He was good with words, my father was, and if you didn't know him well you'd believe him.

I took the Winchester and crawled out from under the wagon; I climbed up on the seat and looked in. It was too dark to see anything, but they heard me jack a shell into the chamber. I said: 'Let her alone. If she has another baby, I'll kill you.'

My mother said, 'Daniel!'

I said, 'You hear me, Pa?'

He had heard me, all right. He was breathing the way a man does who has been running and then can't run any more. Finally he said: 'All right, Daniel. Go back to sleep.'

So I went back under the wagon, but I didn't sleep. I would have killed him and he knew it, and after that he was afraid of me. Before the sun came up I shot a buck, and when I cut his throat and saw the dark red blood on the grass I wished it was my father's.

I'm not sure why my mother stayed with him except that habit is a binding thing, and I suppose she still loved him the way a woman like her loves a man whether he's worth the loving or not. And I suppose she thought of Ben and me, or perhaps she could never bring herself to the point of making the break. But when we came to Howard Valley, our lives changed. It was a red-letter day, the day we saw the valley.

Our horses were old and thin and not much good any more; our wagon was held together by a little hope and prayer and a lot of wire. It

3

had taken us all morning to make the climb to Juniper Summit. My mother drove, as she usually did. Ben sat on the seat beside her, a smile fixed on his wax-like face. He seldom talked or cried, but he could always smile.

The road had been bad all the way up the mountain, narrow and rough, with an occasional boulder big enough to break a wheel. I walked beside the wagon to help out if my mother got stuck. She stopped often to rest the team, and several times I took the crowbar from the wagon and worked a boulder out of its nest and rolled it down the mountain.

My father was ahead of us, carrying the rifle and pretending he was Jim Bridger or Kit Carson. He always pretended. It was part of the lie he lived. I don't think he ever faced reality even in his own mind. I suppose it was the only way he could live, the pretending, the strutting, the constant quoting from the Bible or Shakespeare or Seneca or whatever he could call to mind at the moment.

He stopped on the summit ahead of us, the rifle at his side. He raised a hand to the brim of his battered old hat and stood there looking at the valley we could not see. We had a history book in the wagon I had read from cover to cover, and when I looked at my father I was reminded of the picture of Balboa gazing at the Pacific for the first time. I'm sure he was thinking of the picture when he struck the pose.

He knew we were watching. We were not an

appreciative audience, but we were better than no audience at all. He turned toward us and made a sweeping gesture with his right hand, calling out, 'We have reached the valley!' as if he had come to the Promised Land after all the years of wandering.

My mother stopped the team to rest them again, for the road ahead was steep. I glanced up at her, but she didn't see me. She was staring at my father, who had resumed his Balboa pose. She was still young—thirty-seven—but she looked much older. Her face was thin and brown from the weather, and there were deep lines in her forehead and around her eyes.

She said something to Ben and smiled, and though he smiled back he didn't say anything. I knew he was hungry. We were all hungry, and there was only a little bacon and flour and coffee left in the wagon.

I walked around to the tailgate to see if the chicken coop was all right. I knew it was, but I couldn't stand there and look at my mother and Ben. We might reach the point where we would eat the hens, I thought. If by some miracle we didn't, we would have them to start with, them and the old team and the plow tied to the side of the wagon. Even if we found the land which they had told us in Boise we would find, we didn't have enough to make a go of it.

I knew there was no use in telling my father that. He would say in his grand, confident way that the Lord would provide. So far He had, with me giving Him a little help. Perhaps He would here, for I had heard of Jim Perrin and his J Ranch.

I went around the wagon, looking at the wheels. They needed soaking, but there would be no water until we reached the creek which they had told us flowed down from the Blue Mountains to the lakes. I hoped the wheels would last that long. I had learned to hope. Disaster might come, but if it didn't we'd survive, somehow. We had before; we would again.

When I came around to the front of the wagon, my father had turned, calling out: 'Wagon west. We're almost home.'

Home! A hell of a word to us who had never known a home except the wagon. But he liked to use it, dangling it in front of us the way you'd dangle a baited hook in front of a fish in a deep, clear pool. But because something had worked in the past, that was no guarantee it would work in the future. I don't know if my father had thought of that or not, but I had, and I knew that if I couldn't get a job with Jim Perrin I wouldn't stay. Not even for my mother and Ben.

She spoke to old Coaly and Nell; they leaned into their collars and the wheels rolled again. I walked beside the wagon, climbing with it, watching the white dust that was lifted by the wheels and dripped off in a constant stream and then drifted away to sink slowly to the

6

earth again.

The long grade was behind us. I glanced at the ribbon of road that we had been following since dawn through a rough, broken country that was largely desert covered with sagebrush and rabbit brush and a few scattered junipers. I could see a long way back across a jumbled world of dry canyons with here and there a patch of green marking a water hole or a live stream.

The Blue Mountains were to the north, rugged and far-reaching, and I knew that somewhere, lost from sight beyond those pine-covered peaks, there were mining camps. I would go to them and find work if Jim Perrin failed me.

I'm not sure why I counted so much on Perrin. Because I had heard a good deal about him, I had formed a mental picture of him as a big man, a powerful man, one who shaped life to his own design. His fame had spread far beyond this isolated corner of southeastern Oregon. People talked about him because he seized their imaginations, a man who had accomplished what most of us dream about and never do.

Several years before, Perrin had driven a herd northeast from California, coming in when the country was empty. He had built his big white house and planted his poplar trees, unafraid of anything or anybody. Every fall he drove a herd of steers to the railroad at

Winnemucca. He was successful, so successful that folks said he had buckets filled with gold buried in his yard because there was no bank in Howard Valley.

I was looking at the ground, thinking about Jim Perrin and telling myself that my future was with him because he was the kind of man I wanted to be, when the wagon stopped, and my father said: 'Here it is, the end of the trail. Look at it, Martha. Look at it, Ben. This is where we'll live our lives out.'

I raised my eyes, expecting to see more desert, more deep, dry canyons that curled away into the distance, hiding their bottoms from us. But it wasn't like that at all. Big! That was the first thought I had. The big range. The slope below was somber gray, like the country behind us, but beyond the grade the valley floor ran out for miles and miles, level and green; for it was May, and life had stirred.

The big range! A valley of grass, the Blue Mountains to the north, and out there somewhere to the west, beyond the distant line of rimrock, there was more desert. Garnet Mountain lay to the south, white-haired this early in the year, a tremendous bulge in the earth that went on and on until it was lost in distance. But here was the valley and grass and water, the green line of willows marking Jasper Creek, the lake I had heard about, so far away it seemed no more than a tiny pool. But from what they had told us in Boise, I knew it was large.

I don't know how long I stood there, just looking, awed by the size and the promise of it. Even then I had the feeling that our lives would be changed. Suddenly I was aware that my father was talking in his grand way.

'Long ago Seneca wrote: "Happy is the man who can endure the highest and lowest fortune. He who has endured such vicissitude with equanimity has deprived misfortune of its power." I have done that. Now I will be happy. You will be happy too, Martha. I'll dress you in silks and satins. I'll build the finest house in the valley. The Lord has brought us home.'

I looked at him, big and craggy-faced with an impressive, foot-long beard sprouting from his chin. If I hadn't known him for more than eighteen years, or if I hadn't heard those rosy promises before, I would have believed him. My father was at his best when he talked, and he loved to talk.

I said, 'Will you work?'

When I talked to him like that, he took on the appearance of a saggy balloon. He knew what he was. My mother said sharply, 'Daniel!' But I didn't look at her. I kept staring at my father. He raised a hand to his face and stroked his beard, then he gave me his back and looked out across the valley.

'Of course I'll work,' he said, 'and so will you.'

'Yes,' I said. 'I know I will, but Seneca didn't

9

say anything about the man who lived happily off the labor of his son.'

My mother said again, more sharply this time, '*Daniel!*'

'It's all right, Martha,' he said. 'What is behind is behind. Now that we have reached the vineyard, we will labor. We will camp at the foot of the grade tonight. We will reach Howard City tomorrow, and I will see this Virgil Lang we were told about in Boise. We will establish our credit. We'll buy grain. It is not too late to plant that good land along the lake.' He turned and gave my mother his confident smile, his big head thrown back. 'Wagon west, my wife; wagon west,' and he strode on down the slope.

'Daniel, you shouldn't talk that way,' my mother said.

'I've just started to talk,' I told her. 'We've been silent too long.'

'I'm tired of sitting, Daniel,' she said. 'Will you drive for a while? I'd like to walk.'

She got down. I climbed to the seat and took the lines. I asked, 'How are you making out, Ben.'

'Fine,' he said, and kept staring ahead, smiling the way he always did.

We never spoke a cross word to him, although I didn't know why. At eighteen I was not fully matured, not the man I thought I was, but I had done a man's work for a long time and I had received a man's wages. I had been in

10

man fights; I had learned to do the dirty things you have to do to stay alive in the savage wilderness we called the frontier.

As I drove down the steep slope, holding back the team and with one foot jammed on the brake, the thought occurred to me that my judgments might not be as final or as perfect as I liked to think they were. It was an unpleasant thought, and I tried to avoid it. I did not want to explore the possibility that I owed something to my father. I preferred the simple process of telling myself that I hated him, that I had already repaid whatever debt I owed him for the biological accident which had made him my father.

Whatever love and goodness and decency were a part of me I owed to my mother. I had told myself that over and over, but still I had to admit that it was my father who had given me the education I had. A strange thing, I suppose, to talk correctly and live among people who knew nothing about the rules of grammar. And it was a stranger thing to live among people who had never heard of Seneca or Shakespeare or Emerson, yet I could quote them, too.

To me something for my belly was more important than anything my father had furnished for my mind; so, according to my standards, I had given him far more than he had given me. Still, there was some uneasiness in me, and I knew my mother would speak to me again.

11

The only love I felt was for her and Ben, and that made me their debtor. I glanced at Ben many times that afternoon, so silent and detached. I had not entirely lost the ability to cry, for that much of my boyhood still clung to me, and looking at Ben always made me feel like crying. I could not rid myself of the thought that he lived with the angels, and that it would not be long until he would be among them, and he would be happy.

We made a dry camp that night at the foot of the grade. My father had shot a sage hen and we would eat. The day had been clear and cool, but a wind sprang up when the sun went down, so we found a ridge that gave us protection. While I took care of the horses and brought in wood for the fire from a dead juniper, my father took off through the sagebrush, saying he might find more game.

An old story. He would sit out there, hidden from us until the camp chores were finished, then he would come back to eat. My mother cleaned the sage hen and made biscuits, saving the last of the coffee for breakfast. I brought in another load of wood and dumped it beside the fire. Ben was sitting on a blanket beside a wagon wheel.

'How do you feel, Ben?' I asked.

'Hungry,' he said.

'I'll bet you are,' I said, 'without any dinner. I am too.'

My mother rose and, turning to me, put her

12

hands on my shoulders. She said, 'Daniel, don't talk to your father the way you did up there on the summit.'

'It's the truth,' I said.

'We don't always have to give voice to the truth. We have to forgive and try to understand.'

'I can't understand laziness,' I said, and knew I was letting her see the bitterness that I had tried to keep hidden from her. 'I'm not lazy, and that's one thing I'm proud of.'

'I'm proud of it too,' she said. 'Wonderfully proud. I want to be proud of you as long as I live. Don't do anything to change it. Ever.'

'It'll be the same here it's always been,' I said. 'You know that.'

'You'll see we don't starve.' It was not often that she smiled, but she did then. 'We all reach for a star, Daniel, and when we find that it's beyond our fingertips we cover up to hide our failure. We can't change your father, so we have to take him the way he is.'

'I don't have to take him,' I said roughly. 'We can't change him, but he can change himself.'

'Daniel, Daniel,' she whispered, 'you're young. You don't know. You think you do, but you don't.'

She kissed me on the cheek, the first time she had done so for years, and then she turned quickly from me and started poking at the pieces of sage hen in the frying pan. I looked down at her bent back, and I remembered the wedding picture she kept in a velvet-covered box in her cowhide trunk. She had been young and very pretty, and she had been in love.

I thought of the star she had reached for, only to find that it was beyond her fingertips. She had covered up in her way, still loving and still hoping, and I suppose she prayed that somehow the good Lord would change my father. But I wasn't going to need any prayers. I was going to reach my star. By myself, or maybe with Jim Perrin's help.

Mother got a tin plate and put a biscuit and a piece of sage hen on it. She took the plate and a cup of water to Ben, then, raising her hands to her mouth, and cupping them, she called out, 'Supper's ready, Bartram.'

He came in, striding through the sagebrush, the dying sun at his back, his long shadow leaping before him. Tonight, I thought, he's probably been Hannibal, dreaming of the conquest of Rome.

CHAPTER TWO

I was not sure there was ever a point in a man's life when he could say with certainty that his boyhood was behind him. With some, I suppose, the immaturity of childhood was never left fully behind. My father was forty; he

14

was a big man; he had a handsome beard; and he had made my mother pregnant at least twelve times. To me none of those things were the proper measures of manhood.

For some reason I was thinking along those lines the first morning we were in Howard Valley more than I ever had before, perhaps because I was haunted by the feeling that our lives were about to be changed. Because we were in Jim Perrin's country, I was certain something would happen.

We ate a slim breakfast, my mother using the last of the coffee and almost the last of the flour. She saw to it that Ben had his share. She had less than hers, and when the last crumb had disappeared I was still hungry. I knew that she was, too.

My father took the Winchester and said he would go on ahead, adding that there should be antelope in the valley. My mother had finished packing the dishes and pans and knives and forks. Then she went to my father, who stood beside a wagon wheel, and she looked at him in a way I had never seen her look at him before. At that moment I was not exactly sure what it meant.

'I want to make something clear, Bartram,' she said. 'This is your last chance.'

I had never heard her talk that way before. Neither had my father. He looked hurt, as he did quite often. He stared down at the ground, his blue eyes as sad as a wounded deer's. He

15

said, 'I haven't deserved *this* one, Martha, but, believe me, I shall not need another.'

'Our grub's almost gone,' she said, 'and there isn't much money left in the box. We've lived off Daniel for a long time, and now he's old enough to start making his own life. That leaves it up to you, Bartram. You have me and Ben to think of.'

He gave me a speculative look, then turned his eyes to my mother. 'Daniel is eighteen. He owes us his wages until he's twenty-one.'

'No!' my mother said sharply. 'That's why I'm saying this. He'll be getting married and having his own family soon. If we don't hold him back, he may go a long ways.'

'Of course he will. We'll all go a long ways.'

'But not by reaching for the pot of gold at the end of the rainbow,' my mother said patiently. 'I didn't sleep last night. I thought about what you said up there on the summit, about clothing me in silks and satins. And then I thought about all the promises you've made since I've known you, but not once have you put food in our mouths with a promise.'

My father lifted the rifle and stepped away from the wheel. Reaching for his dignity, he clothed himself with it, saying in his grand way: 'There is an old proverb, "Begin your web, and God will supply the thread." We will begin our weaving here, Martha.' He turned and walked away.

My mother shook her head, watching him. I

16

saw her lips moving and I knew she was praying, but whether it was for him or herself I didn't know. By the time I had harnessed the team and hooked up, she had packed the last of the camp gear. She climbed into the seat and I lifted Ben up to sit beside her.

'I'll see Jim Perrin right away,' I said. 'I'll get a job, but I'll bring my wages to you, not to him.'

She looked down at me, her face thin and tired, and for the first time in my life I could see no hope there. She said, 'You're counting a lot on this man Perrin, aren't you?'

'He's big,' I said. 'I want to be like him.'

'But bigness isn't always greatness, Daniel,' she said. 'Bigness is physical, and greatness is a matter of spirit. You have the right kind of spirit. You'll never be beaten. That's what's the matter with your father. He was beaten once, and he lost something he's never been able to regain.'

She spoke to the team and the wheels rolled. I walked beside the wagon for hours, the sun climbing into a clear sky while the barren slope of Juniper Ridge dropped behind us. The sagebrush thinned out and we were in the grass, the road shallow wheel ruts in the sod.

The wind sprang up, chill and penetrating. My mother got a blanket out of the wagon and wrapped Ben in it. Then she drove with one hand and hugged Ben to her with the other. I asked myself if people ever got used to

17

hardships, even when they had never known anything else. It was bad enough to be hungry; it was bad enough to be cold; but it was worse to be both, and still worse when there was no prospect of relieving either.

I didn't want to think of my father, but I couldn't help it. What my mother had said about my father being beaten once and never regaining something he had lost stayed in my mind. I wondered about it because I had never heard her say it before. I didn't know much about where my folks had come from or what their background had been, and when I asked I received evasive answers that told me nothing.

They must have known better days. I had glimpsed a blue silk dress in my mother's cowhide trunk that rustled when it was touched; I had seen the little velvet-covered box that held a gold wedding ring and a tintype of my mother when she was young and pretty and smiling—not the thin ghost of a smile that I had seen so many times, but rich and full-lipped, as if life was something to enjoy and not an existence to be endured with all her hopes placed on the hereafter which my father described so glowingly.

My father had nothing left from his old life, whatever it had been, except the heavy box of books which he had made me read, often beside the uneasy light of a campfire. The Bible. Shakespeare. The writings of Plato. Seneca. Marcus Aurelius. Emerson. Thoreau.

Useless, I thought rebelliously, useless in a raw land like this where a good team and sharp plow and a Colt .45 were the tools a man needed. And greatness of spirit, greatness that could not be beaten. Then I wondered what my father had been like when he was my age, and what he had lost that he had never been able to regain.

I put my father out of my mind, and I was aware of the vastness of the valley. Land and sky, level, grass-covered land that ran for miles on all sides of us, and a sky that was unmarred by clouds except a few wispy white ones which hung above the Blue Mountains to the north. I could not see the lake, but the green willow line of the creek was directly ahead of us.

Presently I made out a cluster of buildings that would be Howard City. Here was where the storekeeper, Virgil Lang, lived, and I knew my father placed his hopes in Lang just as I did in Jim Perrin.

The miles fell behind us slowly with the hours. The town took shape, and I saw that it was smaller than I had supposed, hardly a town at all. There was one large building with a false front that was Lang's store. A porch ran the full width of the building, and there was a hitch pole in front. A barn stood on the other side of the street, a corral behind it.

Another road ran north and south beyond the store and barn, cutting across the road we were on at a right angle. Two large 'For Sale' signs stood on the corner lots across the north-south road. The other buildings were sheds. The creek was another fifty yards to the west.

It was late afternoon when we reached the town. I thought Lang was a fool to call a settlement like this Howard City. Fool or not, he was unquestionably optimistic. I saw that a number of lots had been staked out along the street, all of them holding 'For Sale' signs.

My father had been ahead of us all day, but he waited for us now, and when my mother pulled up in front of the store, he said: 'I'm going to have a talk with Mr Lang. You wait here.' He jerked his head at me. 'I want you to come inside.'

Without waiting to hear what I had to say, he swung around and stepped up on the porch. A waste of time, I thought; but when I looked at my mother she nodded, so I followed my father inside, not knowing why he wanted me. The interior of the store seemed dark after being outside in the sunlight. I blinked, smelling the strange combined odors of leather, onions, lard, vinegar, and all the other countless commodities that were kept in a general store.

When my eyes became accustomed to the thin light, I saw that counters ran the full length of the big room. On the east side there were the usual shelves holding bolts of cloth, and farther back were saddles and guns and kegs of nails. The groceries were on the west side, and a number of barrels and boxes were piled haphazardly in the wide aisle between the counters.

A fat man came out of the back, calling cheerfully, 'Good afternoon.'

My father said, in his impressive voice: 'Good afternoon, Mr Lang. My name is Bartram Nathan. A friend of yours in Boise, Henry Latimer, told us you would welcome settlers in Howard Valley.'

'That I do, Mr Nathan,' Lang said with great heartiness, 'that I do.'

He waddled toward us, a man as tall as my father and so soft that his belly wobbled as he walked. He had droopy jowls and thick lips, the lower one hanging pendulously so that it did not quite meet his upper one and exposed his wide, tobacco-brown teeth. In spite of his heartiness, I didn't like him; it was an instinctive feeling without any real reason, for I had heard nothing against the man.

He shook hands with my father, who nodded at me, saying, 'This is my elder son Daniel, Mr Lang.'

He offered his hand and I took it, finding it soft and damp. He said, 'Glad to know you, Daniel.' Then he turned his pale blue eyes on my father. 'How do you like our valley, sir?'

'I'm in love with it. A remarkable sight from the summit east of here. Though I have been all over the West, I have never seen anything else like it.'

'And you never will.' Lang's eyes flicked to me as if making an appraisal, and swung back to my father's face. 'You want land, I presume?'

'That's why we're here. We don't have much money, but we have a plow and a team and our hands. If the land is good—'

'It's good,' Lang interrupted. 'Make no mistake about that. We have a number of folks who have settled in the valley, and all of them are doing well. I suggest you take land south of Howard Lake. The water has been receding so that some of the lake bottom is exposed. You simply plow and plant, and come fall you'll harvest a bountiful crop.'

'It sounds like the answer to a dream, Mr Lang.' My father stroked his beard, assuming his grand pose. 'I should tell you that our food is gone and we have no grain to plant. My purpose in stopping here is twofold. I wanted advice on where to settle and I want to establish credit. By fall, if the land is as good as you say, we will be in position to pay our bill.'

'A grubstake,' Lang said. 'Is that it?'

'Why, yes, if you want to phrase it that way.'

'Friend Latimer is generous with my credit.' Lang laughed. 'I presume he promised you I'd fix you up.'

'Not exactly a promise ...'

Lang raised a fat hand. 'I understand, but I must warn you that this valley is not a safe place for a family. You have a wife?'

22

'She is outside in the wagon. I have another child, a five-year-old boy.' My father stroked his beard again, standing very straight. 'What is this danger you hint at, Mr Lang?'

'The Piutes are uneasy. If you came from Boise, you must have heard about the Bannocks. The contagion has spread to our Indians.'

'We are not afraid.'

'That's fine,' Lang said, as if he knew better. 'Most folks are. There is also danger from Jim Perrin, who fancies this valley belongs to him.'

'The land belongs to those who possess it and work it,' my father said. 'I am reminded of Thomas Paine's words: "Tis the business of little minds to shrink, but he whose heart is firm, and whose conscience approves his conduct, will pursue his principles unto death."'

'Well said,' Lang murmured. 'I think we can get together, friend. Come back to my desk. If you will sign a note, we will make up your order, provided you accept my conditions.'

My father glanced at me, and I could see the triumph that was warming him. Lang's 'conditions' would not prevent us from eating for the next few months. 'Go outside, Daniel. Your mother may want something.'

I went out into the sunlight, pulling my hatbrim low to shade my eyes. I didn't like it, but it was of no use to object. My father would take all he could get, and if anyone worried

23

about debt it would be me or my mother.

I stepped down off the porch and walked to the wagon. I said, 'Virgil Lang is a trusting man,' and told her what had happened.

'It isn't enough to starve,' she said with more bitterness than was usually in her voice. 'Now we must be in debt.'

'We'll fight Indians and Jim Perrin,' I said. 'Well, he didn't want me in there when Lang told him about his conditions.'

My mother looked out across the valley, and I thought for a moment she was going to cry. You can hope for so long, and then the hope dries out and becomes thin and brittle with the seeds gone, but still you cling to the pod because there is nothing else.

'It is a beautiful valley, Daniel,' she said. 'It's worth fighting for if we must fight.' Her face was red with the cold, and she looked down at Ben and hugged him a little tighter. 'It will be a chilly night with nothing to break the wind.'

I got out my pocket knife and began to whittle on the hitch pole, thinking that my father was reaching for the star again; but it would still be out of his reach no matter what the Indians or Jim Perrin did. He was counting on me, and that was a mistake. I was going to work on Perrin's J Ranch even if I got nothing but a place to sleep and three meals a day.

The minutes ran out and I lost track of time. The wind died down and quite suddenly the afternoon turned warm, even with the sun

24

dropping low in the west. I heard a rider coming in from the south, and I stepped to the corner of the building. He was a cowboy, a small man riding a sorrel at a brisk pace. I knew that the J Ranch was south of the valley, and my heart began to pound. Maybe he was one of Perrin's men.

I went back to the hitch pole and waited. A moment later the rider reached the corner of the store and reined toward me. I saw that the sorrel was branded with a big J on the left shoulder. He pulled up and stepped down, giving me a nod, and then glanced at the wagon and at my mother, who was still in the seat.

I said, 'Howdy.'

He stood motionless, a small dark man with a heavy mustache and the most penetrating black eyes I had ever seen. He was quite young, under thirty, I judged. He was not carrying a gun, and he was wearing ordinary range clothes, yet he was not an ordinary cowhand.

Something about him hit me hard, and I was puzzled by it. I had the odd impression that he was a big, powerful man, yet all I had to do was to look at him to see that he was six inches shorter than I was, and he couldn't have weighed more than one hundred and forty pounds.

He said, 'Howdy, son,' in a voice that was neither friendly nor hostile. He looked again at our rickety wagon and our skinny horses and shook his head, frowning as if he guessed why

25

we were there and not liking it.

'You're from J Ranch, aren't you?' I asked, and in spite of all my efforts I couldn't keep the eagerness out of my voice.

'Why, yes, I am.' He gave me another, sharper look, as if he were only then really aware of my presence. 'Does it make any difference?'

'It does to me,' I blurted. 'I want a job riding for Jim Perrin.'

A smile touched his lips, a pleasant smile that was almost boyish. 'Why do you want to ride for Jim Perrin?' he said. 'Looks to me like you're strangers here. I'm surprised you've heard of Perrin.'

'Just drove in a while ago,' I said. 'We wintered in Boise, but I heard a lot about J Ranch and Jim Perrin. I guess everybody's heard of him.'

'What have you heard, son?'

'That he's a real big man.' The words rushed out of me. If I could get him interested, I thought, he might take me to Perrin. 'And he's got a big spread. Built it himself. Brought his herd up from California six years ago when nobody much was here, and everything he's done has been right.'

'Funny how talk goes.' He shook his head. 'I'm sorry, son, but there isn't any job for you on J Ranch. Where's your dad? I suppose you have one.'

'He's inside talking to Virgil Lang about

settling south of the lake,' I said, hoping he wouldn't see how disappointed I was.

He frowned, silent for a moment as he teetered back and forth on the toes of his small, expensive boots. I had noticed them when I'd first seen him, for they were not the kind of boots you see on the average rider. They had cost him two months' pay, I thought.

'Your father would make a mistake settling there,' he said gravely. Then, stepping around the end of the hitch rack, he moved toward the store.

I caught up with him. 'I'm Daniel Nathan. I want to see Mr Perrin. It's kind of hard to tell you how I feel, but it's like a dream you keep having over and over until you know it's what you've got to do.'

We stopped, for my father and Virgil Lang had come out of the store. We stood not more than six feet from them, and when I looked at Lang I thought he was going to faint. His fat face was white, and then it turned sort of gray, as if a sickness had suddenly seized him. He breathed, 'Perrin.'

'I came to give you a warning,' the cowboy said, and it took a moment for me to realize that I had been talking to Jim Perrin himself. 'Now listen to me, Lang. Don't send anyone else to settle south of the lake. All the bottom land that is being exposed belongs to me. I'm claiming it by riparian right because I own the south shore, and all of it to the center of the

27

lake is mine.'

'Claim it and be damned!' Lang shouted. 'It ain't yours, by God, and if people live there you can't do nothing about it.'

'I'm holding you responsible,' Perrin said slowly in a tone that sent a chill down my back. 'Because strangers who come here don't know how it is, you're to blame, not them. There's plenty of land on this side of the lake, thousands of acres.'

'You can't keep driving me!' Lang almost screamed. 'I'll beat you into the dirt, Perrin! I'll kill you!'

Perrin gave him a contemptuous grin as if he were nothing more than an annoying fat fly, then swung around on his heel. Lang dived through the door, moving fast for a man of his size, and came back with a shotgun in his hands. Perrin had reached the hitch pole, his back still to Lang.

My father was close to Lang, but I knew he wouldn't do anything; and I had the horrible feeling that I couldn't do anything, either, that I was too far away and Perrin would get a load of buckshot in his back.

I suppose it was only a fraction of a second that I stood there paralyzed while Lang raised the shotgun to his shoulder, then I moved, jumping at him, my right hand swiping at the barrel. I knocked it down, the blast hammering against my ears, then I had hold of it and twisted the gun out of his fat hands.

Perrin wheeled and ran back. I threw the shotgun as far as I could, and yelled at my father, 'You could have done that!' I'd have hit Lang in the face if my father hadn't jumped in front of me, and then Perrin had me by the arm and shook me.

'It's all right, boy, it's all right.' He let go of me and looked at Lang; then he laughed, a soft, amused laugh that sounded kind of crazy at a time when he had almost been killed. 'Virgil, do you know what would have happened if you'd murdered me? My boys would have put a rope on your neck and dragged you behind a horse. Don't try it again.'

Lang backed into the store. My father said, 'Now Mr Perrin ...'

'All right.' Perrin silenced him with two words. 'If you settle south of the lake, you'll be on my land. Understand that.' He turned to me and held out his hand. 'I didn't tell you I was Jim Perrin, but you know now. I'll see you in a few days. You'll have that job if you still want it.'

I shook his hand. He gave mine a quick tight grip, his eyes boring into me, and I had the feeling that he was reading my mind. I said, 'I still want it.'

He swung around and walked back to his sorrel. Our horses had lunged into their collars when the shot had been fired, but my mother had held them. Perrin raised a hand to his hatbrim. He said, 'I'm sorry about that,

29

ma'am.' Then he mounted and rode away.

My father said, 'Daniel, you will *not* work for Perrin.'

'You've made a lot of mistakes,' I said, 'and this is another one,' and walked to the wagon.

CHAPTER THREE

My father remained in front of the store, torn, I suppose, by the desire to discipline me and the knowledge that he couldn't. I had never really defied him before, but I was going to now, and he must have known it.

I was not sure why or how I had finally reached that point except that it had been coming for a long time. If enough feathers are piled on a man, they make a great weight; they can smother him; and I had a breathless feeling as if I were being smothered.

Lang came out of the store and walked to the wagon. He looked up at my mother, trying to smile, but he had not entirely recovered his self-control. He said: 'I haven't had a woman-cooked meal for a long time, Mrs Nathan. I'd be honored if you'd come in and cook for me and your family.'

You don't think of a fat man being sly, but Virgil Lang was sly. He knew we were hungry. Still, he didn't want us to think he was being charitable, so he had chosen his words carefully, making it sound as if my mother would be doing him a favor.

She hesitated, and I could see that she had the same instinctive dislike for Lang that I had. She burst out, 'You would have killed Perrin if it hadn't been for Daniel!'

'Yes, and I'm grateful to your son for keeping me from doing something I'd regret later,' Lang said earnestly. 'But, believe me, I have reason to hate Jim Perrin. You will too, if you live here in this valley—but I'm not trying to excuse myself for what I did a moment ago.'

'I'm hungry, Mamma,' Ben said.

'Drive around to the back of the store, Mrs Nathan,' Lang said. 'I'll go in and start a fire in the range.' He nodded at me. 'You can unhook and put the team in the barn. You'll find a pump and trough behind the barn, and oats in a bin.'

Lang turned and walked back into the store, my father following him. He had not waited for my mother to say she would cook a meal; he had properly measured our hunger. Pride was not important when bellies were as empty as ours.

My mother glanced at Ben and then at me. I said, 'It's a free meal,' and walked around the store. My mother slapped the horses with the lines, and I heard the tired squeal of the wagon as the wheels began to turn. When I rounded the rear corner of the store, I was surprised at two things: a tall pile of unplaned lumber and a shed filled with farm machinery. There must be settlers in the country, although we hadn't seen a plowed field or a shack or any stock from the time we had topped Juniper Ridge.

I waited until the wagon reached me. I gave my mother a hand, then I lifted Ben from the seat and swung him down to the ground. A lean-to had been built behind the main store building, with a stovepipe that served as a chimney sticking up through the roof. Lang's living quarters, I guessed; and now, looking at it closely, I saw smoke trickle out of the end of the stovepipe.

My mother took Ben's hand, and they walked across the dusty yard to the back door. I unhooked the horses and led them around the store and on through the barn to the trough at the back. I pumped until the trough was full, then I put a hand on the spout and backed the water up and drank. It was good cool water, the best I had tasted for days.

I led the animals into the barn and tied them in stalls. After I had stripped the harness from them, I found the oat bin and gave the horses a double feeding. They hadn't had oats for a long time, and it would probably be a longer time before they had any again. There were several other horses in the barn, two of them bulky Percherons, the rest saddlers.

I went back to the wagon. There was another pump behind the lean-to. I got our bucket out of the wagon and filled the water barrels, which were almost empty. By the time I finished, it was almost dusk. Lamplight from the lean-to flowed out through the windows and made long yellow fingers on the white dust.

For a time I just stood there, watching the scarlet sunset die. Clouds, hugging the western rim, turned dark as if the fire had gone out, and purple twilight deepened until it was fully night. I asked myself how many people had followed the sunset since time had begun, and then, quite suddenly, I felt happier than I had for years. I had seen Jim Perrin. He did not look as I had supposed he would, but I liked him, and he had promised me a job.

The back door swung open, and my father called, 'Daniel, supper's ready.'

I returned to the pump and filled the washpan. I hung my hat on the nail and sloshed water on my face. It felt good to my parched, wind-burned skin. I dried myself with a dirty towel that hung from a nail beside the door, and went in. The rest were already sitting down. I took a chair beside my father and began to eat.

'It's a fine thing to be able to put our knees under a table again, Mr Lang,' my father said, 'and it's a fine thing to have a friend like you. I feel the way Abraham must have felt when he obeyed God and left his land and his relatives and his father's home and came to Canaan.'

Lang helped himself to the fried ham and passed the platter to my father, nodding as if he understood. 'And, you'll remember, the Lord promised to bless him, and make his name so great it would be used for blessings, and to bless those who blessed Abraham.'

My father was surprised, for he seldom found anyone who could match his knowledge of the Scriptures. He said, 'The Lord never fails to keep His promise. He will bless us, too.'

Lang, taking three biscuits from the heaping plate and passing it, said, 'Of course He will,' as if he personally had the inside track to the Lord's ear, and I felt he was equally sure that the Lord's vengeance would be visited upon Jim Perrin.

I ate until I had to loosen my belt. I had forgotten how good it felt to have a full belly again. Besides the ham and the biscuits, we had beans, coffee that was black and strong, with brown sugar for sweetening, tomatoes, and a pitcher of syrup. My mother had made a pie of canned peaches. It had been months since we had tasted pie of any kind.

Ben yawned and rubbed his eyes. He said, 'I'm sleepy, Mamma.'

My mother rose. 'If you'll excuse me, I'll put Ben to bed and then I'll come back and wash the dishes.'

'You'll find a lantern on the floor behind the stove.' Lang then nodded at me. 'Daniel, will you take the bucket and fill the reservoir? If the tea kettle is empty, fill that, too, and put it on the front of the stove.'

Though it was a small chore to do in return for a meal, I was irritated, for I sensed that Virgil Lang was a lazy man who would never do anything he could get someone else to do. I obeyed, finding the reservoir on the back of the stove empty. Then I stoked up the fire and returned to my chair.

Lang brought a box of cigars to the table and offered my father one. When he shook his head, Lang helped himself, smelling the cigar and rolling it between his fingers and then biting off the end, all of it a sort of ritual designed to kill time until my mother returned.

When she did, Lang said: 'I won't attempt to justify myself for what I tried to do this afternoon, but in all fairness to myself I want to tell you why I hate Jim Perrin. He came to this country driving a herd of Shorthorn heifers and some bulls from California. That was six years ago. I had already settled south of the lake, on Thunder River, with a small herd and a few horses. I had two buckaroos working for me. Since I was the first in the valley except for the soldiers at Camp Howard, I had my pick of the grass.'

He took the cigar out of his mouth and stared at its dull glow, frowning. 'Perrin settled on the river about twenty miles south of me. I knew he was there, but I didn't worry because there was grass enough for all of us. Then one day my men asked for their time and rode out of the country. A week later Perrin showed up

35

at my camp with six of his men. He said he would buy me out. I told him I wouldn't sell.'

'He couldn't make you,' my father said.

Lang laughed shortly. 'The strong have ways of making the weak obey, my friend. I was alone. There were seven of them. One was a big Mexican vaquero named Pedro García. He took a knife out of its scabbard and began playing with it. They were armed. I wasn't. Perrin said he guessed I'd change my mind. He offered me $10,000 for my squatter's rights and my cattle.' Lang shrugged. 'I took it and left the country.'

'A good price,' I said.

He put his cigar back into his mouth and scowled at me. 'Would any amount of gold have been a good price?' He shook his head. 'Not when you've found the place you want and someone who is strong drives you away. No, Daniel, it was not a good price.'

'Why did you come back?' my mother asked, turning from the stove to look at him.

'I suppose that's something no one would understand.' He pulled hard on his cigar, his fat face mottled with the bitterness of memory. 'I didn't come back until last year. I had heard a few settlers had come to the valley, and I had also heard Howard Lake was receding. I knew that the dry lake bottom would be the best land in the valley and that Perrin had no right to it. I freighted supplies in from The Dalles and I started my town because I believe in the country as a place where folks like you can find a good home. There's not much land left in other parts of the country, land that can be had for the taking.'

'I know that,' my father said.

Lang rose and walked into his bedroom. My mother had turned again to her dishpan on the back of the stove. She said, 'We don't want land if we have to die for it, Bartram.'

Lang returned with some paper and a pencil. He said, 'Good land is worth fighting for, Mrs Nathan.'

'You didn't fight for yours,' she said sharply.

'I didn't have any chance to win, but times have changed. A number of settlers are making their homes along the lake, families, not just single men like I was. Perrin can't treat them like he did me, although he tries to run a bluff, as you saw this afternoon.'

Lang sat down and drew a crude map, making an oblong circle that was Howard Lake.

'The good land is along the south shore of the lake,' he said. 'Perrin's headquarters is here.' He made an *x* and a long line that he called Thunder River, which emptied into Howard Lake, and drew in Garnet Mountain east of the river. He made some marks to indicate the rimrock to the west. 'Perrin has a fine ranch, a twenty-mile strip of choice valley land. He should be satisfied with what he has, but he's greedy for land whether he owns it or not.'

He looked at my father, the cigar tucked into one corner of his fat-lipped mouth. 'I didn't advise you to settle on land that is covered with tules. In time the marsh will be drained and made to produce, but you don't have time. You need a crop this year, and I'll furnish you with seed, food, and enough lumber to build a small house and barn as I promised.'

'I told you we have nothing but our hands.' My father threw me a glance that showed his uncertainty about me. 'Nothing but our hands and a poor team and a plow.'

'You need hands on a plow,' Lang said. 'You signed a note. That's enough to satisfy me.'

'You want us to settle on land that Perrin claims.' My mother had turned from the stove again, her eyes bright with the anger that had been building in her. 'Land that has not been surveyed. Land that we cannot secure title to.' She shook her head, her lips tightly pressed. 'We want no part of it, Mr Lang.'

He laid his pencil down. 'Mrs Nathan,' he said earnestly, 'I will support you in every way I can—if you will settle south of the lake. If not, I will give you nothing.'

'Then we'll get nothing,' she flared. 'There are other places in this valley where we can settle.'

'But no land as good as you will find south of the lake.'

'Why don't you tell us the truth?' she demanded. 'You want us to fight Perrin. Isn't that it?'

'Yes, that's it. You and the others will form a buffer against his greed.' He tapped his chest. 'But I'm the one who's taking the risk. I may lose everything I'm loaning you.' He shrugged. 'Well, I'm willing to take that gamble because I believe in the country. My reward will come later. Someday I'll have a town. Other settlers will move in, but unless Perrin is held to the land he claims now in time he'll have all the valley.'

'You say you're taking the risks,' my mother said hotly, 'but you're only risking your money. We're risking our lives.'

Lang shook his head. 'No ma'am. Jim Perrin will not hurt families. He'll try to apply pressure just as he did this afternoon; but there are a dozen or more families settled on the marginal land, and he has not harmed any of them.' He picked up his pencil again. 'Here are the Ferguson boys. Young and hardworking and tough enough to stay.' He made an *x* at the southeast corner of the lake, then another west of it. 'The Allisons live here, a man and wife and their girl Debbie.' He made a square west of their place. 'Here is a spot where you can settle.' He made a series of *x*'s on around the south shore. 'These are your neighbors, good people, Mr Nathan. You'll like them.'

'We'll settle there.' My father glanced at me

again. 'We couldn't ask for anything better.'

My mother had finished the dishes. 'I'm going to bed,' she said, and walked stiffly from the room.

'Have breakfast with me,' Lang called, but she went on out, saying nothing.

When the door closed, my father said apologetically: 'She's tired. We've come a long ways.'

'I understand,' Lang said. 'Now then, I'll tell you what we'll do. I have a team and lumber wagon which you are welcome to borrow. We'll load your wagon with your supplies.' He tapped his pencil on the table. 'Can you build your house?'

'We're not carpenters,' my father said ruefully.

'Then hire the Ferguson boys. They'll put up a good house for you. Meanwhile you and Daniel can plow the land and sow your grain. Have the Fergusons make a boat for you. You can get a good deal of your living from the lake if you want to hunt. Ducks and geese by the millions.'

'The Promised Land,' my father said reverently.

'It certainly is,' Lang agreed. 'Now I must warn you again about the Piutes. They're uneasy. Some of the Bannocks have drifted over here and infected our Indians with their discontent. However, I don't think there is any danger because your neighbors will unite against them, and we have the troopers at Camp Howard.'

'The Lord will protect us,' my father said.

'And one more thing.' Lang made a small *x* west of Thunder River just above where it emptied into Howard Lake. 'A woman named Liz Hammond lives there with her girl Cissy. They live well, although they have no visible means of support. Daniel should be warned against them.'

My father was horrified. He looked at me and began stroking his beard. He said: 'Daniel is a good boy. He will not be bothered by temptations of the flesh.' Then he shook his head. 'It is a terrible thing to find the devil entrenched in this beautiful valley.' He hesitated, and then asked, 'Is there a preacher here?'

'No.'

'Then I will fill the need. Now I know why the Lord brought me to this valley. I will bring the Gospel to your people.'

I got up and went out. I made my bed under the wagon, but I couldn't sleep, for I was thinking about what Lang had said. I refused to believe that Jim Perrin was the kind of man that Lang claimed, yet I could not entirely rid myself of my father's teachings that a rich man could not go to Heaven. He had said over and over that we all must choose between God and mammon, and if a man chose mammon there was no hope for him. But I liked Jim Perrin and he had promised me a job. I would take it, regardless of the choice he had made.

A long time later the back door of Lang's lean-to closed, and presently I heard my father getting into the wagon. My mother said, 'Bartram, will you let that man make slaves of us?'

'Not slaves,' he said. 'This will be our home. I told you that yesterday when we first saw the valley. Like the Israelites who wandered so long before they reached the Promised Land, we have wandered and the Lord has brought us here for a purpose.'

'But can't you see?' my mother said fiercely. 'Lang wants to use us against Perrin because he hates him. He's a wicked man, Bartram.'

'His motives are not pure,' my father acknowledged. 'I have given much thought to evil. No philosopher has ever explained its presence in the world, but it can be turned into good. It takes a servant of the Lord to transform it. I am that servant.'

My mother was silent then, for she could never argue against my father. Presently I heard him snore, but I doubted that my mother would sleep. It was a good thing she didn't know about the Piutes.

Then I wondered if my father really believed all that Lang had said in a burst of anger? But how could anyone tell what was in another's heart? I thought of Lang saying he believed in the country so much he would risk the supplies and lumber which we needed. Was it really that, or was it the crazy, vindictive streak which made him come back to the valley, hoping to destroy Jim Perrin?

I couldn't believe in Lang, and I couldn't believe in my father, yet I was fair-minded enough to realize I was prejudiced because I wanted to work for Jim Perrin. I went to sleep, and I dreamed the Piutes came and scalped my mother and Ben. I woke, trying to scream, but no sound came from my throat. An agony of horror was on me until I was finally aware that it was only a dream, and I relaxed.

It would not be our neighbors who would save us, I thought, or the troopers at Camp Howard. It would be Jim Perrin and his buckaroos, and I slept again.

CHAPTER FOUR

Darkness still lay upon the valley when we got up. The air was chill and damp. Fog hugged the ground, a white blanket that would sweep around us and then thin out into wispy, shifting tendrils that gave a weird, distorted appearance to the wagon and buildings. Overhead, the stars glittered in vast, untouchable space. My father, in a rare moment when he had been unable to think of something to quote, had called the stars God's

43

lamps. I liked to think of them that way.

Lang had lighted a lamp in the kitchen and started a fire. My mother left Ben sleeping in the wagon and went into the lean-to. I lighted our lantern and walked around the store building to the street. Suddenly the fog became a cold, damp blanket again, and I had the startling sensation of being lost with a store behind me and a barn in front. I went on slowly, and almost bumped into the wall of the barn before I realized it was there.

I fed our horses, then Lang came in, calling cheerfully, 'Good morning, Daniel.'

'Good morning,' I said, and would have gone back to the wagon if he had not asked me to give him a hand with his horses.

When we finished, he nodded at the Percherons, saying: 'As soon as we eat, you can harness them up. The lumber wagon is on the west side of the barn. You can load up and get started. I'll help your father with the supplies.'

The fog had thinned out when we started back to the store. An impulse made me say: 'We're not a good risk. Why are you doing so much for us?'

He put a big hand on my arm and made me turn to look at him. 'You thought I was lying last night when I said I believed in the country, didn't you?'

I didn't have the courage to tell him the truth, so I said: 'I'm not sure. But Pa isn't much for hard work, and I'm going to get a job with

44

Jim Perrin. That's why I say we're not a good risk.'

'I know, but you see, I need a man like your father.' Lang dropped his hand from my arm. 'He talks well, and a talker has his place. I won't let your folks starve, if that's what you're getting at.'

'That's it.'

'You're a smart boy, Daniel, about the smartest boy I ever ran into. I guess you're the working man in your family, so you've had to grow up faster than most boys your age.' He raised a hand to his face and rubbed his chins, his stubble making a sandpapery sound under his fingers. 'You've learned to be suspicious of people who do good turns for strangers. That's the trouble, isn't it?'

'I guess it is,' I admitted.

He shook his head. 'Don't be suspicious of me, Daniel. Now, you go to work for Perrin. He'll treat you fine and pay you well, and after you know him for a while, he'll tell you about his dream. You listen to it, Daniel, and think about it, and then come to me and listen to my dream.' He walked on toward the store, and I kept pace with him. Then he said: 'Any man who is worth a God damn has a dream. Call it something else if you want to. A goal in life. Or ambition. I don't care what the phrases are. They all mean the same thing.'

He was silent while we went around the store to the lean-to. The fog had momentarily

45

thinned again, and the first gray hint of dawn was in the sky. I blew out the lantern and took it to the wagon. I heard Lang pump a pan of water, and when I reached him, he had finished washing and was drying on the towel.

'Daniel,' he said, 'your father has his dream, too, although I don't suppose you ever thought of that. He's still a young man, relatively speaking, I mean. It may be that he'll find something here he has been looking for all his life.'

I pumped a pan of water, not saying anything, but I thought of what my mother had said about reaching for a star. It was another way of saying the same thing Lang had said, and in spite of myself I was uneasy. Perhaps I was too close to my father to understand him; perhaps my judgment was too severe. Still, after the way we had lived, it was unreasonable to think that anything could change him.

Lang stood by the back door, watching me, the lamplight from the lean-to window mingling with the gloomy dawn light. He said, 'You have your dream, too, haven't you, Daniel?'

I finished washing and, throwing the pan of water into the dust, turned to the towel. I said, 'Yes,' and let it go at that, not wanting to tell him what it was. He wouldn't understand any better than my father would have understood. I wanted to work for Jim Perrin; I wanted to be

46

like him because he had succeeded. Then, for some perverse reason, the thought came to me that my mother was right in saying greatness was a matter of spirit, and I had no way of knowing what sort of spirit was in Jim Perrin.

'We make mistakes, Daniel,' Lang went on. 'The younger we are, the more sure we are we're right, and our mistakes are bigger because of our certainty. You see, my dream is contrary to Perrin's. Time will prove one of us wrong and one of us right. One of us will die and one of us will survive, and that's the way it should be. Individuals aren't important. It's the big thing that counts, and I'm thinking about the big thing.'

He went into the kitchen, leaving me standing there, not sure in my mind what he considered 'the big thing.' My mother came out and asked me to wake Ben and dress him. Breakfast was almost ready.

None of us talked during the meal. Even my father seemed preoccupied with his thoughts, and I puzzled over what had passed between him and Lang after I had gone to bed. My mother had fried bacon and flapjacks, and she set a heaped platter on the table. Lang insisted that she sit down while he kept the flapjacks coming. I don't know how many I ate, or how many cups of coffee I drank, sweetened with brown sugar, which was a luxury to us.

I left the table, my stomach full. It had been a long time since we'd had two good meals in a

47

row. For that I could be grateful to Virgil Lang, and as I walked to the barn and harnessed the Percherons the thought occurred to me that a man's mind and even his conscience were influenced by the condition of his belly. Lang understood that.

I did not see Lang again until I had finished loading the lumber wagon. He left the lean-to and waddled across the back yard. The sun was up now, but shadows still lay against the eastern slope of the valley, as if reluctant to admit that day had come again. Here and there fog clung to the earth in low pockets, motionless white banks in the chill air.

Lang pointed to the wheel ruts that led south. 'Just follow the road, Daniel. Turn west when you come to the Ferguson place. Stop at the Allisons'. Frank will go with you and show you where your folks will settle.'

I climbed up and sat down on the lumber, the lines in my hands. I said, 'All right.'

'Watch out for my horses,' he said. 'The Piutes are supposed to be on the reservation, but some have drifted down into the Garnet Mountain country. They're like all Indians. They'll steal every horse they can.'

'All right,' I said again.

He laid a fat hand on the wheel. 'Perrin promised you a job, so you'll see him soon. He'll bring you a present; probably a horse and saddle.' He frowned against the bright morning sunlight, then he asked, 'Wasn't it the

48

ancient Greeks who said to beware of those who brought gifts?'

'I think so,' I said, and spoke to the team.

Lang removed his hand and stepped back. 'Get another load tomorrow. If you see the Ferguson boys, speak to them about building your house.'

I didn't say anything. The Percherons were leaning into their collars, and the heavily loaded wagon groaned as it began to move. I did not look back. Afterward, headed south with a cold wind blowing in from the lake, I thought about Virgil Lang and the sly way he had of putting things, the poison of hate which he so subtly injected into his words.

Well, if Jim Perrin brought me a horse and saddle, I'd take them. I couldn't see much difference between that and Lang's way of buying a family's loyalty with supplies and grain and lumber. Even giving him the benefit of the doubt, and granting that he was honest in opposing Perrin, I couldn't forget that he had tried to murder Perrin the day before.

The road ran due south, and presently I saw the lake, unbelievably blue in the middle where it was deep, and shading out to a drab, muddy color along the south shore where it was shallow. The east side was a tule marsh, dark green, and as I came closer I saw there was more tule on the north and west sides, and a few patches on the south shore.

Three hours after I left Lang's place I

reached the east edge of the lake, the road bending a little to follow a bench that was covered by heavy sod. At a distance I had not been able to judge the size of the marsh. Now I was astonished when I saw how big it was. Thousands of acres, I thought, cut here and there by narrow channels that worked back and forth through the tule. A man in a boat could get lost in them with no landmarks to guide him.

I pulled up. The Percherons did not need rest, for I had let them take their own lumbering pace, but I wanted to look. It was a new and startling world to me. Short-eared owls flew out of the grass just ahead of the team, giving out a strange call that sounded like 'keeyow.' A meadow lark was singing somewhere to my left. A moment earlier a flock of quails had taken flight with a great beating of wings.

All were birds I was familiar with, but out there in the deep channels cutting through the tule were birds I had never seen before. I did recognize the mallard ducks and the great trumpeter swans and Canadian geese. Some of the others I guessed were ducks smaller than the mallards; but many were entirely strange, like the nosy long-billed birds that flew by calling 'cur-lee.' Here was a bird paradise which would be gone in a few years if settlers drained the lake, or if it continued to recede.

Suddenly I was aware of the jangle of chain

harness. I glanced ahead. An empty lumber wagon was coming toward me. I waited until it pulled up alongside my wagon, the driver working hard on a chew of tobacco, his eyes boring into mine. He said, 'Howdy.'

'Howdy,' I said, and waited, thinking he was a settler headed toward Howard City for a load of lumber.

He motioned to the Percherons. 'Lang's?' he asked. I nodded, and then he said, 'Settler?' and I nodded again. Not a wordy man, I thought. He was middle-aged, short and heavy-set, with a scraggly beard on his face. I didn't have the feeling he was hostile, but, on the other hand, he was far from friendly.

He leaned forward and spat over a wheel into the grass. He wiped a hand across his mouth, then said in disgust: 'Fool. Another damned fool. But you're pretty young.'

'I'm not a fool,' I said indignantly. 'I'm going to work for Jim Perrin.'

He choked, and for a moment I thought he had swallowed his quid of tobacco. When he could talk, he sputtered: 'If you're aiming to work for Jim, you'd best get that outfit back to Lang's and find yourself a horse to fork. Jim, he don't cotton to settlers stealing his land.'

'Maybe there's two ways of looking at this land-stealing business,' I said.

'Yeah,' the man snorted. 'Jim's and Lang's. Thought you said you was a settler.'

'My folks are. They're coming with a load of

supplies. I'm just hauling this lumber for their house.'

'Jim's gonna like that, kid. He sure is. Well, you tell your dad he's doing Jim a favor by working the old lake bottom. Courts are almighty slow, but they'll get around to saying that the marginal land is his, and where will your pa be then?'

'Up a tree, I guess,' I said. 'You going after some of Lang's lumber?'

'Not by a damned sight. I wouldn't buy a hunk of cheese and some crackers from that son of a bitch if I was starving to death.' He motioned toward the Blue Mountains. 'There's a sawmill up there on the other side of the fort. Jim hauls his own lumber. Never gets enough, Jim don't. Builds and builds, makes fences, drains swampland. He's a working son, Jim is.'

'My name's Daniel Nathan,' I said.

'I'm Billy Ralls.' He leaned toward me and held out his hand. I shook it and said: 'I'll see you on J Ranch, I guess. Hope so, anyhow.'

'Mebbe.' Ralls shook his head. 'Don't see why Jim wants to hire a settler pup, but he's a real smart hombre, Jim is. He don't make mistakes and he don't do nothing without knowing why. Well, got to move along.'

He drove on then, leaving me puzzling over what he had meant. Anybody who had gone up like Jim Perrin had was smart. I didn't question that, but I couldn't see why he had hired me except for the obvious reason of needing another man to work for him. There would always be work on a spread as big as the J Ranch.

I got the Percherons under way again. An hour later the road swung west around the corner of the lake, and I saw the first settler shack I had seen since I had come to the valley, as small and square as a box, with a dirt roof. The Ferguson place, I thought, but I didn't see anyone and I didn't stop.

Now I understood what Lang had meant when he said not to settle on land that was covered by tule. Here the ground was bare, sloping gently toward the water a quarter of a mile away. Some of the land had been worked between the shack and the water, and already the sprouting grain gave a faint green hue to the black soil.

A mile farther west I reached another shack. Allison's place, I thought. When I came opposite it, a man stepped out of a shed behind the house and called to me. I stopped, and he walked toward me, a lanky, bent-shouldered man who showed in his plodding walk the bone-deep weariness which was in him.

When he reached me he held out a big-knuckled, calloused hand. 'I'm Frank Allison,' he said. 'You fixing to settle here?'

I gripped his hand. 'My folks are. They're coming behind me with their wagon. I'm Daniel Nathan.'

'Git down.' Allison glanced up at the noon-high sun. 'It's eating time. We don't have much, but you're welcome to share what we have.'

He helped me unhook. There was a pump and a log trough between the house and the shed. Allison worked the pump while I held the horses, then we put them in the shed beside his team, a span of horses almost as old and skinny as ours.

When we started toward the house, Allison said: 'Sure wish I had a team like Lang's. They're kind o' slow and they eat like hell, but a man could get a lot of work out of 'em.' He made a clucking sound and jerked a hand back toward the shed. 'I spend more time resting my team than I do working 'em.'

I dragged a toe across the dirt. It looked as if it had dried out not long ago. There were cracks in it deep enough to bury my hand without touching bottom. They made a strange, rectangular pattern, and the dirt which had obviously been mud a few weeks before had curled up at the edges of the cracks so that each block had the appearance of a drab, outsized platter.

'Looks like good soil,' I said.

'It is,' Allison said. 'Of course, it's hell when it rains. When you start here, the first thing you do is to run a few ditches toward the lake to drain off the surface water, but the beauty of it is that the ground never dries out underneath.'

He looked at his field, the sprouted grain making it faintly green. 'Gonna take a lot of work to make a home here.'

I thought of my father. I said, 'I guess a man who won't work will soon starve out.'

'He wouldn't even start.' Allison scratched his long jaw, still looking at the field. 'Well, we have a lot of winter and not much summer, but I figure we'll get a crop. Of course, Jim Perrin claims it ain't farm land. Some fellow at the fort tried raising stuff and had a fizzle, but it don't prove nothing. The land around the fort ain't much good.'

'Perrin given you any trouble?'

'No. Just says this is his land and we'll lose it when the courts get around to deciding on it. That may take years.' He tipped his head back, looking south across the great sweep of grass to the brown hills. 'That's his all the way to hellan'gone, but this marginal land was under water when he came. I figure it belongs to us that's settled it.'

'That's what Lang says.'

Allison nodded. 'Yeah, and Lang claims to be our friend. Well, looks to me like what happens to us in the long run depends on how good a friend he is. If he gives us credit so we can buy grub, we'll make out. Otherwise we'll starve before we get started.'

A girl appeared around the corner of the house. She called, 'Dinner's ready.'

'Debbie,' Allison said, and walked toward

55

her. 'This here is our new neighbor, Daniel Nathan. His folks are coming.'

She gave me a kind of curtsy, smiling shyly. 'How do you do, Mr Nathan.'

I touched the brim of my hat. 'I'm pleased to meet you, Miss Allison.' I said it awkwardly, for I hadn't been around girls of my age very much, and I couldn't keep from being embarrassed when I was.

'I'm Debbie,' she said.

'I'm Daniel,' I said.

She hesitated, her lips slightly parted, standing there like a bird about to take flight. She was sixteen or seventeen, I thought, a full head shorter than I was, and quite slender, with blue eyes and light brown hair. She was wearing a calico dress that had once been red-and-white checked, but strong soap and many washings had stolen the color so that now it was a sort of dingy gray, the red checks barely distinguishable.

Suddenly Debbie whirled, calling, 'Come on in,' and disappeared into the house.

Allison gave me a sharp glance, as if trying to measure my feeling about her. I knew my face was red and I was ill at ease. I resented his look because I thought he was sizing me up as a potential husband for Debbie, hoping he could get rid of her so there would be one less mouth to feed.

'We'll wash up,' he said shortly, and walked on around to the front door of the house.

56

He went inside and, returning with a bucket of water, filled the washpan that was on the bench by the door. We cleaned up and went inside. Allison said: 'Ma, this is Daniel Nathan. He's gonna settle with his folks next to us.'

Mrs Allison turned from the stove and gave me a big smile. 'How do you do, Daniel,' she said. 'I'm glad we're going to have close neighbors.' She paused, her smile fading, and then added, 'I mean, nice neighbors.'

'I'm pleased to meet you,' I said.

I hung my hat on a nail by the door. Perhaps she wouldn't think we were nice neighbors after she met my father, but I was sure she would like my mother and my mother would like her.

Mrs Allison was the same height as Debbie, but she was three times bigger around at the hips and her breasts drooped tiredly, although I suppose they had once been as firm and pointed as Debbie's. Mrs Allison's hair was white, adding years to her appearance, and her dress was as dingy as her daughter's. In another twenty years Debbie would look like her mother, I thought in a sudden burst of bitterness.

Hard work, doing without the things that a woman wants, yet still holding to the foolish hope that someday life would be kinder. It had been that way with my mother, and as I sat down at the table I thought that probably

57

every woman who lived along the lake was a good deal like her, but it wasn't right, not in a country like ours, where wealth was all around us.

We didn't talk as we ate, although I knew the Allisons were curious about us. They would find out later, I thought, and they could form their own judgment without being influenced by what I might say about my father.

It wasn't much of a meal, but better than I had been used to: biscuits, beans, and stewed prunes, and good sweet water from the well. I looked around the room as I ate, trying to be casual, and hoping they wouldn't notice.

A curtain was drawn across the middle of the room. The beds were behind it, I knew. In this part of the cabin there were only a few pieces of crude furniture: the table covered by a strip of scarred yellow oilcloth, a range that was scrubbed clean, and a couple of benches. Pots and pans and dishes were on some shelves behind the stove along with a few cans and sacks of food. The Allisons had a home, for the time at least, but they had not yet lifted themselves above the poverty level that had been our way of life as long as I could remember.

'We'll have a garden come fall,' Allison said after a long silence. 'I hope we'll eat better next winter, the Lord willing.'

Debbie laughed, her glance touching my face briefly. 'If my back holds up,' she said.

'Debbie's the gardener,' Allison said. 'I've been trying to get the crop in and cut a few posts on the hills south of us and hunt a little. I don't seem to have time to do all that needs doing.'

'That's one good thing about this country,' Mrs Allison said in her comfortable way. 'Between the deer and antelope and ducks and geese, we've had meat most of the winter.'

Debbie laughed again, a little forced, I thought, for there was no reason to laugh. She said, 'And fish when Jim Perrin isn't looking.'

'Do all the fish belong to him?' I asked.

'He thinks so,' Allison answered. 'He's quite a fisherman, and we have to go on his land to catch anything.'

We had finished eating and I got up. 'Lang told me you would show me where to settle,' I said.

Allison hesitated, glancing at Debbie, and I was afraid he was going to say that he was too busy, that Debbie could go with me. Instead he nodded and rose. 'I'll ride over with you. Ain't far.' He hesitated again, scratching his long jaw. 'The best claims have been taken, but the quarter-section next to us will do.'

'Isn't it all the same?' I asked.

'Except for the tules,' he said. 'Your land has some, but there is one advantage to it. You can keep your boat close to your buildings, so it ain't much chore to go after a duck or goose. Most of us keep our boats there. I hope your pa

59

won't kick about that.'

'He won't,' I said, 'but why can't you keep your boats here?'

'Too shallow. You're in the mud for fifty yards or more, but the water's deep among the tules. A long channel goes through 'em clean up to the shore. You can trap muskrats if you want to. Lang will buy the pelts. Don't pay much, but it helps.'

I took my hat off the nail. 'Thank you for the dinner,' I said to Mrs Allison.

She seemed startled by this small courtesy, then she smiled. 'We were glad to have you, Daniel. I hope you'll come to see us often.'

Debbie, still sitting at the table, gave me a straight look, her face grave, and I sensed that she was lonely. I couldn't understand it, because I was sure there were few girls in this country, and if she gave Jim Perrin's riders any encouragement she could have some of them calling on her.

'We have a schoolhouse about three miles west of here,' she said. 'Sometimes we have parties there because it's the only place big enough. I hope you'll come.'

'I will,' I said, and left the house, thinking she was a bold girl but still not a flirt.

Allison helped me hook up. He sat on the lumber beside me as we drove out of the yard. He cleared his throat, looking at me as if there was something on his mind and it was important for him to say it right.

'Debbie is all we have,' he said finally. 'She's a good girl and she works hard and she doesn't have much fun. I guess it's natural for parents to want their children to have something better than we've had, but I don't know.'

I couldn't tell what he was getting at, so I didn't say anything. He got a pipe out of his pocket and filled it. He had some trouble lighting it, for the west wind was keen, but presently he got it going. Then he went on: 'We won't let Perrin's buckaroos come to see her. They've tried, riding in and doing their best to impress her with their fancy horses and geegaws and all, but they ain't the kind of men we want her to marry. Besides—well, Perrin's our enemy any way we look at it.'

He was silent for a long time, pulling hard on his pipe, the skin on his forehead curled up in a worried frown. 'Then there's the Ferguson boys who want to shine up to her, but I'd kill them before I'd let her marry one of them. They're mean, just animal mean.' He choked, his face getting red. 'It's damned bad luck to have them for neighbors.'

'Lang said to get them to build our house,' I said.

'They're good carpenters,' he admitted grudgingly, 'but don't get 'em unless you can pay 'em. Never owe 'em a penny. Virgil claims we need fighters, but that's one thing he's wrong on. If we ever have any shooting trouble with Perrin, it'll be on account of the

61

Fergusons. They eat his beef regular, so I suppose he'll wind up hanging 'em.'

I began to understand why they had made it plain I was welcome to call on Debbie. I would be a sort of barrier to the Fergusons. Allison was not a fighting man, and it was evident enough that he was afraid of the Fergusons. I didn't say anything, although I did think of telling him I was going to work for Perrin. If I did, I would have their door slammed in my face, and I didn't want it to be.

I liked Debbie, liked her well enough to want to see her again, and I was surprised at myself. I had never had time for girls, and I had never had money to spend on them. Maybe I would have both now, I thought; then I tried to put it out of my mind. No sense in dreaming about the first girl I'd seen.

We were silent until Allison pointed to a ridge that was directly ahead of us, running north and south and dropping off sharply at the edge of the lake. Tule made a dark splotch along the foot of the ridge, and I could see several boats pulled up on the bank, awkward flat-bottomed affairs that would be hard to handle.

'You'll raise your crop this side of the ridge,' Allison said. 'I'd advise you to build on top. You'll have to go deeper for water than most of us, but on the other hand there's grass on the ridge, so you won't be in the mud when it rains, like I am.'

I nodded, liking it. I wasn't very good at measuring land with my eyes the way some men are, but I judged we'd have eighty acres that could be farmed between the ridge and the stakes that marked Allison's boundary. It was more than my father would work.

'Purty wet along here,' Allison said, 'but it'll dry out sooner'n you think after you run a few ditches. You can get some of it planted this spring along the edge of the grass where it's tolerable dry. Well, I'd best hike back.'

I pulled up. 'Thanks for coming and showing me where to stop.'

'Glad to.' He stepped down. 'Best put up some stakes. None of us know just where our corners are, but you can step it off purty close. Fellow named Nolan lives west of the ridge. He'll be a good neighbor.'

'There's something I ought to tell you about my father,' I said. 'He's not a good worker. He's a preacher.'

Allison laid a big hand on the wheel, looking steadily at me. I liked him. I seldom felt that way about a man I had known for only a few hours. I was cynical about most people, perhaps because of my father, or possibly because I had run into too many men who had tried to cheat me when I worked for them. But there was something about Frank Allison that set him apart from the average man, a straightforward, guileless quality that he could not have disguised if he had wanted to.

'We need a preacher,' he said after a moment's silence. 'We've all missed having regular service since we got here. There's always young folks wanting to get married, and now and then somebody dies, and there's others that need their faith bolstered by a minister. It'll work out, Daniel. We do a lot of swapping, you know. We have to.'

Nodding, he turned and plodded back toward his place. I drove on to the top of the ridge, looking westward at the faint patches of green where grain had been sowed. I could see a few shacks along the lake shore like Allison's; and the lake, deep blue out there in the middle, so wide that the north shore was made vaguely indistinct by distance.

To the south cattle were grazing near the base of the hills. Beyond was massive Garnet Mountain, and west of it there was a break in the hills that I knew was made by Thunder River. J Ranch was somewhere upstream. I wondered how soon I would see Jim Perrin. Would he come for me, or would I have to go to him, and would he keep his promise if I did?

The big range! All of it to the south belonged to Jim Perrin. It should be enough to satisfy anyone, and then I had my doubts about him. I despised a greedy man. Maybe Virgil Lang, with his talk about believing in the country as a place for little people, was right, and maybe Perrin was wrong if he was thinking only about himself. But I would go to work for him, regardless of my doubts. My folks needed my wages to live, and only Jim Perrin could pay wages in this country.

I got down and unhooked the Percherons; I stripped harness from them and watered them at the edge of the lake, then staked them out on the grass fifty yards to the south. I unloaded the lumber, and presently I saw our wagon, at first beyond the Allison place. It moved at a snail's pace; it stopped at Allison's and I knew my folks were getting acquainted with their neighbors.

I wondered what Debbie would think when she heard my father's fine talk. No matter how I felt about him, or whether I stayed here with my folks, I couldn't be entirely apart from them whether I worked on J Ranch or not. Debbie and everybody else along the lake would have their opinion of me shaped by what they thought of my family.

I gathered some cow chips and built a fire, and near sundown our wagon pulled up the ridge and stopped beside the fire. I stood there watching my father put his Winchester down, leaning the barrel against a wheel. For once he wasn't posing; he seemed very subdued. He had no fine words, no classic to quote, no Scripture. He just looked up at my mother and said simply, 'We're home.'

I thought of Virgil Lang saying, 'It may be he'll find something here he has been looking for all his life.' I hoped it would be true; I had never hoped for anything as earnestly as I hoped for that.

CHAPTER FIVE

We went to bed before the sun was down; we were up before it showed in the east. I led the Percherons down to the edge of the lake and watered them below the boats that were on the bank, and when I returned my mother had breakfast ready. Coffee, strong and black, for now we had plenty of it, and we did not need to scrimp and save as we had for so long.

While we were eating, I asked my father, 'Did you see the Fergusons?'

He shook his head. 'No, they were not home when we passed their place.'

'Allison said not to hire them unless we could pay them.'

He hunched over the fire, shivering a little, for a fine, cold mist was blowing in from the lake. He drank his coffee, looking at me over the rim of his tin cup, and for some strange reason he seemed at a loss for words. I didn't understand it, for he could always talk if he couldn't do anything else.

He put his cup down. 'I can't build a cabin,' he said. 'I can't even build a shed for the horses and our chickens. We have to have a corral. Lang promised me a few cows. We need a fence. Lang said it was the only way to keep Perrin's cows out of our grain.'

'But we don't have enough money to pay the Fergusons for all that work,' I said. 'Hold them off until I talk to Allison again. Maybe he can figure something out, swap work or something.'

'All right.' He filled his mouth with bacon and chewed on it, his beard fluttering with the movement of his jaw, then he asked, 'When are you going to work for Perrin?'

'I don't know,' I answered, surprised that he was not making an issue out of my leaving.

The sun was still not up when I drove down the east slope of the ridge a few minutes later. I thought about my father, knowing that the barrier which had grown between us would always be there. I would never respect him as a son should respect his father. He had always been an opportunist just as he had been with Virgil Lang, taking the food and lumber and grain and not worrying about the debt. But the thought haunted me that I was not being fair in my judgment of him, that Lang had been right in saying the younger we were, the more sure we were that we were right, and that our mistakes were bigger because of that certainty.

Perhaps a man could change. I wanted to think my father could. Maybe he had leaned on me too long, and now that he knew I was leaving he might go to work. He might believe what my mother had said about this being his last chance. I was sure of one thing. He could not face life without her.

I reached Lang's store shortly before noon, knowing that I was hoping for a miracle, and I had no faith in miracles. Lang came out of the store and said he would have dinner ready as soon as I took care of the Percherons. I unhooked them and led them around the store building to the barn; I watered them and gave them a double feeding of oats, a little ashamed because I was using Lang's horses and I could not even feed them our own grain.

By the time I had loaded the wagon with lumber again, Lang called that dinner was ready. Beans, biscuits, coffee, and a can of peaches, plenty of everything, and as I ate I wondered if our starvation time was behind us.

'Did you see the Fergusons?' Lang asked.

'No. Allison warned me about them. He said that they were living off Perrin's beef and that if we ever have any real trouble it would be on account of them.'

Lang's expression soured. 'Frank Allison's a good man but he's soft. The only settlers along the lake that Perrin is afraid of are the Ferguson boys. Allison won't admit it, and I suppose the others won't, either, but if it wasn't for the Ferguson boys Perrin would have cleared the lake shore of every damned farmer I've sent out there.'

I didn't argue with him, and I realized that Allison might be prejudiced against the

68

Fergusons because he was worried about Debbie. Still, Perrin had apparently not resorted to violence. He seemed willing to wait for a court decision, and there was no sense in forcing the issue. If the Fergusons were stealing Perrin's beef, no one could blame him for taking the law into his own hands.

Before I left, Lang said: 'I don't know how much lumber your pa will need, but you keep coming back till you get enough. You'll need grain for seed, and some wire. You can cut juniper posts on the hills south of the valley.'

I thanked him and drove away. Dusk was working across the valley when I reached our place. I saw that my father had run some ditches toward the lake, because the mud at the north end had been stirred by the hoofs of our horses. Probably Allison had been over, I thought, for my father was not practical enough to think of it.

When I reached our wagon, I saw that two men were there, saddle horses standing ground-hitched a few feet from our fire. As I got down from the wagon my father said, 'Daniel, these are the Ferguson boys, Ernie,' nodding at the shorter one, 'and Carl.'

I shook hands with them, both making a show of their strength when they gripped my hand. They were in their early twenties, not as tall as I was, but heavier built. Both carried guns. They were dark-complexioned, their skins swarthy, their square heads anchored to their shoulders by short, muscular necks. They had flat noses and thick lips, and they looked enough alike to be twins.

Both of them appraised me the way a buyer studies a horse that's for sale, cold and calculating and frankly unfriendly. I didn't like them. I told myself it was because they were dirty, greasy stinking dirty, and even there in the open the stench of months of accumulated sweat was sickening.

As much as we had drifted, my father had always insisted that we keep relatively clean. To him cleanliness was next to godliness, and I mean that literally. But in all honesty I had to admit that my dislike for the Fergusons was, in part, based on what Frank Allison had said about them.

After they had looked me over, Ernie, who apparently was the leader of the two, turned to my father. He said: 'As I was saying, we're the only carpenters along the lake. We've built most of the houses, and you can see from them that we put up a good tight building.'

'We don't have much money,' my father said. 'Not enough to pay for all the work that we need to have done.'

Ernie threw out a big hand. 'To hell with that. Pay us what you can. Owe us the rest.'

'I don't like to be in debt,' my father said uneasily.

'Why, damn your conscience,' Ernie said in a bullying voice. 'You're in debt to Lang, ain't you?'

'That's different,' my father said.

'No different.' Carl laughed, a rumbling sound that came from far down in his belly. 'It's this way, Nathan. We've got to stand together against that God-damned bastard of a Perrin.'

Frightened by his laugh and loud voice, Ben began to cry. My mother picked him up. She said sternly, 'We don't like to hear that kind of talk, Mr Ferguson.'

'You'll keep a clean tongue in front of her,' I said, 'or you can get out of here.'

Carl wheeled on me, his big hands fisted. He wanted to fight: he was like a proddy bull that feels the challenge of a younger animal. He said, 'You fixing to clean my tongue, kid?'

I could handle my end in most fights, but this would be against both of them, and I didn't have any illusions about myself. I just wasn't man enough to do the job. I would have tried, though, if Ernie hadn't said irritably, 'Shut up, you God-damned fool.' He turned to my mother. 'I'm sorry, ma'am. We ain't around ladies very often, and Carl plumb forgot.' He faced my father. 'We've got some things to do this week, but Monday morning we'll be on hand. By that time you'll have the lumber you need. Come on, Carl.'

He stalked to his horse and swung up. Carl hesitated, reluctant to leave without a fight, his black eyes pinned on my face. Ernie called irritably, 'Get into your saddle, Carl, or by God I'll get down and kick you into it!'

Carl shrugged, grinning a little as if finding pleasure in anticipation, then he walked to his horse and mounted. After they had ridden away, my father said in a low tone, 'I have read the Bible more times than I can remember, but I have never found in it a logical explanation for the Lord putting men like that on the earth.'

I was sweating and trembling a little, relieved that the fight had not been forced upon me, but I knew that it would come. This had been a postponement. Nothing more. My mother said, 'Don't let them do a lick of work for us, Bartram.'

'They'll come back,' he said. 'How can I stop them?'

'You've got a Winchester,' I said. 'They aren't so tough a bullet won't cut them down to size.'

He looked at me disapprovingly. 'Vengeance is the Lord's...' He stopped and bowed his head, and I thought he was recalling the scene on the porch of Virgil Lang's store when Lang had come so close to killing Jim Perrin. He said, 'Yes, maybe that's the only way they can be dealt with.' Then he looked directly at me, frightened and worried. 'Frank Allison was right about them. They're mean, animal mean.'

I took care of the Percherons and ate supper,

72

and it was completely dark before I had finished unloading the lumber. After I went to bed, I realized how deeply the fear of the Fergusons had gripped Frank Allison, how any man who had a daughter as attractive as Debbie would worry about living next to men like the Fergusons.

I thought, too, of my father, who had not strutted or posed before them. They would not be fooled by it. Well, no one else along the lake would be fooled, either. Folks like the Allisons were earthy people who could intuitively distinguish between sham and reality. My father had lost out more than once in the past because he had been unable to overcome his desire to dramatize himself. There was one thing in his favor. The people needed a preacher, and that would give him a chance to make himself respected, if he was smart enough and humble enough to take advantage of it. I knew he could lay aside his posing and be himself. I remembered a few times when he had. They seemed a long time ago, for I had been younger then, memorable occasions when we had sat around our campfire and talked about some of his books that he had made me read.

I hauled another load of lumber the next day, and when I returned I found to my surprise that my father had actually plowed a small piece of land at the edge of the grass. While I ate supper, he told me with pride that

73

there would be preaching at the schoolhouse on Sunday. Debbie had walked the length of the lake to tell the folks. They would bring food, and we would have a picnic dinner after the service.

I don't know whether he realized how much depended on it. I looked at my mother, and in the murky light of the chip fire I saw that hope was high in her again, hope that our wandering was behind us and that she would have a home at last. But it was more than that, I knew. She must have watched him plow, a prayer in her heart that he had at last reached the point where whatever pride remained in him would finally force him to make something of his life. But I had no real faith that it would.

The next day was Saturday. I hauled a load of grain, wire, and nails, and I had brought a posthole digger and an auger to bore holes through the juniper posts through which we would string the wire. Bitter disappointment had been in me all day because I had not heard from Jim Perrin. Lang had asked me about it, taunting me when I had admitted I had not seen Perrin.

I tried to rationalize, telling myself that maybe my place was with my folks, that I had been wrong in wanting to work for Perrin. When Monday came I would return Lang's Percherons and take our horses and go after juniper posts. It would mean moving the cover off our wagon and unloading our things. We could make out, for we had done so before when we had needed the wagon. But my rationalization did not restore peace of mind. I had trusted Jim Perrin too much; I had dreamed of working on J Ranch too long.

That night I carried water from the lake. We heated some in our copper boiler, and we took baths, Ben first, and then my mother. My father and I walked to the edge of the lake and stopped beside the boats, my father carrying the Winchester. He didn't need it, but I suppose it was habit, or maybe he was identifying himself with Daniel Boone again.

He had done more work in these three days than he had done in the past year, and he was tired. It wouldn't last, I thought, and I was ashamed because I couldn't share my mother's hope. We didn't say anything for a while; we just sat there on the grass staring at the lake, which was pale silver in the moonlight. My father was very thoughtful, and I suddenly realized he was thinking about tomorrow's sermon; then my mother called, and we started back to the wagon.

'I shall read from the Second Book of Samuel,' my father said. 'About David and Bathsheba, and how David sent Uriah to his death. I shall preach on temptations of the flesh.'

I did not know why he told me, but the bitterness of memory burned my mind. I was remembering the time my mother had called him a monster, a liar to God and man, and how I had taken the Winchester and climbed up on the wagon seat and told him to let her alone. He should know about temptations of the flesh, I thought.

We took our baths, shivering in the night air, and I went to bed at once, slowly getting warm again under my blankets. I wondered if he still wanted my mother, or if the flame had died in him. Or did it ever die in a man until he was old and nothing was left? I clenched my fists, thinking of Debbie Allison and knowing I was no better, and hating my father because somehow he had made it seem wrong and dirty.

Then I remembered Lang talking about Liz Hammond and her daughter Cissy. He'd said they should be driven from the valley, and suddenly I knew why my father had decided to preach about David and Bathsheba and the temptations of the flesh. His sermon would be popular because the women would welcome it and the men couldn't say anything against it or they'd give themselves away.

I was curious about whether Liz Hammond and her girl Cissy would be in church. Probably not. The hand of every settler's wife would be lifted against them. If the Hammond women did come, they would be either very brave or very stupid.

We put on our best clothes in the morning. My mother got a suitcase from the wagon that

76

had not been opened for months. She took out a poplin dress, the one good dress she possessed, and my father put on his black suit, wrinkled and smelling of moth balls, and so old it was more green than black. He brushed his hair and beard and polished his shoes. I shaved, then put on a clean shirt and my best pair of pants, and my mother dressed Ben.

In spite of myself, when I looked at my father I had to admit that he was a fine-looking man. He seemed confident and sure of himself, and I couldn't tell, even as well as I knew him, whether he was posing again, or whether he honestly felt that he was going to be himself and make a place in the valley.

The Allisons came by for us, a basket of food with a white cloth over it in one corner of the wagon bed. We rode to the schoolhouse with them, my father sitting beside Frank on the seat, his Bible on his lap. I sat in the back beside Debbie, who was wearing a starched gingham dress, of white with pink dots, that rustled when she moved. She was uncommonly pretty, I thought, with her light brown hair done up in curls. She must have worked on it half the night.

I wanted to talk but I couldn't. I glanced at her covertly, and sometimes I caught her looking at me, and then she'd turn her head quickly, her cheeks flushed. Finally I said it was a nice day, and she said she thought so too. I said it was a pretty valley, and she said she thought so too. When a meadow lark sang from somewhere out in the grass south of us, I said it was nice, and she agreed that it was. Then I stopped trying. I was as big as a man, but that morning, sitting beside Debbie, I was just an awkward kid.

My mother sat in the front of the wagon, Ben on her lap. Mrs Allison was beside her, and they chattered all the way to the schoolhouse, about cooking and sewing and the climate, about what would grow in the garden and what wouldn't. It was good for my mother, the best thing that had happened to her for a long time. I looked at my father's straight, broad back. He's got to make a living for her, I thought. He's got to.

We were early. I helped Frank with the horses, and when we went into the schoolhouse my father had taken his place in the front of the room behind the teacher's desk, his Bible open before him. There were a number of crude benches and desks, a dozen battered books on a shelf, and a globe that my father had set in a corner. I suppose it wasn't much of a schoolhouse, measured by some standards, but it was as good as anything I had seen.

People began coming then, the Nolans and the Cartwrights and the Morrises and some others whose names I could not remember. We were introduced to them, and then, just before the service started, two women came in. They were dressed in silk with cartwheel hats decorated with purple plumes, and immediately the too sweet smell of their perfume flowed out from them and filled the room.

Everybody stiffened, the talk dying as suddenly as if someone had given an audible order. My father went back to the desk. Two girls who had been sitting in front got up and moved to the back. The women who had just come in sat down in the vacated seats directly in front of my father. They were, I knew, the Hammonds.

I was standing along the side, for there weren't half enough benches, and all the men and boys were standing. Frank Allison, next to me, whispered to Nolan, 'That bitch has sure got her gall.'

Grinning, Nolan whispered back, 'That ain't all she's got, from what I hear.'

My father said, 'Let us pray.' He folded his hands and looked upward, and his rich, deep voice rolled out of his great chest, as soothing as the tone of a fine organ. 'Our Father Who art in Heaven, forgive us our sins, both of the flesh and of the spirit. Point the way for us that we may be children of Thine. Amen.'

He had his tuning fork in his hand. He looked at the faces before him, and I saw that he was troubled, and I sensed a humility in him I had never felt before. It was the first time I had any hope that my mother's faith in him was justified; it was also the first time that I had the slightest inkling of the hell he had suffered through the years while he had strutted and posed, plagued by the knowledge that he was a futile man, a failure.

'We will worship the Lord in song,' he said, 'first with "Rescue the Perishing."'

He struck the tuning fork on the desk and, giving us the pitch, led out. We all followed, making the room ring. From where I stood I could see the side of Cissy Hammond's face. She was singing with us, her cheeks glowing with the fine warmth that was in all of us. We sang several songs, and then my father read from the Second Book of Samuel just as he had told me he would.

After that he preached, walking back and forth across the front of the room, gesturing in the dramatic way he had. He would look up at the ceiling, or he would stare at us, pointing an accusing finger. Heaven was waiting for us if we overcame our lust, and hell was waiting if we didn't; Heaven with its golden streets and trumpets and white-robed angels, and hell with its fury, its fire eating at us and yet not destroying us, for this was eternity.

He talked of the everlasting wrath of God and of how it would be visited upon us if we did not repent of our sins and come to Him on bended knees; he talked about the Devil, who had a thousand disguises, attractive disguises that we would not recognize unless we were on guard. I saw the glorious beauty of Heaven and felt its peace; I heard the crackle of the flames in hell and smelled the brimstone; and I had the feeling that the Devil was a woman in a silk dress and a cartwheel hat with a purple plume, who smelled too sweetly of perfume.

I had not heard my father preach for a long time, and never as he did now. He worked harder than he had at his plowing; sweat burst through his skin, making his face shiny in the sunlight that came through a side window. He seemed to be standing there with the radiance of God upon him. Sincere? At the moment I could not doubt it, although four days before I would have said he wasn't. Something had happened to him.

When he finished, we sang another song and he dismissed us with a benediction, but he was not ready to let us go. He held up a hand, silent for a moment, and then said solemnly: 'I want to serve you in any way that I can. I pray that we may live together as God's children. And this I know: If we pray for strength, we will receive; we will overpower our enemies however strong they may be.' Then he looked squarely at Liz and Cissy Hammond. 'Go in peace. The Lord will forgive our sins if we ask Him, no matter how great they may be.'

We broke up then. I worked my way to the door. I had to get out. I couldn't stay. I had seen a miracle. For the first time in my life I had felt God's presence, but I couldn't understand; and I certainly couldn't understand my father.

81

I felt guilty as hell. I had been wrong and my mother had been right. My faith had been as small as a mustard seed.

CHAPTER SIX

Outside, men had gathered in little groups. I walked around the schoolhouse, not wanting to talk to anyone. Then I felt a woman rub against me. I whirled around, knowing who it was before I saw her. It was Cissy Hammond. She must have taken a bath in her perfume.

She was younger than I had thought, probably not much older than I was, blue-eyed, with a soft peach-bloom complexion and curls of bright yellow hair along her forehead that were visible under the brim of her huge hat.

She took my hands, smiling at me. 'You're the preacher's boy, aren't you?'

I heard the silk of her dress rustle; I saw the bold, high mound of her breasts that I had felt a moment before, and the curves of her hips and the slim ankles below the hem of her skirt. I was hot and cold all over, and I knew how David had felt when he had stood on his roof and looked at Bathsheba.

'Yes,' I said, and the whispered word did not sound like my voice.

'I'm Cissy Hammond,' she said, still smiling.

'I live with my mother on the other side of Thunder River. Come and see us.'

Then she dropped my hands and went on to the horse shed, her hips swaying in a titillating rhythm. Her mother walked past me, as attractive and slender as Cissy. She nodded at me, maintaining her composure with an effort. Foolishly I asked, 'Aren't you staying to eat with us?'

She stopped and looked at me, and I saw she was close to crying. She said: 'You're young and not very wise. I'm much older, but I'm not any wiser. They've tried me and Cissy, and condemned us on the grounds that, like Bathsheba, we took off our clothes to attract the eyes of David.'

'The Bible doesn't say that,' I said, but I don't think she heard me.

She flung out a hand toward the schoolhouse. 'All women are Bathshebas under the right circumstances, but they won't admit it, and all the men are Davids. If it hadn't been for him, Bathsheba wouldn't have sinned, but I doubt that your father ever thought of that.'

She walked on toward the buggy where Cissy was sitting with the lines in her hands. Liz got in and they drove away, and I knew they would never come to church again.

When I turned, I saw that several of the men had moved around the corner of the schoolhouse and were watching me. Frank

Allison walked toward me, his face showing his distaste. He said harshly: 'You didn't know, Daniel, but those two women are nothing but God-damned whores running a hog ranch. They're a disgrace to the valley.'

'Who would know that but the men who have gone there?' I asked.

Anger stirred in him. 'We've all heard the talk. There must be fire where there's so much smoke. Matt Cartwright lives across the river from them, and he says Perrin's riders come and go all night.'

I thought of Matt Cartwright, little and stooped and henpecked, and his wife who had taken as much space to sit down as two ordinary women would need. I said: 'Maybe he's been to see the Hammond women. Maybe that's how he knows.'

'Not Matt,' Frank said. 'He's told us what he's seen. That's all. It's a bad thing, Daniel, a bad thing to have temptation flaunted in our faces like this.' He scowled, his eyes on the Hammond buggy that was moving away across the grass. 'Of course, none of us are beyond temptation. There's been talk of tarring and feathering them, but their house is on Perrin's land. He'd raise hell if we did anything.'

I was angry then, angrier than I should have been, I suppose, but I felt sorry for them. I remembered Liz Hammond's contorted face. She had wanted to cry, and she would when she was away from the other women's condemning eyes. I admired anyone with courage, and Liz Hammond had her share.

'If anybody needs to come to church, it's the sinners,' I said. 'And maybe those women aren't such sinners after all. Let the one pick up the first stone who is without sin.'

He stared at me, appalled, and then his expression softened. 'You know your Bible, Daniel.'

'My father used it to teach me to read,' I said.

He swung sharply away from me toward the front of the schoolhouse, and then turned back. 'Don't say anything to Debbie or her mother about talking with the Hammond women. Debbie wouldn't understand.'

Before long he'd get around to asking me to marry Debbie, I thought angrily. She must have something wrong with her if her father had to drag a husband in by the ears, but I nodded and let it go at that. No use making him mad at me.

I followed Frank to the other side of the schoolhouse where the women were setting the food out on the grass. Mrs Cartwright asked my father to give the blessing, and we began to eat. All the children except Ben were running around and yelling like a bunch of Piutes on the warpath. Finally one of the Cartwright boys stepped in a bowl of beans and fell flat on his face. His mother gave him a whack, and he ran off bawling. After that they settled down.

I sat by myself with my back against the schoolhouse wall, having an idea that Debbie was watching me and wanting me to sit with her. I suppose she had some sort of prior rights based on discovery, but I perversely withdrew from all of them.

I was sore about the whole business. Nothing made me madder than folks taking a holier-than-thou attitude. The more I thought about it, the more I was convinced that Mrs Allison had suggested the sermon topic to my father, knowing that the Hammond women would be there. Probably every wife along the lake was afraid of them.

I didn't want to admit it, but Cissy Hammond had got hold of me in a way I didn't like. It would be a long time before I forgot the way she'd rubbed up against me, and then held my hands, and smiled at me and asked me to come to see them. Maybe I would, I thought. I would if I wanted to. Being the preacher's boy wouldn't stop me.

We took a long time to eat. The women had supplied enough food for twice the people who were there: beans, fried duck, and a big beef roast that Mrs Cartwright had brought. Her husband came in for some joshing about the roast, several of the men asking if it was slow elk and Cartwright swearing it was venison, which we all knew it wasn't.

One of Jim Perrin's steers, I was sure, which

didn't make Cartwright's gossiping about the Hammond women look any better to me, although I knew there was no absolute standard by which an act could be judged. According to Cartwright's sense of morals, stealing from Jim Perrin wasn't a crime.

It seemed queer, after being so close to starving, that suddenly we had all we wanted to eat. Everybody had put himself out, and to make up for it I suppose there would be some slim meals for the next few days. But no one worried. It was an escape from loneliness, and all of them had a good time, saturating themselves in talk and laughter after a sterile winter.

One of the boys had brought a ball, and they got a game going behind the schoolhouse. Nolan asked me if I wanted to play, and I said no. He frowned and walked away, and I knew I was getting off on the wrong foot with all of them, but I didn't care. I kept thinking of the Hammond women, and the sourness grew in me until I was poisoned with it.

The girls got together at one corner of the schoolhouse, whispering and giggling. Debbie in the middle. They'd glance covertly at me and one of them would say something to Debbie, and they'd all giggle.

They could say and think what they wanted to for all of me. Then I got to wondering if Cissy Hammond ever came to their parties, and I decided she didn't. I made a resolve to bring her to one of them. I'd give these people a topic of conversation that would last them until Christmas.

Frank Allison put his plate down and rose. He said: 'We've got a little business to talk about before we light out for home and start the chores. I guess I don't need to say we're all mighty happy that we have a parson among us, and a mighty good one at that. Never heard stronger preaching of the Word than we had this morning, Brother Nathan.'

A lot of them shouted, 'Amen,' and nodded and smiled at my father. He stroked his beard, pleased with the praise and preening like a peacock. He said, 'I pray that I was guided by the Spirit to say something that will make better Christians of all of us.'

He was posing again, the humility gone from him. I thought: He's backslid. He's right where he was four days ago. I felt sick.

'We ought to have Bible study before church,' Frank went on. 'Maybe Brother Nathan can arrange it. I reckon we all need it, especially our young uns we've been neglecting something fierce since we've come to the valley. Let's get here about an hour earlier next Lord's Day.' He scratched his jaw. 'Now there's one more thing. We ain't had a house raising for a long time. The Nathans have their lumber, and I thought it'd be a good thing if we gave 'em a hand. We're all busy, but I figure we can take a day off without no hurt. We ain't in shape to

88

pay him any cash, but if Brother Nathan's willing to preach for us the least we can do is to help out.'

'You bet we can,' Matt Cartwright shouted. 'I'll be there by sunup.'

'Fetch a hunk of that venison of yourn,' Nolan called. 'It'd go good about noon.'

'I'll come and help Mrs Nathan,' Mrs Cartwright said. 'We'll see you're fed if you'll get their house and barn up.'

I thought of the Ferguson boys, but apparently no one else did. Our neighbors would do well to fetch their Winchesters, but because they knew the Fergusons better than I did I didn't think it was my business to mention it any more than it was my business to ask if the Hammond women would be welcome, come Sunday.

We broke up after that, but Mrs Cartwright remained to talk to my father about her five younger children who hadn't been baptized. She was fretful about one of them dying and being lost. She just couldn't bear it, she said, if one of her children went to hell when salvation could be had. My father said he would see about the lake. Maybe it was deep enough close to shore for baptizing. It would be attended to, some way, even if they had to go out into the lake a piece. Next Sunday he'd give the invitation.

Watching Mrs Cartwright, I thought of Liz Hammond saying that every woman was a

89

Bathsheba under the right circumstances, and then I looked up at the dried-up husk of a man she had for a husband, who wasn't above butchering one of Jim Perrin's steers, and I had a feeling my father was going to be tempted.

I sat beside Debbie when we drove home, but neither of us said a word. I had an idea she knew I'd talked to Cissy Hammond. Somehow Debbie seemed plain and a little dull, and I was ashamed of myself because I couldn't keep from comparing her to Cissy, who would have talked an ear off if she had been in the wagon with me, Cissy in her silk dress and the cartwheel hat with the purple plume and the perfume I could still smell.

When we reached our camp, I got down and Debbie said shyly, 'Come over and visit with us whenever you have time.'

'I will,' I said, not having the slightest intention of keeping my promise.

They drove away after a lot of 'Thank you' and 'What a wonderful, spiritual day it's been' and 'Goodbye.' Then my father looked at me, his great head thrown back. He said harshly, 'You didn't mix very well with the young people, Daniel.'

'Kids,' I said contemptuously. 'Boys playing ball and girls giggling like a bunch of fool geese.'

'Debbie is a fine girl,' he said. 'We're neighbors. It would be well if you paid her some attention.'

They'll force me into marrying her if I stay here, I thought wildly. They'll hammer at me from all sides.

I said: 'Sure, a fine girl. They're a fine lot, all of them, a smug, self-righteous bunch that'll steal Jim Perrin's beef and use the tallow to grease their runners so they can slide into Heaven.'

'Daniel,' my mother said reprovingly.

My father took a long breath, staring at me the way he often did when he couldn't understand the way I felt or the things I said. A little afraid of me, too. Then he shook his head. 'Don't judge, Daniel.'

'But you judged!' I cried. 'And they judged. Have you forgotten Mary Magdalene?'

My father looked at my mother helplessly. 'What's got into him?'

'The Hammond women,' she answered. 'Mrs Cartwright told Liz Hammond not to show her face in church again.'

My father stroked his beard, looking at me and then at my mother. Finally he said: 'I didn't know. That was wrong, even as bad as they are. I'll pray for them, and I'll go see them.'

'And have the Cartwrights gossiping about you,' I said. 'It won't do and you know it.'

'That's right,' my mother said. 'It won't do. They'd never let you preach to them again.'

'But I'll pray for them,' he said. 'I'll wrestle with the Devil for their souls. It may be the

91

Lord will work through them.'

Without another word he turned and walked toward the lake, his Bible under his arm. He sat down on the grass and stared out across the water. My mother sighed and, dropping down in the shade of the wagon, took Ben on her lap.

'I thought for a while this morning that he was going to change,' I said. 'Really change.'

She smiled a little. 'He has, Daniel. Someday you'll understand. This is the place he's been looking for. He will never dress me in silks and satins, but that isn't important. He'll give us a home and we'll have enough to eat.' She looked at him, her lips quivering. 'Hell purifies, Daniel. He would never admit it, but I know. Now he can be himself.'

Then, completely rebellious, I said, 'If Jim Perrin doesn't come for me, I'm going to him.'

She nodded as if she understood. 'You'll be nineteen in a couple of weeks, Daniel. You have to live your own life. I guess it's time you were starting.'

When I took the horses to water, my father was still sitting there at the edge of the lake, so lost in thought that he didn't see me. I was curious about what he was thinking. Perhaps of Mrs Cartwright, or Liz Hammond, who had sat directly in front of him. He must have smelled her perfume all through the service.

Then I remembered him saying that the Lord might work through the Hammond women. I puzzled over it, but I had no idea

92

what he had meant. The Lord, I thought, was scraping the bottom of the barrel if He had to use the Hammond women to accomplish His purposes.

CHAPTER SEVEN

The next morning was cloudy, daylight coming slowly, as if the sun was reluctant to drive darkness from the valley. The west wind was saturated with moisture, smelling strongly of sage. It had rained on the desert during the night, and it looked as if it would rain in the valley before noon. I was not sure Cartwright and Frank Allison and the rest would come. Perhaps their talk had been empty promises.

But they kept their word. The Cartwrights had the farthest to come, and they were the first to arrive, bringing a big chunk of beef with them. Then the Allisons, Debbie and her father. My mother would need help getting dinner for so many, Debbie said, and she wanted to help. She brought two prune pies with her, sweetened from their dwindling stock of brown sugar. She had made them herself, she said, speaking loudly enough for me to hear.

Other men arrived, all of them bringing their hammers and saws. Cartwright had a level. He took charge, bustling around like a terrier in a crowd of mastiffs. He picked out the site for the house a little north of the wagon, pointed to where the shed and corrals should be, then he drove his wagon up to where the house was to go and asked us to unload the four big rocks he had brought for the corners.

I liked Cartwright a little better after that. I had not thought about the rocks, although I knew the floor could not rest directly on the ground. If one of us had gone after the rocks, half the day would have been wasted, but Cartwright had foreseen that. I helped Frank Allison unload them, wondering how a little man like Matt Cartwright had been able to lift them into the wagon bed. Maybe his wife had helped him, a thought that weighed uneasily upon my mind.

Cartwright got us organized at once, hurrying around as busy as an undersized bull in a clover patch. My job was to rip some of the boards into narrow slats to cover the cracks in the walls. Within a matter of minutes we had a great clatter going, and Cartwright, overseeing the placing of the rocks, would call out: 'You're still a little high on your corner, Buck,' or, 'Frank, you dug too deep. We'll have to roll that rock out and throw in some dirt.'

Suddenly Frank Allison shouted, 'The Fergusons are coming,' and the racket stopped as suddenly as if Cartwright had given the order.

The Ferguson boys were still fifty yards to

the east, riding in at a gallop. I dropped my saw and ran to the wagon. No one had brought a gun, or at least none was in evidence, and as I reached inside the wagon for our Winchester I realized I should have mentioned the Fergusons the day before.

They were scared, or I should say we were, because I was as scared as anyone. I glanced at the women. Debbie's face was so pale that I thought she was going to faint, and even Mrs Cartwright, whose tongue had been wagging steadily, just stood there staring at the Fergusons as if she had lost the power to stir her mountain of flesh.

I moved around to the back of the wagon so that the Fergusons wouldn't see me. I had the smell of trouble in my nose, and although I didn't have much idea how far it would go I was convinced that the Fergusons would have our crew headed home in about a minute if I didn't get the drop on them.

The Ferguson boys reined up about twenty feet from the men who had bunched behind my father as if expecting him to make a stand. My mother, with Ben in her arms, stood with Mrs Cartwright and Debbie beside the fire. Ernie Ferguson leaned forward in his saddle, a hand gripping the horn, his dark eyes on my father.

'You son of a bitch,' Ernie said. 'I told you last week me and Carl would be over Monday morning to build your house. What'd you fetch these bastards in for?'

95

My father had never been one to face up to trouble. He always found ways to duck it, or let me handle it, but now he didn't look around for me. I was never more surprised in my life. He stood motionless, tall and square-shouldered, his long legs spread.

'If you can't keep a decent tongue in your head, Ferguson,' my father said evenly, 'get out of camp. We will not have that kind of talk before our women.'

Matt Cartwright stepped up beside my father, his puckered little face upturned to stare at Ernie. 'You heard Brother Nathan. We don't need your help. Get out.'

He had his share of guts, Matt Cartwright did. I was surprised at that, too. So was Ernie. He laughed, staring down at Cartwright. He said, 'You've been drinking rattlesnake milk, Matt. You want to be careful about that. It's plumb poison for a gent your size.'

The other night when I had found the Fergusons here, it had been dusk. Now, in daylight, I had the feeling I was looking at two gorillas. Carl's meaty lips were drawn away from his brown teeth. He said: 'Brother Nathan! You hear that, Ernie? Brother Nathan.'

'Yeah, I heard,' Ernie said. 'Well, Brother Nathan, we do the building hereabouts. You let these knuckleheads put up your house and it'll be down with the first strong wind. Now get 'em out of here and me'n Carl will

96

go to work.'

'No,' my father said, 'I told you I didn't have enough money to pay you.'

'This is a house raising,' Cartwright said. 'We ain't getting paid. We're just being neighborly. If you want to help, all right. If you don't, get out. We've got work to do.'

Ernie put a hand on the butt of his gun. 'I said we were doing this job. We'll get paid for it, too. Now drift, the whole kaboodle of you.'

No one moved; no one said anything. The only sounds were the heavy breathing of the men and Mrs Cartwright. Then I stepped away from the wagon and cocked the Winchester. The shocked expression on the Fergusons' faces when they looked at me made me want to laugh. I suppose I was almost hysterical. I wasn't any part of a hero and I knew it, but I had to act like one.

'Get out of camp,' I said. 'You pull that gun and I'll kill you.'

Ernie didn't say anything. I had my rifle lined on him, and I guess I looked wild enough to make him think I'd do what I said. Carl was the one who worried me. I had to keep my eyes on Ernie, so I couldn't watch Carl.

The more the seconds piled up, the more scared I was. My belly felt as if it held a cold stone and I thought my knees were going to buckle under me. Our wandering had brought us up against some tough men, but none quite like the Fergusons. Frank Allison had used the right words when he'd said they were 'animal mean.'

I was still watching Ernie, but I caught the movement of Carl's hand as it moved to his side and gripped the butt of his gun. He said: 'It's the Nathan pup, Ernie. Maybe I'd better plug him.'

'That won't save your brother's hide,' I said. 'I'm a good shot.'

'Maybe he is.' Ernie licked dry lips. 'This ain't the right day to find out.'

'Why, hell, Ernie...' Carl began.

'He's got that rifle on me, not you,' Ernie snapped. 'Let the bastards build their house. Let it fall in on 'em. Let the roof leak. Come on. We've got our own work to do.'

Ernie wheeled his horse and galloped down the ridge. Carl stared at me, and then he grinned. 'You stick around here, bucko,' he said, 'and we'll sure tangle.' Then he rode after Ernie.

I eased the hammer down and leaned against the wagon wheel. Suddenly I realized I was panting, and cold sweat had broken out all over me. Debbie walked toward me, her eyes wide. She said softly, 'Daniel, that's the bravest thing I ever saw.'

I leaned the rifle against the wheel. I said, 'I don't feel brave.'

The rest of them nodded, and I knew that as far as they were concerned I was a man and not a boy. Perhaps they understood why I hadn't wanted to play ball the day before. None of us had noticed Jim Perrin. We had been too preoccupied with the Fergusons to see him ride up.

Now Perrin said: 'You did a better job than you know, Danny, but the Fergusons are tough boys. You'll need to watch them.'

'I didn't hear you ride up, Mr Perrin,' I said.

He stood holding the reins of his sorrel, smiling as if pleased by what he had seen. A buckskin stood behind him, a long canvas-wrapped package tied across the saddle. Mrs Cartwright let out a scream, said, 'Perrin,' and fainted.

'My God!' Cartwright cried, and ran to her.

Perrin shook his head, the smile dying. 'I should have hollered, but I wanted to see if anybody was man enough to stand up to the Fergusons. It's time somebody did.'

My mother and Debbie were fanning Mrs Cartwright, and her husband held her hands and kept saying, 'Melissa, Melissa, you *can't* die.'

She came out of it a moment later and sat up. 'I'm ashamed,' she whispered. 'I haven't fainted for twenty years. I sure am ashamed.'

'It was enough to make anyone faint,' my mother said. 'I don't know why I didn't.'

Debbie, her face still pale, said, 'I don't know why I didn't, either.'

Perrin had moved back to the buckskin, leaving the reins of the sorrel dangling. He

99

untied the package and brought it to my mother. 'We butchered Saturday, and since I was coming over anyhow I thought maybe you could use a quarter. I didn't know you folks were having a house raising, but I guess I couldn't have picked a better time to bring it.'

He didn't know, I thought, that the Cartwrights had brought another piece of beef that he had raised. My father was standing now. He said courteously: 'Thank you, Mr Perrin. We're beholden to you.'

'Not at all,' Perrin said. 'I came to get Danny if he wants the job I promised, but if you need him—'

'We can get along,' my mother interrupted. 'He wants to work for you more than anything else in the world. We won't keep him from doing what he wants to do.'

Perrin glanced at me, the smile returning to his lips. 'That's queer, Mrs Nathan, because he'll have hard work and small pay, but if it's what he wants I guess he ought to have his chance.'

Debbie was staring at me, open-mouthed. She cried out, 'Daniel, you can't ...'

'I can,' I said.

I kissed my mother on the cheek and patted Ben on the head and walked away, saying nothing to my father. I had to get away. I knew what they were all thinking, but I didn't care. Perhaps I would never belong to my family again, or to the settlers who were my people.

Then I knew they weren't really my people. Well, I didn't care, one way or the other. I kept telling myself that. I didn't care. This was what I wanted. Jim Perrin had kept his promise. I didn't need to beat down my pride and go to him.

I stood beside the sorrel, my back to the others. A moment later Perrin came to me. He said, 'The buckskin and saddle are yours, Danny.'

'I'll pay—'

'I'm giving them to you. Forget the pay. It's a small thing for me to do in return for what you did for me.'

I had not given much thought to saving his life on Virgil Lang's porch, but now I understood. I said, 'I didn't do—'

'Danny, it isn't anything to talk about, so let's not talk about it.' He stepped into the saddle. 'Climb up and we'll ride.'

I walked to the buckskin, a close-coupled young gelding that looked as if he had all the stamina in the world. The saddle was new, a center-fire California rig, handsomely decorated with an impressed design of leaves and flowers. I ran my hand over the leather, knowing it had cost fifty dollars or more, a far better saddle than I had ever dreamed of owning.

'Climb aboard,' Perrin said, a little impatient now.

I had put my foot in the stirrup and swung

101

up, when I heard my father call, 'Mr Perrin.'

I looked at him, my hand clutching the reins so tightly that the leather bit into my palm. He had his head back, posing again, and I remembered my mother saying the evening before that now he could be himself. She had been wrong, at least in part.

'Well?' Perrin asked, his tone sharp-edged.

My father stared at him, not nearly as pretentious and important-looking as he wanted to appear. He couldn't quite maintain his swagger when he had to tip his head back to look at a man on horseback. Not when he was talking to Jim Perrin, who at that moment seemed very formidable.

'I wanted to tell you that my son is not yet twenty-one,' my father said. 'Until he is, his wages belong to me.'

I could have struck him then. He wasn't trusting me, and he had to let Jim Perrin know. But worse than that was the unmistakable fact that he hadn't changed. For days now I had been pulled and hauled between dislike for my father that was based on his laziness and futility, and the natural hope that at last he would justify my mother's faith in him.

'I'll bring my wages to Ma,' I said, my tone sapping some of the importance out of him.

'That's fine, Danny,' Perrin said. 'As for you, Nathan, I wish I had brought my spyglasses. You're so small I can't rightly see you without them.'

He swung his sorrel and rode south. I caught up with him and came alongside, my face red. I was more ashamed of my father than I had ever been, but I owed him one thing. Now I had no regrets about leaving.

Only a moment before I had been forced to reassure myself by mentally declaring my independence, by telling myself I didn't care what anybody thought. Now I really didn't. I was just glad to get away from them. My father had cut my ties as effectively as if he had literally slashed them with a knife.

Perrin angled southwest toward the gap in the hills that marked Thunder River. Then, after a long silence, he glanced at me, his face grave. He said: 'In spite of anything you've heard, Danny, I want you to know that I will not do anything to hurt the settlers. Of course, that includes your folks. In fact, I'd like to be neighborly; but most of them hate me, and all of them are suspicious of me, so it seems better to let them alone.'

'Why do they feel like that?' I asked, knowing the answer to my question, but not sure that Perrin would meet it squarely.

'Several reasons,' he said. 'One is the lies that Lang tells them. He's a coward, so he tries to use other people to do something he's not man enough to do. And I suppose it's just human nature for people who have never succeeded at anything to hate a man who has.' He glanced at me again, adding apologetically, 'I don't mean to insult your father, but if a man has been successful he doesn't come here looking for something for nothing.'

I thought of saying that a man wasn't always to blame for past failures, but I didn't want to argue with Perrin, and as far as my father was concerned Perrin was right. Instead I said: 'There's another reason. They're afraid you'll take their land.'

'They have reason to be afraid of that,' he said quickly. 'They have all been warned. Until the court decides who owns the marginal land, I won't do anything to make them move. It's possible they may live there for years, but when they do have to go it will be a tragic day.'

Perrin had been fair, I thought, and if Virgil Lang had not been trying to strike at him he would have told the settlers to make their homes north of the lake. I could not in any way blame Perrin, and I was sure he was sincere in saying he would like to be neighborly. Bringing the quarter of beef to my folks was proof enough of that. Still, the idea that a man could not choose both God and mammon was rooted strongly in my mind.

Without thinking of how it might strike Perrin, I said: 'Why don't you let them have the land? I mean, it's not a case of you really needing it, is it?'

He gave me a sharp look, apparently surprised by my question, and perhaps not sure in his mind whether I was condemning him or not. He said: 'No, I don't need it, Danny. Not the way you mean, and I suppose that's the way they look at it. In fact, men who don't have anything always raise that argument when they are struggling with a man who does have something.'

Perrin frowned, his eyes on the long sweep of the grass in front of him. I had the feeling he had debated the issue in his mind many times. Suddenly he motioned toward a set of ranch buildings to our left, set at the base of the hills.

'That's what I call my Valley Ranch,' Perrin said. 'It works better to have several divisions. J Ranch is in the middle. I'm very proud of what I have accomplished in the six years I've been here. I was twenty-one when I drove my first herd to Thunder River. I've spent a good deal of money buying men out who had nothing to sell except their squatter's rights. I have offered to buy out the settlers on the marginal land. Not that I owe them a nickel. It's just simpler in the long run to do it that way.'

He glanced at me again as if measuring my reaction to what he had said. It was rather strange, I thought, that he wanted me to understand. After all, I was a boy who wanted to work for him, and he was doing me a favor by giving me a job. Bringing me a horse and saddle was more than a favor, and I was sorry I had raised the question.

'I think it's natural for a man to take pride in

his accomplishments,' Perrin went on. 'Little or big, it's still natural. You have every right to be proud of what you did at Lang's the other afternoon. Regardless of what my life is worth, it was something to be proud of because it took courage and quick thinking. It was the same with the Fergusons just now. The rest stood around like a band of sheep, but you did something. That's the way it is with me. I've done something and I'm proud of it.'

With most men it would have been bragging; with Jim Perrin it was a simple statement of fact. I was more embarrassed than ever. I thought of how my father had posed and strutted when he had never done anything worth while that I could remember, but Jim Perrin didn't need to strut and pose.

'I'm sorry—' I began.

'Never apologize, Danny.' Perrin laughed softly. 'I wouldn't apologize to anyone. Someone said your friends don't need apologies and your enemies won't believe you. I'm talking this way because I want you to understand how I feel. I hope we'll be working together for a long time, and if we do we might as well start off being honest with each other.'

My throat closed up on me. I had been a damned fool to ask why he didn't give the marginal land away, but I couldn't put my tongue on the words that would tell him.

'There's just one thing you need to understand about a country like this, Danny,'

Perrin went on. 'We're a hell of a long ways from a railroad. I suppose in time a railroad will be built into the valley, but it will be another fifty years. Meanwhile the little man doesn't have a chance to make a go of it. A country like this calls for a big operation. I've done well. So has Clark Pritchard on the other side of Garnet Mountain with his Rainbow, and Barney O'Hara who's west of us. He has the Box O. There are a few more outfits around, but we're the biggest.'

It was reasonable, I thought, and I nodded agreement. Men like Perrin and the others he had mentioned weren't worrying about their next meal; they weren't depending on Virgil Lang to see them through until their crops were harvested—if they ever had crops they could harvest.

'What I'm getting around to saying is this,' Perrin said. 'Law should protect both a man's person and his property. I have never taken anything that didn't belong to me, and I haven't asked a man for something that belonged to him. As far as the marginal land goes, I'll take the court decision when it comes. I won't fight for it if it isn't mine, but if it is I certainly won't give it away. That's fair, isn't it?'

'Sure,' I said quickly. 'I didn't mean—'

'I know, but like I said, I want you to understand. The time may come when you can save all of us a lot of trouble and maybe

107

bloodshed. For the sake of the settlers, I hope they will sell to me and move out, or go to work for me. I've offered them jobs, which they won't take. But if they stay, they're only building up to a terrible disappointment. They can't win. Maybe Virgil Lang will, but the settlers won't.'

He laughed ruefully. 'I was crazy to go to Lang the other day. I knew I couldn't change things, and my threats don't really amount to much. Some of my friends—O'Hara, for instance—talk about violence; but that isn't the answer to our problem, so we'll just have to go along like we have. I've overlooked some things that perhaps I shouldn't, but it seems better to try to get along.'

I knew what he meant. I sensed that he was a lonely man, hated even when he offered friendship, hated for no good reason.

We rode in silence then. Presently we reached Thunder River, a swift, clear stream flowing between walls of willows, and we turned south along it. The sage-covered hills closed in, the river cutting a narrow passage between them, and then the valley widened, with a mile or more of meadow on both sides. Here and there haystacks made brown dots against the green grass, hay that would be carried over for winter which might be more severe than the last.

Near noon we came to J Ranch. I had expected to see something big, but not that big.

A huge barn, a number of outbuildings, and innumerable corrals. I had never seen anything like the corrals. They were built by setting juniper posts taller than a man's head close together in pairs and threading willows between them which were tied in place by leather thongs. Later I heard they were called stockade corrals, and were peculiar to this country.

But it was the ranch house that caught my attention, a huge, two-storied structure that was painted white. A row of young poplars stood along one side of it. The yard between the trees and the house was covered with grass. Everything about the place was clean and attractive, contrasting sharply with other ranches I had seen. Most cattlemen cared little either about grass around the house or about paint on its walls, but Jim Perrin wasn't like most cattlemen.

I think he got pleasure out of the surprise which I must have shown in my face. He said with the quiet pride characteristic of him, 'We lived in a willow shelter the first winter, with a brush roof covered with clay.' He shrugged. 'Well, we didn't freeze, but it wasn't my idea of a headquarters; so when we built, we built for a long time ahead. I expect to spend a lifetime here, Danny.'

We put our horses in a corral. Then he said: 'Come into the house. Wang will have dinner ready. I caught some trout last night.' He glanced sideways at me. 'You know, Danny, it isn't right for mortal man to live as near to Heaven as I do. Sometimes I think it's too good to last.'

He swung toward the house, his face troubled, and I wondered what was in his mind. I said, 'A man makes his heaven or his hell.'

'That's right, but not many men ever find it out. When we came here, I had pictured in my mind what I expected to find, and I found it. I like to fish, and here they are, right in front of my door.' He laughed, the troubled expression gone. 'I remember that I rode on ahead of the herd with Pedro García. I was planning then where to build my house, but Pedro had gone down to the river. He yelled at me, "*El río*, she is full of fish." After six years, it's still full of fish.'

We walked between two young poplars and went up the path to the front door. Perrin opened the door and stood aside for me to go in. I took two steps into the big living room and stopped, for I had been used to only the most primitive kind of living, and here was luxury beyond anything I had imagined.

A big fireplace took up most of the north wall. A hot iron had burned the J brand a dozen times across the edge of the mantel. My feet seemed buried in the high-piled Brussels carpet. The room was filled with expensive furniture; walnut chairs and velvet-covered love seats and a massive leather couch. A marble-topped table stood in the middle of the room.

I suppose I remained there a full minute, drinking the magnificence in, not sure it was real. I had never seen a room like it; I had never thought there was such a room outside a city. Then I saw the picture of a girl above the fireplace, glass-covered and bordered by an ornate gilt frame. As if drawn by some hypnotic influence, I walked toward it.

She was beautiful. That was my first impression. Her eyes were wide-set above a nose that had just a hint of a pug tip; her lips were full and rich, her chin wide and dimpled. As I looked at the picture, I sensed something in her face that was more important than beauty, a strong face filled with vitality and sheer love of living. Then, quite suddenly, it came to me. The girl had what my mother called 'greatness of spirit.'

'I built this house for her,' Perrin said in a low voice. 'I furnished it for her. Will she like it, Danny?'

I hadn't realized he was standing beside me. Now I glanced at him, surprised at the tension that was in him. I said: 'Of course she will. If she doesn't ...'

'We're getting married this fall,' Perrin said. 'I've been putting it off because of the Indian scare, and, well, it just seemed like there was so much work to do I could never get away.' He took a long breath. 'She's got blue eyes and red hair. Her name is Shamrock O'Toole, and she's as Irish as Dublin; but she'll slit your throat if you call her Irish, so I call her Rocky.'

I only half heard. I could not take my eyes from the picture. I think that was the moment when I fell in love with the girl who was to be Jim Perrin's wife.

CHAPTER EIGHT

After dinner Perrin took me to the ranch store and introduced me to Alec Brown, a middle-aged man who had a soft voice and friendly gray eyes that were almost hidden under the canopy of his massive black brows. He had a wooden leg. Perrin later told me that Brown had lost his right leg three years before when his horse had fallen under him.

They had taken him to the army post in a jolting wagon. The sheer agony of the ride must have come close to killing him, but he had survived both the ride and the operation, and Perrin had given him the job of running the store.

'Give him a change of everything, Alec.' Perrin nodded at me. 'Let him burn your old clothes, Danny. I'd say you just about had your money's worth out of them.'

He left then, leaving me standing there

feeling like a beggar. Alec looked me over, clucking the way a setting hen does when she's worried about something. Finally he said: 'Well, sir, you're a long drink of water if I ever seen one. Looks to me like you ain't been eating real well lately.'

I wanted to tell him that there had been damn' few times in my life when I had eaten well. But I didn't. He was a kindly man, and there was no sense in getting started on the wrong foot with him, so I said, 'No, I haven't.'

'I can fit you for length, but you'll have to fill out a mite. Ain't nobody on J Ranch as skinny as you are.' He brought underclothes, pants, shirt, and socks, and laid them on the counter. 'Let's see how good a fit these are, son.'

'I'll take them to the bunkhouse—' I began.

'Son,' Alec said, 'there ain't a woman within ten miles o' J Ranch, and there won't be till Jim fetches his bride here. So take 'em off, hod dang it!'

I obeyed, wondering if there had ever been a time before in my life when I'd had new clothes from the skin out. When I was completely naked, Alec shook his head again, and made the funny clucking sound.

'Never saw so many ribs in my life,' he said, 'except four years ago when we had a tough winter. Every cow we had looked like you, but they fattened up come spring. Reckon you will, too, after a month or so on Sam Boon's cooking.'

113

I was just a maverick to Alec Brown, I thought, a stray that Jim Perrin had brought in off the range. As I put on the new clothes, I said, 'I'll pay for these some day, if you're worrying.'

'I ain't.' Alec hobbled around the counter and picked up my discarded clothes. 'I let Jim do all the worrying. He don't make nothing on what he sells. Just figures to get his money back. You don't need to worry, neither. Half the boys are in debt to him.' He looked at my shirt where my mother had patched the patches so many times that there was almost nothing left of the original cloth. 'Yes, sir, you got your money's worth out o' them duds, all right.'

He carried my clothes into a back room, and when he returned I had finished dressing. He looked me over, nodding as if satisfied. 'You'll be quite a man when you get some meat on your bones.' He laid out a change of clothes, then pointed to a shelf of hats. 'Try 'em on. I never guess on the size of a man's head.'

It took time to find a hat that fitted me, more time to find a pair of boots, and when I walked to the counter to pick up my change of clothes I felt as if the floor was coming up to meet me with each step. My old boots had been as worn as my shirt, the heels run down until they were hardly heels at all.

I piled the shirt on the pants and the undershirt, the drawers on the shirt, and then the socks. I looked at Alec, hesitated, and then

114

blurted, 'I want a gun.'

'Now ain't that like a younker?' Alec scratched his head. 'Well, I've got a Colt .44 and a belt you might as well have. Belonged to a gent who left in a hurry last fall. Rolly Dillon wants it, but he's the kind who oughtn't never to have a gun.' He waggled a finger at me. 'But don't figure on packing it, son. There's two things Jim don't like for a man to have when he's working. Whisky's one. A gun's the other.'

He must have thought I was the harmless kind. He hobbled into the back room and returned with the gun and belt. The fellow who had left in a hurry had been a gun slinger, judging by the stiff cut-away holster and filed-down front sight of the Colt. The loops of the belt were filled, but the gun was empty. I checked the action, almost bursting with the pride of ownership.

Alec said: 'There's times when a man needs a gun. We've got a few rattlesnakes hereabouts, crawling ones and two-legged ones. Trouble with the two-legged ones is that a man can get himself killed trying to stomp 'em. You ever handle a six?'

'No,' I said as I thumbed five shells into the cylinder, leaving an empty under the hammer.

'Jim's right handy with a gun,' Alec said, 'but don't ask him to teach you how to use it. Just wait till you know Lane Sears pretty well, then ask him. Lane's the foreman, and he don't like to have a man on the pay roll who can't defend himself.'

'Thanks,' I said, laying the belt and gun on the clothes, and left the store.

The bunkhouse was empty when I went in, but I found a corner bunk that apparently wasn't used. I dropped my bundle on it, slipping the gun into the holster and hiding the belt between the shirt and the pants.

Perrin was working on a drainage ditch between the barn and the river. I found a shovel in the barn and crossed the meadow to him. When I reached him, he said, 'I guess you feel a little awkward in those boots.'

'They'll break in,' I said, and wondered if I'd ever have enough money to buy a pair like his.

He looked across the meadow, wiping his face with a red bandanna. 'Danny,' he said, 'if you've got the idea some boys have that working on a ranch is a picnic, get it out of your head. My men aren't above building fences or breaking their backs keeping the ditches open.' He made a sweeping gesture that included all the meadow. 'This was marsh when we came, and it'll go back to marsh if we don't keep working at it.'

'I've worked on ranches before,' I said. 'I didn't ask you for a job because I thought I'd have a picnic.'

'Good.' He nodded approvingly. 'Always something to do. More marsh to reclaim.' He motioned toward the ridge east of the house. 'Fences to build.' He jabbed a forefinger at the nearest haystack. 'Hay to put up. Working on J Ranch is more than riding and branding calves and driving a herd to the railroad.'

He went back to work. I learned something about Jim Perrin that afternoon. He demanded much from his men, but no more than he demanded from himself, and he never asked a man to do a job he could not or would not do himself. Jim Perrin was no aristocrat of the saddle, and that, I thought, was one reason he had made the success he had.

We quit near sundown and walked back across the meadow. The crew had already ridden in, and by the time we reached the corrals the men had put their horses away and were washing up in front of the cookshack. As I crossed the dusty yard with Perrin, the cook came out and began beating the triangle with lusty strokes.

Perrin introduced me to the crew, beginning with the foreman, Lane Sears, a tall man with the longest, droopiest mustache I had ever seen. His blue eyes were very pale, bleached, I suppose, by years of being out in the sun and wind, and his skin was so darkly tanned that it seemed as if the mahogany hue must go right on into the muscle and bone of his long body.

Sears shook hands with me, a slow grin coming to lips that were almost hidden by his huge mustache. He said, 'Glad to meet you, Dan,' in a friendly voice. He wasn't one to bully his men, and I had the impression he was

117

a mild, slow-tempered man. It seemed inconceivable he was an expert with a gun.

We went on down the line of men, several of them swarthy-faced vaqueros who had come north with Perrin six years ago. One was Pedro García, the man who had scared Virgil Lang out of the country simply by drawing a knife. They were all friendly, all but the heavy-set, scowling man at the end of the line who wasn't much older than I was.

'Danny, meet Rolly Dillon,' Perrin said. 'He came up the trail with us when he was just a kid.'

Dillon made no effort to shake hands. He stared at me as if resenting my being there, and I felt like a fool, standing with my hand extended. I dropped it, sensing his enmity. There was no reason for it. We had never seen each other before, but he hated me. I could see it in the ugly curl of his mouth, in the wicked expression of his green eyes.

There was a moment of uneasy silence, with all the men looking at Dillon. He liked that, I thought. Suddenly I was angry. I suppose I was hurt as much as anything, for in that one instant Dillon had destroyed something which was very precious. I had felt that these men would be my friends, that I was being welcomed to J Ranch, and now Rolly Dillon was pushing me out of the circle.

I started to turn away when he said, 'You don't think you'll ever make a buckaroo out of this nester kid, do you, Jim?'

It was the way he said it, more than what he actually said. With that question, asked in a contemptuous tone, Dillon had shoved me across the line, cutting me off from the fraternity into which I was being welcomed, and making the settlers I had left that morning my people. And I had been foolish enough to think they were not my people, that this was where I belonged.

Perrin started to say something, but I have no idea what it was. I didn't let him say it. I turned on them. 'I thought this outfit was different, but it isn't. Every spread I've worked for had somebody like Dillon I had to lick. Then they'd bring out an outlaw horse I was supposed to ride. All right, go saddle your horse!'

Dillon let out a whoop as I whirled back to him. 'Lick me, are you—' Then I hit him. I guess I was a little crazy, and sick because I blamed Perrin and was disillusioned about him. Anyhow, I was beyond thinking. All I wanted to do was to fight Dillon and beat him.

He was heavier than I was, and stronger, but I had considerable reach on him. More than that, he had no real reason to fight. I did. If I let him whip me, I'd have to saddle up the gelding Perrin had given me and ride back to the lake.

Dillon couldn't have stopped me unless he'd knocked me cold. I rocked his head with a right and then a left, and I caught him squarely on

119

the nose with the third blow. He was swinging all the time, but his punches were short.

I hurt him. Blood burst out of his nose in a gush. Then he lunged at me, his arms outstretched, trying to get me by the legs and drag me down so he could use his greater strength and weight. I rammed my knee up into his face, and I had a brutal sense of satisfaction when I heard the crack of the blow and the sound of his teeth snapping together.

He went down on his face, soddenly. He must have been knocked out, or close to it. Perrin's voice came to me, 'He's done, Danny.' But it was too late to stop me with words, and no one tried to hold me. I suppose they thought I'd quit, but I wanted to kill him. I picked him up and threw him against the side of the cookshack. He hit full length and bounced off and lay still. Even then I would have jumped on him and kept beating him if Perrin hadn't grabbed me by the arm and shook me. Lane Sears got me by the other arm.

Perrin shouted, 'All right, Danny, *all right!* He's done fighting.'

Sears said, 'Go over to the pump and wash up.'

I rubbed a hand across my face. I was sweating, and now I began to tremble. Someone, García, I think, pumped a pan of water and threw it on Dillon's face. I walked over to the pump, and when the pan was back on the bench I filled it and washed. By the time

120

I had dried on the roller towel, Dillon was sitting up and wiping a sleeve across his bloody nose.

'If'n you don't come in here,' the cook yelled from the doorway, 'I'll throw it out.'

We filed in, leaving Dillon sitting there, his eyes still glazed. We sat down, Perrin with us, and began to eat. Afterward I learned that Perrin usually ate by himself in the house, but tonight I suppose he thought he had better stay with us.

No one paid any attention to me. Presently Dillon came in and found a place at the other end of the long table from me. When we were done, we drifted outside, most of the men going into the bunkhouse.

I walked across the yard to a corral and stood there by the gate, my stomach feeling as if it were full of rocks. Perrin had gone into the house. Then I was aware that Lane Sears stood beside me.

'We don't have an outlaw horse to ride, Dan,' he said gently. 'Jim don't keep outlaws on J Ranch. He's a good man to work for—the best there is—but he don't like hot tempers and he don't like fights.'

'What was I supposed to do?' I said. I still felt that Perrin was to blame. 'Dillon had no cause—'

'I know,' Sears said, 'but you didn't give Jim time to handle it. He would have, if you'd let him.'

I had been wrong, I thought. Then I remembered the gun, and what Brown had said about two-legged rattlesnakes, and I wondered if he had meant Rolly Dillon. I said, 'I got a .44 from Alec Brown, but I've never carried a gun. He said you'd show me how to use it.'

Sears was silent for a full minute. He brushed his mustache absently, as if thinking about something that had happened a long time ago. Finally he asked, 'And why do you think you'll need a gun on J Ranch?'

'I've had trouble with the Fergusons,' I said.

He nodded as if not surprised. 'Everybody except Rolly Dillon has trouble with the Fergusons. All right, I'll teach you how to handle a gun, but not here. Jim figures that guns, like whisky, just make trouble. But I'll show you. It'll have to wait, though. We'll be starting spring roundup in a few days.'

He walked away and left me standing there. The sun was down, the last of its light on the very top point of Garnet Mountain, and dusk was a lavender curtain that was being drawn across the valley. I turned around and walked to the bunkhouse.

I expected to be fired. Perrin ran his ranch and his crew, and he wouldn't stand for anyone getting out of line. If I had waited a few seconds ... Then I reached the bunkhouse door. Dillon was sitting on the corner bunk where I had left my clothes. He had thrown them onto the floor and was holding my .44, the belt on the bunk

122

beside him. He was looking at the gun, but I'm sure he knew I was there.

'Lane, I want you to tell me something,' Dillon said. 'Alec's had Mason's gun ever since Jim ran him off the ranch. Why did he give it to this God-damned nester kid when he knew I wanted it?'

I started for Dillon, and we would have picked the fight up again if García hadn't got in front of me. Sears yelled: 'Stay where you are, Rolly! We've had all the ruckusing we're going to have for tonight. Now, pick up Danny's clothes.'

Dillon looked at me and laughed. 'Sure, I'll pick 'em up.' He reached down and grabbed my clean shirt and threw it past me into the yard.

'You're acting like a damned fool,' Sears said.

He shoved Dillon back onto the bunk, took the gun away from him, and slapped him across the face. He picked up the belt, jerking his head at me. 'Gather up your duds, Dan.'

For a moment I stood looking at Dillon, who was grinning at me, a little lopsided, for one side of his mouth was bruised. This is just the beginning, I thought. It was the same as it had been with the Fergusons. I'd made another enemy.

I left the bunkhouse, picked up my shirt, and walked across the yard to the house. Sears fell in beside me, and when he reached the poplars he said: 'Here, take your gun belt. Alec done right giving it to you, but I ain't sure Jim will savvy. Put your shirt on top of it.'

I obeyed. When we went into the house, the gun belt was hidden. Perrin was squatting in front of the fireplace whittling some shavings. He looked around when he heard us, and rose. Sears said to me, 'Sit down,' and crossed the big room to Perrin, his boots silent on the thick rug.

I dropped into a leather chair, holding my pile of clothes on my lap. Sears said something to Perrin in a low voice. Perrin was facing me, but I could see no change of expression on his face. Sears said, raising his voice: 'You've got to fire him, Jim. He's no good. He hasn't been since his dad cashed in.'

'I can't fire him,' Perrin said. 'You know that, Lane. We might be able to do something for him as long as we keep him, but we can't if we let him go, and you know what will happen.'

He walked out of the room, telling me to stay where I was. Sears followed, shaking his head. Perrin was gone about ten minutes. When he came back, he didn't mention Dillon. Instead, he asked, 'You've been raised to take care of yourself, haven't you, Danny?'

'I guess I have,' I answered.

'Your father has a good education, hasn't he?'

'Yes.'

Perrin walked across the room to the fireplace, but he didn't light the fire he had started to build. He stood there, his head tilted back, looking at the picture of the girl he was going to marry. Then he reached for his pipe that was on the mantel and filled it and turned around.

'Strikes me that somewhere between jobs you've picked up a good deal of your father's education,' Perrin said.

I nodded, having no idea what he was driving at. Perrin lighted his pipe. He said: 'You're going to sleep upstairs. There's an extra room beside mine. My office is up there, too. It'll be handy. I've been thinking about this ever since I met you at Lang's the other day. I'll need help with my bookkeeping. That's one part of ranching I don't like.'

Then I knew what he had in mind. For some reason he couldn't get rid of Rolly Dillon, and he felt an obligation to me, too. This was his way of keeping peace. But in all the time I lived on J Ranch, I never once worked on Jim Perrin's books.

CHAPTER NINE

I had never worked as hard in my life as I did during spring roundup, and I had never enjoyed myself as much. We started at Giant

Springs Ranch, which was at the south end of the valley. Perrin divided us into two crews, one to work the hills and desert to the west, the other Garnet Mountain on the east.

Lane Sears ran the west outfit, Perrin the Garnet Mountain crew. Rolly Dillon was with Sears and I was with Perrin, so we didn't see each other until we finished roundup at the Valley Ranch. I suppose Perrin thought we'd forget our trouble, so he had purposely arranged it that way.

I'd have been glad to forget it, but I was sure Dillon wouldn't. Because no one said anything about it, when Sears's crew finished its side of the valley and joined us at Valley Ranch I still had no idea why Dillon felt the way he did.

I saw him that night, our eyes meeting across the campfire, and I knew I was right. Dillon would never forget, and I was depressed by the feeling that the day would come when I would have to kill Rolly Dillon or he would kill me.

As far as the work was concerned, it was no different from other roundups I had been on. We worked the daylight hours, we never had enough sleep, we were never rested. The weather turned hot, and the cattle began drifting higher up on the shoulders of the mountain. We had to search every gorge, every brush thicket. Around the branding fire it was the same as it was at all branding fires: stamp irons glowing in the coals, the constant bawling of cows and calves, ear marking, the

126

sizzling hair and burning hide as the stamp iron, cherry red, was slapped onto the calf's flank, and dust everywhere.

No, the work was no different than it had been on other ranches, but there was a world of difference in the feeling inside me. Always before, every job had been temporary, but now I belonged. Perrin would find other work for me when the roundup was over. I was sure of that the night he showed me the room in the big house where I was to sleep. I was still sure of it the day we finished roundup.

I liked every man in our mountain crew from big Pedro García with the soft voice that seemed strange coming from so huge a man on down to little bald-headed Ole Larsen who did the cooking for us. They found out the first day I could do everything that was expected of me reasonably well. If I made a mistake, Pedro or Perrin pointed it out. No scolding, no ridiculing, just the mild-voiced advice of expert buckaroos to a new hand who still had a few things to learn.

Rolly Dillon seemed entirely out of place in Jim Perrin's outfit. I wondered about it and found no answer except what Perrin had told Sears that first night in the big house, that he couldn't fire Dillon.

There was something else that worried me— the strange, violent fury I had experienced when I'd fought Rolly Dillon. I hadn't known I was capable of feeling it. I thought about it

127

often when I crawled into my blankets at night, bone-tired. I had not been scared as I had the time I had held the Winchester on the Ferguson boys. The only feeling I could remember distinctly was my crazy desire to kill Rolly Dillon.

I tried to analyze the reason for it. There was an inherent violence in the land itself. Perhaps it had taken hold of me. Or perhaps it was Perrin and the fear I would lose the thing I had dreamed about so long and just attained, a job on J Ranch. Or maybe it was because I had cut myself off from my family. I could not, under any circumstances, go back to my father.

The answer, I decided, must be a combination of all these things, but the answer, in itself, was not important. The fact that I had been possessed by an unreasoning, killing rage was. I remembered clearly that after I had picked Dillon up and thrown him against the side of the building and he lay on the ground, knocked cold, I had wanted to jump onto him, to drive the last bit of life from his body.

More than once during that month I woke up at night, tormented by the thought that I might have killed a man I had never seen before. Then I would stare at the stars that my father had called 'God's lamps,' and wonder what sort of man I was going to be. But when I saw Dillon again and met his calculating stare, I felt the month-old tension go out of me. If I ever killed Rolly Dillon, it would be because it was forced upon me.

At noon on the last day of roundup, Perrin called me away from the others. He said: 'This is Saturday. I guess that makes tomorrow Sunday.'

'It ought to,' I agreed.

He gave me that quick boyish grin which came so naturally to him. 'You haven't been to church since you started working for me. Maybe you ought to go in the morning.'

'I'd like to,' I said.

He handed three five-dollar gold pieces to me. 'You're making thirty a month and found. I'll take out half of it for your clothes until you're squared up. If you want to, get a pair of pants from the store that you think would fit your father.'

'He could use a new pair,' I said.

'Now there's something I want you to do for me, Danny. You don't have to. I mean, it isn't part of your job. It's just a favor. I'll start haying right after the Fourth and I need a hay crew. You see if some of the settlers will work for me. There isn't a man on the lake who couldn't use the money, but if I asked them I'd make them mad and they'd turn me down.'

He was right about that. The settlers had listened to Virgil Lang too long. 'I'll ask them,' I said, 'but I don't think they'll listen to me, either.'

'Give it a try,' he said. 'Tell them they'll be working under Lane, not me. Now you hike

129

out for J Ranch. Have Alec give you a haircut. Take a bath in the river and put on your clean clothes.' He grinned. 'We sure look like a tough crew.'

I saddled my buckskin and headed south, saying nothing to the men, who watched me with curious eyes. I cleaned up when I got to the ranch. Alec gave me a haircut, and admitted he was the barber of the crew.

'I ain't no expert,' he said, 'but I make out. Not much an old has-been like me is good for except tending store and barbering.' He cleared his throat. 'How'd you and Rolly get along?'

'All right. I didn't see him until last night.' I hesitated, then decided I'd never find out about Dillon if I didn't ask. 'Why did he jump me that night, Alec?'

He snipped away for a while, then said: 'Well, as near as I can figure out, he was jealous. You see, him and his dad came north with Jim when he made his first drive. Rolly was fourteen then, but he was 'bout as big as he is now. A good hand with horses, Rolly was. Still is. Anyhow, he was the kid of the outfit and I reckon we spoiled him.'

Alec kept on snipping at my hair, thinking about what had happened, I guess. Finally he went on. 'Well, a couple of years ago Rolly's dad got killed on a drive to Winnemucca. They had a stampede one night, and I reckon his horse fell with him. Anyhow, when they picked

130

him up they couldn't find enough to bury. Since then Jim's figured he had to keep Rolly on and look out for him. But Lane, hell, he'd have kicked the seat of Rolly's pants off J Ranch a year ago if he had his druthers about it.'

I still didn't understand why Dillon had picked on me, a stranger he had never laid eyes on before, so I asked the question again. Alec said: 'I told you he's jealous. Didn't want another young feller around here.'

I dropped it then, but it didn't make sense. Only a fool would act that way, and Dillon wasn't a fool, and he wasn't a kid any longer.

I left early the next morning, swinging west of the Valley Ranch. I was wearing my gun, and I didn't want Perrin to see me. I told myself I'd need it if I ran into the Fergusons, but the truth was that I wanted my folks and everybody at church to think I was dressed like a cowboy, and a gun belonged on a cowboy's hip. Maybe not to Jim Perrin, but it did to me.

I reached the schoolhouse just as they were starting the first hymn. The place was crowded, the men and boys standing along the sides and back. Everybody turned and stared at me when I came in. Some grinned. Others shook their heads in disapproval. I knew what they were thinking. The preacher's boy had gone to the devil just as they had known he would when he'd started working for Jim Perrin.

It was different with the boys. I stood beside

131

Jed Cartwright, Matt's oldest, a kid my age but a full head shorter, a wizened, knot-muscled boy who had worked too hard all his life. He stared at me, frankly envious of the gun on my hip. It was the same with the other boys. At this moment I was, in my own estimation, man-sized, and I had the proper contempt for these men that a cowboy has for those who are bound to the soil.

When my father began preaching, I forgot myself. Under the spell of his words, even the boys' eyes turned to him. He had always been a good preacher as far as words were concerned, but to me they were usually as meaningless as the booming of a bass drum. I knew him too well.

But it was different that morning. I thought at first it was because I had been away from him for a month, then I realized I wasn't being fair. He took his text from the Sermon on the Mount; he described how Jesus had fed the multitude; and he went on to the problem of those who faced him. The Lord would provide, he said, for those who gave the Lord a hand.

I had not thought much about my father for the past month. I had been too busy thinking about myself and my trouble with Rolly Dillon. Now, watching him pace back and forth behind the desk and listening to his rich voice, I couldn't help hoping, as my mother had hoped for so long, that at last the years of wandering were ended.

When he finished the sermon and the final hymn was sung, he said: 'I did not preach the sermon that I had planned on preaching today. I intended to talk about the Prodigal Son, but when I saw Daniel come in I knew I could not preach that sermon. He would think I was aiming it at him, but Daniel would never be a prodigal son who would waste his substance on riotous living.'

I whirled and went outside. I was ashamed of myself, ashamed of the gun I wore. I was posing just as my father had posed so many times, and I had hated him for it. But I didn't hate him now, and he wasn't posing. Somehow he seemed different. And then I thought I knew. He had leaned on me, but after I left necessity had made him discover he could do things he had not thought he could.

My father was the first one through the door. He came to me and shook hands, saying, 'I'm glad to see you, Daniel.'

'I'm glad to be here,' I said. 'That was a good sermon.'

It pleased him. I had never before given him a word of praise about anything. The other men drifted out of the schoolhouse, Cartwright and Frank Allison and the rest. They shook hands with me, asking how I liked working for Jim Perrin and what sort of man he was anyhow. That, I thought, was proof enough that they realized they didn't really know him, that they had taken Virgil Lang's word.

When I finished shaking hands, I said: 'Perrin is starting haying right after the Fourth. Any of you men who want work can have it.'

It was blunt, but I saw no reason to beat around the bush. Perrin needed a hay crew and these men needed cash money, so plain common sense said it was a good bargain. But I wasn't prepared for the reception they gave Perrin's offer. They stared at me as if I had committed some treasonable act. It had been enough, I suppose, for the preacher's boy to go to work for Perrin, but to come to church and ask them to work for him was too much.

Matt Cartwright looked at me with frank loathing. 'You haven't been to church for a month, and when you do come you ask us to work for that devil. If that was your only purpose in coming, may the Lord have mercy on your soul.'

My father stood motionless, not knowing what to do or say, and it may have been that the same suspicion that was in Cartwright's mind was also in his. The only man in the half-circle facing me who didn't look as if I were some sort of crawling thing that should get back under a rock was Frank Allison. He said mildly, 'Matt, you're too hard on the boy.'

Cartwright wheeled to face him. 'How could I be too hard on a boy who should stay home to help his father? Comes to church wearing a gun. If that ain't enough ...'

My father surprised me. He looked squarely

at Cartwright when he said, 'Matt, are you in a position to condemn anyone, even if he is the preacher's son?'

'I was wondering the same,' Frank Allison said. 'I haven't had a piece of gold in my pocket for a long time, and even if we get a crop this year where will we sell it for cash money?' He nodded at me. 'You tell Perrin I'll be there on the morning of the fifth.'

'I'll tell him,' I said.

I swung around and walked to my horse. If I stayed there I'd say something I'd be sorry about later, and I didn't want to hurt my father's position with them. Sooner or later he'd have trouble with Cartwright, for that was the kind of man Cartwright was.

The women were coming out of the schoolhouse, Debbie Allison among them. I wanted to see my mother, but I didn't want to talk to Debbie, so I hurriedly tightened the cinch and stepped into the saddle. Then I heard Ben call 'Daniel!' and I looked around and saw him running toward me.

'How are you, Ben?' I said, and waited until he reached me.

He put up his arms and I leaned down and picked him up. He was light, terrifyingly light, and when he hugged me there was no strength in his thin little arms. He said, 'I'm fine,' and when I asked, 'Want me to give you a ride home?' he said, 'Yes.'

So I started east along the road, catching a

glimpse of Debbie, who was walking toward me. I pretended not to see her, and then I forgot about her. Ben looked up at me, the fixed smile on his lips, and it seemed to me his face was thinner and more waxlike than ever.

I remembered how I used to think he was born to be with the angels and would soon go to them. I held him close all the way home, a terrible fear clawing up through me as I wondered what would happen to my mother if Ben died.

CHAPTER TEN

I could hardly believe my eyes when I reached the ridge where I had stopped that first evening with a load of Virgil Lang's lumber. I had used the word 'home' without really thinking. Only a month before, I had resented my father's use of that same word because we had never known a home except for our rickety, wornout old wagon. But now I looked at the tight little cabin, at the shed behind it, and at the chicken pen of woven wire. It was home to my folks and to Ben; it would have been home to me if I had stayed with them.

I lowered Ben to the ground and stepped down, leaving the reins dangling. Ben pointed to an old brindle milk cow that was staked out on the grass south of the cabin. He said, 'Cow,' and I said: 'She sure is, Ben. Does she give milk?' He nodded, and pointed to the shed. 'See?'

'It looks good, Ben,' I said. 'Mighty good.'

I had to inspect the shed, and the chicken pen at one end. He tugged the gate open and went in, the hens eyeing him disapprovingly. A moment later he came out, a brown egg clutched in his hand. He held it up for me to see, and I nodded and closed the wire gate.

I suppose this proved my father's often repeated statement that the Lord would provide. As I walked to the cabin with Ben, I remembered the day we had made the climb to Juniper Summit and I had been filled with so many doubts, even to wondering if we would be forced to eat the hens. I stopped and bowed my head and said a little prayer of thanksgiving. To me it was a miracle.

Our horses were staked out on the grass beyond the milk cow, but Virgil Lang's Percherons and wagon were not in sight. My father must have returned them. I went inside. The cabin was rough, but I couldn't see daylight anywhere in the walls or ceiling. Cartwright and the others had done a better job than the Ferguson boys had said they would.

A curtain at one end of the room hid the bed from the rest of the cabin. The battered furniture that we had hauled over the western half of the United States was all around me: the rickety table, the rocking chair that creaked with every rock, the two cane-bottom chairs, the range, the three-legged bureau with a piece of wood under the corner where the leg was missing, the mirror that gave back a distorted, wavy image. The Winchester my father loved to carry leaned against the wall, a shotgun beside it.

New, bright-colored curtains hung at the two windows. Shelves had been built along one wall. Food was stacked on the shelves in cans and sacks, enough to last for months. Virgil Lang had kept his part of the bargain.

I built a fire in the range and went outside. A fair-sized piece of land at the bottom of the ridge had been plowed and sowed, and the grain was up enough to give a green hue to the black soil. I wondered if my father had done the work, or Frank Allison.

I heard the wagon coming and stepped around the corner of the cabin. My father was sitting beside Allison on the seat, my mother and Mrs Allison and Debbie in the back. As soon as the wagon stopped, my mother jumped down and ran to me. She hugged and kissed me, looking as if she wanted to cry.

'It's been so long, Daniel,' she said.

'I've been on spring roundup,' I told her. 'This is the first chance I had to get home.'

The Allisons got down, Mrs Allison saying, 'You're looking fine, Daniel,' and Debbie said shyly, 'Hello, Daniel.'

I took off my Stetson, embarrassed. 'Howdy,' I said, and glanced at Debbie and then looked away. Kind of pretty, I thought, with her hair done up in curls and wearing a starched gingham dress with red dots, pretty enough for me to be interested in her. I think I would have if she hadn't had a sort of welcome look about her that said all I had to do was ask and she'd say yes.

The women went inside, and Frank Allison took my arm and led me away from the wagon. He said in a low tone: 'Daniel, your folks are making out fine. They've got as good a set of buildings as anybody on the lake, and plenty of grub on the shelves. Your dad's got about ten acres of wheat in that's looking good. It's natural for you to fret some about 'em, but you don't need to.'

I don't know why he said all that, but I had an idea he was working up to something. I said, 'They've got good neighbors.'

'Your father's a fine preacher,' Allison went on. 'We've needed a man like him ever since we came. Now there's something I want to ask you. Mrs Cartwright taught school three months last summer. We have school during the summer 'cause it's hard for the kids to get there in bad weather. Trouble is, Mrs Cartwright ain't much of a teacher. She gets mad, and then Matt sticks his nose in and it goes from bad to worse. I was wondering if your father would take the job.'

I thought about it a moment. He had never taught school, but he could. At least he knew enough book learning to teach, but he wouldn't know how to handle mean boys if there were any.

'He ain't much of a farmer,' Allison said, 'but we're helping him out, swapping work for his preaching. I figure we could pay him a hundred dollars for the term. That's why I'm going to work for Perrin. Debbie didn't go to school last summer on account of she can't get along with Mrs Cartwright, but I'd like for her to have a little learnin'.' He cleared his throat, watching me closely. Then he added: 'I wanted to know what you thought about it before I asked him. Didn't want him to figure he had to say yes because he was beholden.'

To my knowledge my father had never made a hundred dollars in his life. It would be a fortune to him. I said: 'I think he'd be pleased to be asked, but teaching is one thing and preaching is another. I don't think he'd know how to keep the ornery boys in line.'

'Jed Cartwright is the only one he'd have,' Allison said, his lips thinning with dislike for the boy. 'He'd go too, if Debbie went.' He shook his head. 'I'll promise you one thing, Daniel. If Jed acts up, I'll beat hell out of him myself.'

'Then ask Pa,' I said. 'I'm sure he'll take the job.'

Allison seemed relieved. 'Another thing,

Daniel, long as we're talking. Don't get mad at Matt on account of what he said. He's like a feisty dog. A lot of bark but not much bite. I figure about ten of us will show up to work for Perrin, and if I don't miss my guess Matt and Jed will be along.'

'Might be better if they don't come,' I said.

'No, they're good workers. It's just that Matt has to do so much gabbing before he starts thinking.' We walked back along the wagon, Allison calling, 'Ma. Debbie. We'd best be going.'

My mother and Mrs Allison came out of the cabin, Debbie following. She glanced at me and looked away, and then she seemed to make up her mind about something. She walked directly to me, her head thrown back and breathing hard.

'We're having a dance at the schoolhouse Saturday night,' she said. 'Do you suppose you'll come?'

'I don't know,' I said, thinking that if I was as dog-tired every night as I had been on spring roundup, I wouldn't do much dancing.

'Jed Cartwright asked me to go with him,' Debbie said, looking at the ground. 'I didn't tell him I would, though.'

I didn't say anything. I couldn't. All I knew was that this was dangerous ground and I wasn't going to walk on it. Outside of the Fergusons, Jed Cartwright and I were the only boys old enough to think about getting married. Except, of course, some of Perrin's riders like Rolly Dillon, and Frank Allison wouldn't let them come within shooting distance of Debbie.

When she decided I wasn't going with her, she climbed into the wagon and they drove away. Debbie kept her face turned from me. I don't know whether her mother and father heard our conversation or not, but my mother had. She asked severely, 'Why didn't you ask Debbie to go?'

'She's too willing,' I said. 'I'm afraid of her.'

'She'd make you a fine wife,' my mother said. 'I'd like it if you were married and settled down here beside us. I worry about you, being with those—those cowboys all the time.'

'It's where I belong.' I gave her the three gold pieces Perrin had paid me. 'I told you I'd bring my wages to you. This is all the cash I got. The rest of it went on the clothes I bought.'

She stared at the money a long time. I don't suppose she could remember when she'd had fifteen dollars in her hand, and she was probably thinking of things in Virgil Lang's store she would like to buy but was too proud to charge. Then she shook her head and held the money out to me.

'I can't take it, Daniel,' she said. 'Down inside me I know it's a good thing you went away, so I'll try to get used to not having you at home.'

Home! I didn't remember hearing her use the

word before. She couldn't have. How could a wagon be home to anyone? I said: 'You keep it. I don't need money. I get my clothes and meals. I just don't need it.'

She had put an apron over her poplin dress. She dropped the money into her apron pocket and turned toward the cabin. 'I'll get dinner,' she said.

I got the pair of trousers that I had rolled up and tied behind the saddle. Ben was playing in the yard, digging into the dirt with a stick and filling a tin can. I asked, 'What are you doing?'

'Mining,' he said, and kept on digging.

I went inside. My father was sitting in the rocking chair reading his Bible. I said: 'I brought you a pair of pants. I hope they fit.'

He took them and felt of the heavy woolen cloth. He said, 'Thank you, Daniel,' not looking up. He laid the trousers on his lap and went on reading. Then I knew I had done wrong. He was getting along without me and he didn't want my help, but he was not rude enough to give them back. It was the way it should be, and I was glad.

We had a good meal: antelope steak, biscuits, beans, and a dried apple pie. My mother said, 'You're filling out, Daniel. I believe you've gained ten pounds.'

'I haven't looked at myself,' I said, and we laughed.

After dinner we sat around and tried to talk, but it was hard. For once my father had little to say, and when I asked about the milk cow he said: 'I bought her from Morris. I gave him my note for ten dollars. I thought Ben needed the milk.'

'It'll be good for him,' I said, and knew it was time for me to leave.

When I rode away, I looked back once and waved. My father and mother stood in front of the cabin and waved back. Ben kept on mining. I don't think he knew I had gone. It was then that I realized I had done far more than I had thought when I'd left with Jim Perrin.

A month ago my father would have grabbed that pair of pants, taking it for granted as he had taken everything I did for granted. I pondered it as the miles fell behind. I didn't know whether any man could change, or whether the change I had found in my father was real or not. But if it was real, there must have been some violent, soul-twisting cause for it.

Possibly the thing Perrin had said when my father had asked for my wages had caused it. But whatever the cause, it seemed to me there was a new strength in my father, a self-assurance that had not been in him before. Perhaps it was the trust these people were giving him; perhaps he had finally found a place where he was respected for the talents he had.

Then, for some reason, I thought of Debbie. I couldn't come back if she was going to be

144

underfoot and my mother kept nudging me in her direction. If I could make Debbie angry at me … Suddenly I knew how I could, and I swung west toward the Hammond place.

I wasn't particularly proud of the idea, but it was attractive in the way many forbidden things are attractive. In all honesty I mentally admitted I hadn't forgotten the feel of Cissy Hammond's soft body against mine the day she and her mother had come to church.

The sun was well over toward the west when I forded Thunder River that ran wide and clear over a gravel bottom and rode on up the west bank to the Hammond house. It was a square white cottage with a porch across the front, the only house I had seen along the lake shore that was painted.

Cissy was sitting in a rocking chair on the porch. She had been watching me for a long time, but I don't think she recognized me until I reined up and lifted my hat to her and said, 'How are you, Miss Hammond?'

She jumped up, calling, 'Mamma, the preacher's boy is here!'

She was wearing a pink silk dress with a prim lace collar that looked tight enough to choke her. The sleeves came down to her wrists and the skirt was long and full, but now, as she lifted her arm and waved to me, I glimpsed her trim ankles. The dress covered almost all of her body, and yet somehow it didn't seem to. I suppose it was the way the bodice was cut to

145

hug the firm round mounds of her breasts and the way the skirt clung to the curve of her hips.

Here was sin, I thought, and I was sure my folks would call it that, but to me she was the most alluring woman I had ever seen. If it was sin, and I wasn't sure it was, I was in favor of it, and I found distinct satisfaction in the color that excitement had brought to her face.

'What's the matter with me?' I asked. 'You'd think I was some kind of freak.'

Her mother appeared in the doorway, smiling at me. She said: 'You are, Mr Nathan. In the first place I don't think anyone ever called Cissy Miss Hammond before, and in the second place this is our first visit from a preacher's son. Won't you come in?'

'And you're dressed up like a cowboy, gun and everything,' Cissy said triumphantly. 'What more does it take to make you a freak?'

'I don't like it,' I said. 'I don't like it a little bit. I don't go around calling other people freaks.'

'You came around here because I'm a pretty girl,' Cissy said, 'and you've thought about me ever since you saw me at church. Now, get down off that horse and come in. I *told* Mamma you'd come to see me.'

'I am not a freak and I am a cowboy,' I said. 'I'm working for Jim Perrin.'

They both seemed shocked, then Cissy laughed aloud. 'A preacher's son working for Jim, and the preacher's nester.' She threw up her hands. 'Of course you're a freak. You're an A Number One freak. Get off that horse, I tell you, or I'll come out there and pull you off.'

'Hush up, Cissy,' Mrs Hammond said. 'You're embarrassing him.'

Then it struck me funny, and I laughed. Cissy ran lightly down off the porch. Coming to me, she took my hand and gave it a yank. 'Come in, Dan. You'll get sunstroke out here.'

I shook my head. 'I've got to get back. I came to ask you to go to the dance with me at the schoolhouse Saturday night.'

The light went out of Cissy's face. She dropped my hand and stepped back. Mrs Hammond came off the porch and walked toward me, her face grave. 'Why do you ask that after what happened at church? Don't you have any sense?'

'I guess not,' I said. 'I just wanted her to go.'

Cissy whirled to face her mother. 'Let me go, Mamma,' she cried. 'I don't care what happens. I want to go.'

'Mrs Hammond,' I said, 'I'll bust the first man in the nose who insults her.'

Cissy, who hadn't taken her gaze from her mother's face, said again, 'Let me go, Mamma.'

'In all the time we've been here,' Mrs Hammond said, 'no one has ever asked her to go to a dance. I'm afraid for you as much as for her. It—it won't be nice.'

'You'll let me go?' Cissy asked.

147

Mrs Hammond nodded. 'But you won't have any fun. I can tell you that.'

'I'll be here as early as I can,' I said, and touching my hatbrim to them, rode away.

I had plenty of time on my way back to J Ranch to regret what I had done. I hadn't thought it through when the notion had struck me. I had really only wanted one thing: to get Debbie off my back. But there was something else now, a sort of crawling excitement that worked into me and made my heart miss a beat now and then, an excitement that came from the thought of being with Cissy.

There was still another thing—it made me laugh aloud when I thought of it—the looks that would be on all their faces when I walked into the schoolhouse with Cissy, especially Matt Cartwright's. Then I was sorry I had asked her. She had been pathetically eager to go, but I was afraid her mother was right. Regardless of Cissy's morals, if the gossip was true, she didn't deserve to be hurt.

It was dark when I reached J Ranch and put my horse away. When I went into the house Perrin was sitting in front of the fireplace. He looked around when I came in, and his voice seemed a little anxious when he asked, 'Well?'

'Frank Allison says ten men will show up for work on the morning of the fifth,' I said.

He took a long breath and, getting up, reached for his pipe on the mantel. 'You did something I couldn't have done, Danny,' he said. 'Haying has always been a problem because I've had to put my men to work at it when there were other things they should be doing. And all the time the settlers needed the work.'

'I'm not sure they'll come,' I said. 'I'm just saying what Allison told me.'

'They'll come if Allison said they would. Allison's a good man.'

Then I was sorry again I had asked Cissy to go to the dance. It would make trouble, and they might blame Perrin for what I had done.

CHAPTER ELEVEN

Early Monday morning Perrin sent Rolly Dillon and a vaquero named José Otero to the Valley Ranch. Two other riders rode south to Giant Springs Ranch. Both satellite ranches had been deserted during spring roundup, but he usually kept two or three hands at each place except for a few weeks in spring and fall when everyone except Alec Brown and Wang, the Chinese cook in the big house, were on the range.

Lane Sears and Ole Larsen started getting the haying equipment ready. The Fourth was only a few days away. Several men attacked the marsh between J Ranch and Giant Springs. As Pedro García said: 'The marsh, she don't stand still. She pushes you back, or you push her back.'

I could see that would be true. It was a tremendous task to drain the low land on both sides of the river and burn off the tule. I could hardly believe that Perrin had accomplished as much as he had in the six years he had been there.

There was another job that was never finished: the building of fences in the breaks of the rimrock to the west, and high on the shoulders of Garnet Mountain to the east. That fell to me, along with Pedro and Perrin himself.

'The fences serve a double purpose,' Perrin explained. 'In winter they keep the cattle from working back onto the mountain or the desert on the other side of the river. In summer they keep the cattle out of the meadows.' He smiled then. 'Maybe I should say a triple purpose. I own the land along the river. Bought it from the state. Swampland, you know, that the federal government turned over to the state.'

Pedro and I had been loading rocks on a sled and hauling them downslope to the fence Perrin was building. Now we paused, straightening our backs as Perrin threw out a hand in an inclusive gesture, indicating the mountain land that ran for miles above the valley, gentle slopes covered with bunch grass, sheer rock walls that were natural barriers, and the deep, shadowed gorges that must

150

be fenced.

'We can't call this swampland,' Perrin said, 'and it hasn't been surveyed. Someday it will be and I'll get title to it, in one way or another. Meanwhile these fences prove I'm using the land.'

Many times during that week I watched Perrin stand motionless, eyes sweeping the green valley below us, then the gray sage-covered slopes west of the river, and finally the grim rimrock. Or he would look the other way, to the grass-carpeted slopes of the mountain and up the long ridges that ran toward the sky and then broke off in an undulating line with here and there patches of snow that still clung to the brush and rock-shaded spots even in late June.

Thus I discovered another of the many facets of Jim Perrin's character. Before I had ever seen him, I had formed a preconceived mental picture of what he was like. Then I had met him that day in front of Virgil Lang's store, and I discovered I had not been far wrong in anything except size. That wasn't important, because you simply couldn't think of Jim Perrin as a small man, and the feeling grew on me as I worked with him. He could outdo any big man I had ever met.

The qualities I had imagined would be in Jim Perrin were easily seen. Courage was one, although he would have dismissed it with a laugh if anyone had suggested he was a brave man. But the way he had taken Lang's attempt on his life was ample proof of his courage, and not once did I ever know him to give a moment's thought to his personal safety, regardless of the emergency. He was one of those rare men who either did not know fear, or kept it so completely controlled that no one knew he felt it.

Loyalty was another, as demonstrated by his inability to fire Rolly Dillon, even though he knew as well as Lane Sears did that Dillon was not the kind of man he wanted on J Ranch. Such qualities were the ones you expected to find in Perrin, and he never disappointed me or anyone who worked for him.

Not that he was more god than man. He had his failings, and stubbornness was one. He could have gone to the settlers on the lake shore and said that he wouldn't bother them, that he didn't need the marginal land, and that if the courts ruled that it belonged to him he'd deed it over to the people who lived on it. But he was absolutely incapable of doing so.

During that first week we worked together on the slopes of Garnet Mountain, he would stand there as if completely unaware of Pedro and me. In his own mind he was alone, and you could feel the hunger that was in him, hunger that no amount of land would ever satisfy. 'Greed' is an ugly word and the wrong one, perhaps, for me to apply to Jim Perrin. 'Ambition' is better, although it seems to me there is a thin line between them.

But there was something in his make-up that was inconsistent. He was wonderfully kind and generous. He paid his experienced hands forty a month and found, which was more than anyone else in the country paid. I think he knew that Matt Cartwright ate his cattle, but he overlooked it.

When it came to land, everything else was secondary, and I'm sure he never stopped scheming about how to get more. To him money was made for the buying of land, and many times he gave twice what he should for a piece of property when actually he was buying nothing more than a man's squatter's right.

I once said to Pedro that it seemed as if Perrin should be content with what he had. Pedro, whose dark face so easily broke into laughter, turned grave, and I knew he had given it much thought himself. After a moment he said: 'Señor Jim, he is never content. Once he had a dream.' He nodded toward the valley below us. 'That was part of the dream, but only a part. There was no end to the dream.'

That reminded me of what Virgil Lang had said, that all of us have our dreams, Perrin his and Lang his, and that when I learned to know Perrin I was to decide which was the better dream. It was something to think about. Perrin was a better man than Lang, for Lang was driven by hate, and I never knew Perrin to belittle himself by actually hating anyone. But

153

Lang's dream of putting families on the land was the better of the two, and even then, just beginning to know Perrin, I had a feeling that his hunger for land would break and ruin him.

Later in the week I quit thinking about it, for my date with Cissy made me uneasy. I had no intention of backing out. It was simply that I knew I had made a mistake, that I had traded small trouble for big trouble.

I told Perrin Saturday noon that I had a date for the dance that night, trying to sound casual about it. He winked at Pedro. 'Well, now,' he said, 'that's interesting. The only girls in the country are settler girls, and you're the only man working for me who could get a date with one of them. Some of my boys have tried, but they're poison.'

'Señor Dan, he is not poison,' Pedro said. 'He is the great lover.'

I got red in the face and started to say something, but all I could do was stammer. One thing was certain. I couldn't tell them my date was Cissy Hammond. Perrin laughed softly. 'You'd better ride in and get cleaned up, Danny. I want you to look your best if you're going to represent J Ranch.'

'Thanks,' I mumbled, and got on my horse and rode down the mountain.

The afternoon was half gone by the time I was ready to leave J Ranch. I hesitated about wearing my gun, remembering I had made a mistake when I had taken it Sunday. But this

154

was different, and finally I strapped the belt around my waist. It was not likely the Fergusons would pass up a dance.

When I was saddling my buckskin, Alec Brown came hobbling out of the store. He looked at my gun disapprovingly, then he asked, 'You talk to Lane about teaching you how to use that iron?'

'He said he would, later on.'

'Late enough for you to start pushing up the daisies,' Alec grunted. 'Now you look here, son. Wearing an iron is an invitation for trouble, so a man who totes one had better be damned sure he can handle it.'

I knew he was right, but I wasn't going to give him the satisfaction of getting off my horse and taking the gun back up to my room. I rode out of the yard, leaving him shaking his head. It was six o'clock when I forded the river at the Hammond place. Cissy ran out of the house, waving to me.

'Still a cowboy,' she teased, 'with a gun and everything.'

I dismounted, knowing she thought I was playing big just as I had been on Sunday. I said, 'I'll take it off.'

She grabbed my arm and hugged it, laughing at me. 'I was joshing,' she said. 'Come on. Put your horse up. Mamma said for us to take the buggy tonight. Supper's ready. We thought you'd be along about now.'

I stripped gear from my buckskin and turned

155

him into the corral. When I shut the gate, Cissy grabbed my arm again and we walked to the house that way, my cheeks feeling as if they were on fire.

The moment I stepped into the sitting room, I smelled frying ham. Mrs Hammond called from the kitchen: 'Sit down, Dan. Supper's almost ready. Come and help me, Cissy.'

She gave me a curtsy, her cheeks high with color, and it was impossible to mistake the excitement that was in her. 'Excuse me, Dan,' she said, and bounced out of the room. I watched her go.

When I looked around, I was surprised by what I saw. It might have been the sitting room of any modest family in any small western town. There were pictures on the wall, a blue-flowered carpet on the floor, a dainty mahogany table with graceful carved legs, several rocking chairs, and a bookcase against one wall.

I walked to the bookcase. The books were not the heavy tomes my father had hauled all over the western half of the United States. Most of them were novels. I recognized several of the authors: Hawthorne, Cooper, Irving. There were a few volumes of poetry, too: Longfellow, Lowell, Whittier, and some of the English poets.

When I sat down again, I felt vaguely disappointed. My father, with his exaggerated hatred of what he called sin, would have

156

termed the Hammond house a cesspool of iniquity. I don't know what I had expected, but it wasn't this clean, inviting room with white lace curtains at the windows.

A moment later Mrs Hammond called me to supper. Again I was surprised, for it was a good meal of fried ham, golden-hued biscuits, potatoes and gravy, and dried apple butter. I sat stiff with embarrassment, hard pressed by a sense of inadequacy. I had never taken a girl anywhere before, and to have asked one like Cissy ... I wished I was a thousand miles from there. I'd ridden into a bog with my eyes shut.

But if they noticed my embarrassment, and they must have, they ignored it. Cissy chattered along about nothing, as excited as when I had first seen her, and now and then Mrs Hammond asked about Jim Perrin and Lane Sears and some of the others, and I had the feeling she knew them all very well.

When we finished with the dessert, a three-layer cake, Mrs Hammond said: 'The buggy's beside the barn and the horses are inside. I expect you'd better harness up.'

'I'll be ready in a minute,' Cissy said, and jumped up and ran into her bedroom.

Mrs Hammond walked to the front door with me. She laid a hand on my arm. 'Dan, I know how your folks and the other good people along the lake feel about us. I may be wrong living the way I do, but when they close the doors of their church to us I can't believe they are any better than Cissy and me.'

Misery was written on her face. I looked at her, realizing she was close to tears. I had a sudden insight of something that seemed to be truth, of how completely wrong our human values were, and I thought of my father asking Matt Cartwright, 'Are you in a position to condemn anyone?' I wanted to ask her if what they said was true, or if it was all a lie, filth skimmed from the surface of unclean minds. But I couldn't say it.

'Take care of Cissy, Dan,' she said. 'That's all I ask.'

'I will,' I said, and turned and ran toward the barn.

Ten minutes later I drove up to the front door in the buggy. Cissy kissed her mother and crossed the porch and came down the steps in that light way she had. She was wearing the silk dress she had worn Sunday, and a light brown coat and a brown scarf over her blond hair. I spoke to the team, and we wheeled down the slope toward the river. Cissy turned and waved to her mother, then we forded the stream and she settled into the seat disturbingly close to me.

The sun was almost down, our long shadows racing before us. We were silent for a time, then Cissy said, 'I declare, Dan, sometimes I think you can't talk.'

I looked at her and she looked at me and we both laughed. 'I'm tongue-tied,' I said, 'and you're to blame.'

She slipped her arm through mine. 'I guess that's a compliment, a kind of compliment. Well, you don't tie my tongue. I like to talk.'

And she did. After that it was easier. As we passed the cabins that lay between the road and the lake, she told me who lived in each of them, the Cartwrights and the Longleys and others.

'Mamma and I have always wondered what the Cartwrights do in that tiny little cabin with their kids,' she said, 'and Mrs Cartwright as big as Garnet Mountain. The walls have just got to give when they're all inside.'

I laughed and told Cissy about the morning of the house raising when Mrs Cartwright saw Jim Perrin, said 'Perrin,' and fainted. Cissy giggled.

The sun went down, the rose light faded, and the purple twilight was all around us and the wind was sweet with the smell of grass and juniper and sage. It had been a warm day, not hot, but just right, and now, with the night closing in, the warmth of the day still held.

Everything was perfect until we saw the lights of the schoolhouse ahead of us and heard the fiddler's 'Turkey in the Straw.' Then I saw them in the road, waiting, and everything was wrong.

Cartwright shouted: 'Pull up, Nathan! You ain't bringing that floozy to our dance. We have some respect for our women even if you don't for your mother.'

159

There were five of them, all carrying rifles. I pulled the horses to a stop, cold now, cold all over and cold inside, and the same crazy fury that had been in me the night I had fought Rolly Dillon was in me again.

'Turn around.' It was young Jed Cartwright. 'I brought Debbie to the dance. She ain't gonna go on the same floor with that—'

'Shut up.' I said it, but it didn't sound like my voice. I handed the reins to Cissy and stepped down. 'Get out of my way.'

Cartwright moved toward me, and when he was close I saw that his rifle was pointed at my stomach. 'Don't make us trouble, Nathan. We'll kill you if we have to.'

'Get back into the buggy!' Cissy cried. 'I don't care about the dance.'

But I didn't move. My throat was dry; my heart was hammering in my chest as if it wanted to beat its way out. I wasn't thinking clearly; I hardly heard what Cissy had said. Then Cartwright was very close, the muzzle of his rifle within inches of my stomach. He didn't see my hand in time. I knocked the barrel to one side and I hit him with my other hand, a hard fist that had all of my wild rage behind it. Cartwright went down without so much as a grunt.

The others were ten feet in front of me, far enough away so that it was difficult for them to see what I had done, but they must have heard the crack of my fist on Cartwright's chin. Jed let out a scared squall. Then I had covered the ten feet between us and had him by the front of his shirt. I shook him so hard his teeth rattled and he dropped the rifle. I hit him on one side of the head and then the other and he was down.

I didn't know Frank Allison was among them until he struck me with his rifle barrel, not a hard blow, but hard enough to knock some of the anger out of me. He said: 'Easy, Daniel. Let me talk to you.'

Behind me Cartwright was on his hands and knees, groping for his rifle. Cissy cried, 'Dan, he's trying to find his Winchester!'

I backed up and whirled and kicked him in the rump just as his hands closed over the rifle, and he went flat on his belly. I said: 'I've got my gun, Matt. Want me to use it?'

He lay there, too scared to move. My gun was in my hand as I edged toward the buggy. None of them moved except Allison, and he came right up to me. He said: 'I guess you can use that gun, Daniel, if you want to dance bad enough, but it won't do. Have you thought of your father?'

I stood there, breathing hard, my heart still hammering. I couldn't see Allison's face, but somehow I felt that he was trying to be fair. I respected him. He was the only one in the bunch with a spoonful of guts in his whole body.

'No,' I said, 'I guess I haven't.'

Silence then, and I was thinking about last Sunday, and how my father had shown a confidence and self-assurance I had never seen in him before. Allison didn't say it in words. He didn't need to. But I knew. If I forced my way into the schoolhouse with Cissy, my father would never preach there again.

I got into the buggy and took the lines from Cissy and turned around. She didn't say anything for a mile, just sat stiffly beside me. At last she spoke. 'I'm to blame, Dan. Cartwright came to see us last night. He's always bothering Mamma. I got mad and told him you were taking me to the dance. That's why they were waiting for us.'

I wished I'd hit him harder than I had. Matt Cartwright with a wife and half a dozen kids, Matt Cartwright who thought he had a right to judge others and who was worse than the worst of us. Then I realized Cissy was crying, and I put my arm around her and held her hard against me. But all the fun had gone out of the evening.

She stayed with me while I unharnessed the team, holding a lantern for me. She wasn't crying now, but stains of her tears were still on her face. I tried to think of something to say, but I couldn't think of anything.

After I had put the horses in the barn, she said, 'Will you stay a little while, Dan, just a little while?'

'I'll stay as long as you want me.'

'Wait till I tell Mamma. She'll wonder what happened.'

I stayed outside while she crossed the yard to the house, not walking lightly now, just trudging. Presently she returned, blew out the lantern, and hung it inside the barn door. She took my hand and led me around the corral and down the grassy slope toward the river.

We sat down, and for a time we didn't say anything, just listened to the murmur of the water, and the sound of it was good, softening the bitterness that had piled up in me. I had thought of this country as the big range, but now, I told myself, I would rename it the violent land. That was it, a violent, savage land. It had changed me since I had come into it. Virgil Lang. The Fergusons. Rolly Dillon. And now the Cartwrights.

'Dan.'

'What?'

'I want to talk. I've got to tell you that all the things you've heard about us is gossip—just lies. Maybe it's the way we dress, or maybe it's living here by ourselves without a man. Or maybe it's because they hate Jim Perrin and he comes to see us and we sing and make candy and have fun.'

I believed her. I wanted to believe her. Then she said: 'Dan, I'm not sorry we didn't get to dance. You know, your coming here tonight and not being ashamed of me and wanting to take me—well, it's the nicest thing that ever

163

happened to me.'

I wasn't proud of myself. I remembered how I'd thought about Cissy when she had come up behind me that day after church, but I'd been wrong. She wanted to be loved, to be accepted just the way I had wanted to be accepted when I had been introduced to the J Ranch crew and Rolly Dillon had spoiled it.

I put my arm around her and lay back on the grass. Her mouth came down to mine, and it was rich and sweet. Then she lay beside me, my arm still around her, and we stared up at the stars that were God's lamps.

I didn't go to church the next morning. I couldn't.

CHAPTER TWELVE

After dinner Sunday afternoon Lane Sears said: 'Go get your gun. We'll have a lesson.'

From the look on his face I knew something had happened. I went upstairs to my room in the big house and strapped my gun belt around me. Perrin was gone. I think Lane knew he wasn't there, or he wouldn't have suggested a lesson. When I got back to the corral, he was carrying his gun.

We saddled up and rode south until we were out of sight of the house, then swung up a dry wash and followed it until we reached an earth

164

bank ten feet high. We dismounted, and Lane picked up a stick and outlined the figure of a man in the soft earth of the bank.

'Ain't much I can do to help,' Lane said. 'When you get down to cases, there's just two things that count. One is practice. While you're doing it, just remember that the gent who's slow on the draw but shoots straight has a hell of a lot better chance of staying alive than the feller who's fast and can't hit the ground with his hat.'

Lane backed off from the figure on the bank and glared at it as if it were a malevolent being that he must destroy. 'I used to be pretty good,' he said, 'but I ain't had much chance to practice since I hired on with Jim.'

I never heard what Lane's background was before he had come north with Perrin six years ago, but I always thought he had a record somewhere else, Arizona maybe, and was glad to bury himself on J Ranch. I do know that he never left the country as long as he worked for Perrin, with the exception of the fall drives to Winnemucca, and he never stayed more than one night in Winnemucca.

I had seen several gun fights, and I had watched a number of men who thought they were experts entertain a crowd by making a fast draw and kicking a can along the ground, but I had never seen a man come close to Lane Sears either in speed or in accuracy. He shook five bullets out of his gun in less time than it

165

took me to take a deep breath, every one hitting within a three-inch circle of where the man's heart would have been.

My mouth must have hung open and my eyes were probably about to pop out of my head. He gave me his slow grin and reloaded. 'Not bad, considering. Now, like I said, there's just two things that count. You don't often run across a man who's fast and shoots straight too. If you do, you're dead, so don't worry about it. Your job is to shoot straight.'

He slipped his gun back into holster. 'The other thing is something neither me or nobody else is gonna teach you. It's whether or not you've still got your nerve when you're standing up against another man who's got a gun in his hand.' He jerked his head at the figure he had drawn on the bank. 'That bird can't shoot back. Now I've seen plenty of fellers who were hell on high red wheels when it came to shooting at a tree or a tin can, but when they had to swap lead with a gent who wanted to kill 'em they couldn't get their guns out of their holsters.'

He gave me a long look, stroking that big droopy mustache of his. Then he said: 'Danny, you've got it or you ain't. It's that simple. I think mebbe you have, judging by the way you handled Rolly the other night.'

He gave me a lecture on how to carry my gun and how to tie the holster snugly to my thigh. The hard leather casing I had received with the

166

gun was just right, according to Lane. Softer leather would squeeze the gun and slow up my draw. Having that front sight filed down was good too. This Mason fellow had been a professional. At least he'd had the right equipment.

I found out I had been carrying the gun too high. Most men did, Lane said. Kind of stupid when you thought about it. You shouldn't have to raise your hand and then lower it while your wrist straightened the gun. Make it all in one motion, straight up and out, and you squeezed the trigger as the barrel came level.

'I said *squeeze*,' he repeated. 'Not jerk or pull.'

I tried it then, but it seemed awkward with the gun so low on my thigh. I was slow, as I knew I would be, but I got one bullet where I wanted it—inside the three-inch circle where Lane's had gone.

I used up a box of shells, and Lane said that was enough. 'Get down here every Sunday you can, and practice. You don't need me.'

We mounted and started back. Lane was silent quite a while, his lips working as if he were talking to himself. Finally he said: 'Old Alec's purty sharp. He gave you that gun 'cause Jim had told him you were a preacher's kid. In a country like this, a preacher's kid either runs or fights. If he's got sand in his craw, he's gonna need a gun.'

He looked at me, his face gloomy. 'You're

gonna need one all right, and you'd better be sure you learn how to use it. I was down to the Valley Ranch last night. Took a bottle along, figuring it was time Rolly was talking. He done so, after he got oiled up pretty well.'

Lane rolled a smoke and lighted it. 'Jim's a funny one. Sometimes he's as tough as all hell, like when he kicked this Mason hombre off the ranch and kept his gun. But it's different with Rolly. The kid's no damned good, but Jim allows he's got to try to straighten him up. Rolly's got a gun. Mebbe bought it from Virgil Lang. Or the Fergusons. He hobnobs with them considerable. He's practicing, too. Aims to shoot your liver out when he's ready.'

'Why?' I demanded. 'He's got nothing against me.'

'You knocked hell out of him, which is plenty. But Cissy Hammond is the one who started it.'

I guess Lane heard my breath come out of me when he said that. He went on. 'Rolly's been hanging around Cissy for a long time, but her mother don't cotton to him. What it amounts to is that she's trying to keep Cissy out of the business as long as she can, but Rolly wants to sleep with Cissy, not her mamma.'

I could feel the anger working in me again. Lane was lying, but I couldn't say so, not with him being friendly the way he was, so I just rode along, trying to keep a tight rein on my tongue.

'It started the day before you got to J Ranch,' Lane said. 'Rolly rode over to see Cissy, but she wouldn't have nothing to do with him. Then, just to plague him, I reckon, she told him she liked you. Seen you at church, I think it was. Rolly figured you'd got to her, and that's why he acted the way he done. Then, to put the pink icing on the cake, last week she told him she was going to the dance with you. Now he's sure you've slept with her, and sooner or later he'll come gunning for you.'

I couldn't stand it any longer. 'It isn't so,' I said hotly. 'Cissy told me all this talk was just gossip, lies the nester women were telling about her and her mother.'

He gave me a short, scornful laugh. I guess he was wondering how innocent a kid like me could be. He said: 'Cissy does like you, I reckon. And mebbe she wants you to like her. That's why she told you that. As far as I know, she's straight, though I wouldn't bet on it. But how do you think her mother makes a living? And where do you think Jim goes every Sunday? I've been over there more'n once myself. Comes high, but that's all right. It's worth something for Liz to live out here like she does.'

I didn't say anything after that. We just rode along, and Lane didn't mention Cissy or her mother again. Maybe he regretted disillusioning me, and that was exactly what he had done. I would have liked Cissy better if she

169

hadn't lied to me. Then I wondered what she thought of me, satisfied just to lie there in the grass beside the river and hold her in my arms.

I didn't go to church any more that summer. The less I saw of the settlers, the better. I was around them enough during haying. They ate with the rest of us at the long table, but they didn't sleep in the bunkhouse and they didn't mingle with any of the crew except Lane and Ole Larsen, who worked with them.

The Cartwrights would pass within three feet of me without speaking. None of the settlers tried to be friendly except Frank Allison. He told me my father was teaching school and getting along fine. Then he said I ought to go see my folks, and turned and walked away fast as if afraid I'd resent his advice. I did resent it, but not because he was wrong. My conscience had been making me uneasy. I rode to the lake the last Sunday in July, waiting until it was late because I didn't want to run into Debbie.

I kissed my mother, shook hands with my father, and let Ben lead me down to the lake to show me the boat my father had hired the Fergusons to make for him. Then I went back into the cabin and sat down, and I knew they had heard about my date with Cissy.

My father sat in the rocking chair and my mother sewed on a new dress, and the silence was a burden. It was wrong, all wrong, I told myself, and there was nothing I could do about

170

it. They didn't need me any more, but the trouble lay deeper than that.

They believed the worst about me just as they did about Cissy. I would never live their way of life again. From now on our relationship would be superficial, bridged only by social amenities which meant nothing.

I said, 'Your wheat looks good.'

My father nodded. 'Frank says it will make a crop. He's going to harvest it for half.'

'He told me you were teaching,' I said.

He nodded again. 'I believe the children are learning something.'

'Of course they are, Bartram,' my mother said, her voice holding more feeling than the occasion called for. 'Mrs Allison told me just yesterday that Debbie enjoys school more than she ever has.'

Now, looking at my father, it seemed to me I was seeing a stranger. There was no posing, no strutting. He hadn't once quoted Seneca or Shakespeare or even the Bible. That had always been a crutch for him, but he didn't need it any longer. He was playing the soft note of humility. And that, I thought, was at least a new pose far better than the old one of many pretensions.

I rose, knowing I was doing no one any good by staying. I said: 'I haven't been coming to church, but it wasn't because I didn't want to hear you preach. I just thought it was better if I stayed away.'

He got up and stroked his beard. He said gravely, 'I understand, Daniel.'

I gave my mother half of my month's wages. She took the gold pieces without a word. I went outside to where Ben was chasing a butterfly, and when he ran past me I picked him up and held him high above my head. He giggled and kicked, wanting to be put down, and when I lowered him to the ground I felt the same gnawing fear I'd had the last time I'd seen him. He weighed almost nothing, and his face had not taken on any tan, although July had been hot and dry, and I knew he played outdoors a good deal.

My mother and father had followed me, and when Ben ran on across the yard after the butterfly I looked at my mother. Her face was more placid than I had ever seen it. If she worried about Ben, she didn't show it. I suppose she wasn't aware of any change in him, being with him every day.

I kissed my mother and shook hands with my father; I called goodbye to Ben, who kept on chasing the butterfly. As I swung into the saddle, I said, 'I may not get back for a while.'

'Don't feel that you have to come,' my mother said. 'We're getting along fine.'

My father came quite close to my horse and tilted his head back. He said, 'I guess you know Jim Perrin pretty well by now.'

'Yes, I guess I do,' I said.

'I was talking to Virgil Lang last week. He

says it may be two or three years before the court decides about this land. Perrin has money to hire good lawyers, and there are always ways of keeping things like this tied up.'

'He's not holding it up,' I said. 'He'd rather get it settled.'

'And if it is settled in his favor, he'll run us off. Is that it?' When I nodded, he breathed, 'With all his land and all his money, still he would do that.'

I rode away then. If I had stayed, there would have been an argument. But there was something to be said for the settlers' side of it. Perhaps I would have looked at it differently if it was my land, but it did seem to me that Perrin might have made the generous gesture of telling the settlers he would not take the land regardless of how the case was decided. He might have, but he couldn't.

The haying was finished early in August at the Valley Ranch and the settlers went home. Now, in the meadows at all three of Perrin's ranches, new bright haystacks stood beside the old brown ones that had been held over from the previous year.

On several occasions Rolly Dillon had eaten supper at J Ranch. He avoided me, his face dark and sullen, and as soon as he finished he rode away. He had withdrawn, it seemed to me, from the others, most of them men he had known for six years.

I thought of telling him Cissy meant nothing

to me, that I would never see her again, but the thought left my mind at once. I could not abase myself that way. So every Sunday afternoon I bought two boxes of shells at the store and rode south to the place where I had first practiced with Lane Sears. I was improving my accuracy, but I wasn't sure about my speed.

I still slept in the room beside Perrin's, and that, it seemed to me, was not a good thing. I was a sort of half-and-half creature, not really belonging to the crew, and certainly not belonging in the big house with Perrin. But when I suggested moving to the bunkhouse, Perrin said curtly that I was staying where I was.

We were sitting in the living room at the time, and although the evening was warm he had built a fire in the fireplace. For some reason a fire seemed to make him feel comfortable, even though every window and door was open and he had to sit twenty feet from the fireplace.

He was leaning back in one of his big leather chairs, smoking, his eyes closed. I suppose he was dreaming about more land, and my question jarred him. Suddenly he straightened up and looked at me, ashamed, I think, of the curt way in which he had answered me.

'I like to have you here, Danny,' he said. Then, filled with a sudden restlessness, he got up and began pacing around the room. 'I couldn't ask any of the others to move in here with me. It just wouldn't do.'

He stopped in front of the fireplace and stared for a long moment at the picture of the girl he was going to marry. He said in a low tone, 'She's got to like it here, Danny; she's *got* to.' He swung around to face me, pulling hard on his pipe. 'You know, Danny, you're good for me. For one thing, you speak correctly. That's something I've been working on. Rocky's kind of foolish about it.'

He took the pipe out of his mouth, and gave me that quick, boyish grin which always made me feel he wasn't much older than I was. Sometimes I wondered about his age. Despite his grin, he was actually older than his years. I often thought his ambition was too heavy a burden for him, but he couldn't rid himself of it.

'Rocky's had a lot of book learning, too much, maybe,' he said. 'But what worries me is that she'll be lonely. That's why I want you to stay here. You can talk to her, and I'll be too busy to give her the time I should. Maybe you can be a bridge between her old life and the one she'll have to get used to here.'

I rose. 'I'll try, Mr Perrin.'

'Jim,' he said.

I was the only one on J Ranch who didn't call him Jim. From that time I did. I went upstairs feeling uneasy. He didn't know how often I had stood in front of the fireplace, just looking at Rocky's picture. Now, lying on my back and staring into the darkness, I could recall her features: her full lips, the dimpled chin, her wide-set eyes and tip-tilted nose, her face that seemed filled with so much strength and love of life.

So I was to be part of the family, someone who could talk Rocky's kind of talk, a companion to Jim Perrin's wife. It couldn't work. It was crazy. Perrin should know better. But to him I was a kid who could fill a place he couldn't. The trouble was—and it was something I couldn't tell him—I wasn't a kid as far as Rocky was concerned.

Then I fell to thinking about what he had said. In spite of his wealth and success and power, Jim Perrin was a lonely man. It was natural to think he had everything a man could want, but he didn't. I realized then that I had seen another facet of a man who became more complex the better I knew him.

I had always respected him, even before I met him in front of Virgil Lang's store, but now I had a warmth of affection for him I had not had before. With the egotism of youth, I believed I understood him better than anyone else on J Ranch.

In September we quit working on the fences. 'It'll do till next year,' Perrin said. 'Pedro's got some horses to break before we start roundup. You can help Manuel and Harry cut wood. They aren't going to have enough by the time we start to Winnemucca.' He gave me a quick,

176

sharp glance. 'But you won't begin until day after tomorrow. We've got a ride to take first.'

I had no idea what he was thinking about, but the next morning I hooked the bay mare he used for driving to his light, two-wheeled cart and we started north to the Valley Ranch. It was a small copy of J Ranch, even to the poplars around the white house.

We had dinner there, but both Rolly Dillon and José Otero were out on the range. I built a fire and cooked a meal while Perrin took care of the mare and strolled across the meadow until I called that dinner was ready. I suppose he thought Dillon would come in at noon, and he could perform a miracle by bringing us to an understanding, but for my part I was glad Dillon was gone.

After dinner we took off across the sagebrush, climbing toward a ridge that made a straight line across the blue sky. When we got higher, I could see the lake and the cabins that belonged to my folks and the Allisons. Later I could make out the others, even the Hammond place clear over on Thunder River.

I had never mentioned the Hammonds to him, nor he to me, but after what Lane Sears had said I knew where Perrin went every Sunday, usually not getting back until after midnight. I hated what he was doing because I always thought of Rocky, and wondered if she would ever find out.

Presently we reached the top and I pulled up,

the rimrock breaking off below us for a sheer fifty feet. I looked down into the prettiest valley I had ever seen, a willow-lined creek meandering through it with green meadows on both sides.

Rimrock made an almost solid wall around the valley, with here and there a few breaks that were easily closed by fences. A number of buildings stood in the center of the valley, a small frame house and a barn and several sheds and stockade corrals similar to the ones at J Ranch.

I suppose we sat there a full ten minutes, just looking, then Perrin made an impatient gesture for me to start back. 'Paradise Valley,' he said. 'I suppose there are ten thousand Paradise Valleys in the United States, but this one is worthy of the name. Belongs to a man named Joe Ryan. He got here before I did. Has a wife and two boys. Runs about a hundred head of cattle under the Rafter R iron. I've done my damnedest to buy it. Offered him twice what it's worth, but he just laughs in my face.'

His voice was bitter, and when I looked at him I had the feeling that 'greed' was a better word than 'ambition' to describe the land hunger that was in him. I knew that he was thinking that Ryan was a fool to turn down his offer because this was a land for big operators, and in the long run the little fellow was bound to fail. I had heard him say it often enough.

'What about the Indians?' I asked. 'Looks to
178

me as if an isolated family like the Ryans would be the first to be attacked.'

'We won't have any Indian trouble,' he said scornfully. 'Just scare talk.'

I hoped he was right, but I remembered what Virgil Lang had said the night we stayed at his place. I knew Lang scared easily, but the knowledge was balanced by the fact that Jim Perrin didn't scare at all.

CHAPTER THIRTEEN

Winters on Thunder River were unpredictable, some were tough, as the winter four years before had been when, according to Lane Sears, many of the cowmen to the south and west of J Ranch had been wiped out. Other winters were mild, but the trick, Lane said, was to be ready for the tough ones and then be thankful for the mild ones. That was another reason for Perrin's success. He was never unprepared.

Billy Ralls continued to haul lumber from the sawmill in the Blue Mountains as long as the weather permitted. Perrin had ordered freight from Portland to be sent upriver by the steamboat, and had sent wagons north to The Dalles. Now, in early fall, the wagons rolled into the J Ranch yard with supplies for the winter.

Although the long row of wood continued to lengthen, Perrin kept me cutting with Manuel Sandoval and Harry Gillam, so I did not go on fall roundup. I didn't object to that, but I wanted to go on the drive to Winnemucca more than I had ever wanted anything in my life, or so it seemed to me as the fall days dragged out and Perrin said nothing either way.

Then, with roundup finished and a herd of eight hundred steers gathered at Giant Springs Ranch, I was told without any preliminaries that I was to go. Manuel and Harry could finish the wood cutting without me. That afternoon I left J Ranch with Perrin, my gun and belt tied behind my saddle inside my slicker.

I don't think Perrin knew I had the gun. In any case he said nothing about it. I knew that Rolly Dillon had been on roundup, and I was reasonably sure he'd help make the drive. When we reached Giant Springs Ranch that night, I saw I had guessed right. Rolly Dillon was there.

Many times I have seen Perrin ignore situations that were loaded with trouble. He ignored this one, but I think he'd decided that it had to come to a head sooner or later, and he purposely took Dillon and me on the drive so that it would.

That night at supper Lane Sears brought his plate and tin cup and hunkered beside me. He asked softly, 'Fetch your gun?'

'I've got it,' I said.

'Don't wear it. Just keep it handy.'

That was all he said, but it was enough to tell me that Dillon had his gun and that only one of us would be coming back. But nothing happened that night. Before sunup we were on our way, heading the herd south along the western slope of Garnet Mountain. Sam Boon had gone on ahead with the chuck wagon.

The first day of a drive is always the hardest, but it seldom takes long for a herd to shake down. I have a theory that cattle are like people. In a herd you find a few leaders who get out in front and set the pace, but the great bulk of them just follow along as soon as the direction is established.

You can count on a few individualists, the bullheaded ones who take off the wrong way just on general principles. They have to be forced back into line. Then there are the laggards who have to be prodded along, the lazy ones who, if they could talk, would have a fine alibi for not keeping up.

Perrin was riding point with Rolly Dillon. Because I rode drag with Pedro García, we had to deal with the laggards. About the middle of the morning Perrin turned the herd eastward through a gorge that led to the top of the mountain. When, on occasion, the dust cleared, I could see the pass toward which we were headed.

It was a hard day, the only day on the entire drive when we pushed the herd harder than we should, but we had to get over the top and down to the bunchgrass slope on the east side. There Sam Boon was waiting with the chuck wagon beside a fire within fifty feet of a small stream.

The cattle drifted out across the grass, some to graze, some to lie down, and others simply to stand there chewing their cuds. Sam got out a quarter of beef that had been wrapped in a heavy canvas and cut steaks. He made coffee, baked biscuits in a Dutch oven, and by the time the sun slid down over Garnet Mountain we were eating supper.

After that, one day was much like another as we pointed the herd southeast, then almost directly south. A storm hit us shortly after we crossed the Nevada line, but with that exception the days were comfortably warm and clear, the nights cold with the promise of winter.

The drive took more than two weeks, and not once did I ride night herd with Rolly Dillon. Lane Sears saw to that. The same idea was in his mind, I think, that was in mine. Rolly Dillon would not be above shooting a man in the back, and if that shot started a stampede it would be all the better. No one would find the bullet in what was left of a man after eight hundred steers had run over him. But whatever Dillon's intentions were, he never had a chance

182

to kill me that way.

The steers were in good shape by the time we reached the railroad. We had brought them along slowly and carefully, for Jim Perrin was never one to run weight off his cattle. A buyer who apparently had dealt with Perrin before met us a mile out of town. He scratched his head in amazement—Lane Sears said he always did—and wanted to know what Perrin fed them in Oregon that made them grow to such size in three years.

Lane gave me a wink. 'And when them critters get to Sacramento, somebody will be asking the same thing. Of course, there's something in having the right Shorthorn stock, and knowing how to handle 'em, but when you get down to cases it ain't hard to find the answer. No diseases, the best grass in the world, and the right climate.'

'It won't last forever,' I said.

Lane shrugged. 'I ain't so sure, Danny. Jim's got a habit of looking a long ways ahead. I've got a hunch it'll last as long as I'm around. Or you, either.'

Maybe it would at that, I thought. Lane was right about Perrin looking ahead. No doubt that was back of his obsession to own land, or at least to control it. I thought about it as the buyer made his count and paid Perrin in cash. It seemed to me that in time a man reached the point where he had to control his appetite, or his appetite would control him.

Perrin came to where Lane sat his horse beside me. He said: 'I've got to send a telegram. I'll meet the boys in Malone's Bar in half an hour.' He swung around and mounted and rode down the street that paralleled the railroad, carrying the saddlebags heavy with gold.

Lane sighed. 'Well, Danny, you're here, and not a cap's been cracked.'

'Plenty of time,' I said.

He nodded. 'Plenty of time, all right. Let's put our horses up. Then we'll put the feed bag on as soon as we get paid and we'll cut our wolf loose.' He gave me a sharp glance. 'Keep your eyes peeled, Danny.'

When Lane and I reached Malone's Bar, most of the crew was already there, but Dillon wasn't in sight. We had a drink, mine almost choking me because I wasn't used to it. Lane said, 'One's enough for you, Danny,' and I nodded, knowing what he meant.

Dillon came in a moment later, glanced about the bar until he saw me, then came straight to where I stood. 'Whisky,' he said, shouldering in between me and Lane. He downed his drink, then looked at me and grinned. 'Don't bother to draw your time, nester,' he said. 'You won't have no use for it.'

He wasn't wearing his gun. I glanced at Lane, wondering if I could knock some of Dillon's belligerence out of him with my fists. I don't know whether Lane guessed what I was

184

thinking or not, but I have an idea he did, for he shook his head at me.

Perrin came in, carrying one saddlebag, and dumped a pile of gold coins on the bar. He had deposited most of the money in a bank, leaving enough for his own expenses and to pay the crew.

The men gathered around him, Ole Larsen saying, 'I've been thinking about this all summer.'

'All winter, too,' Lane said.

And Pedro: '*Sí*. Tonight Pedro gambles.'

'Hell, you're no poker player,' Lane said. 'What makes you think you are?'

'Save your breath,' Perrin said. 'You'll never convince Pedro he can't play poker.'

Perrin was counting out each man's wages, adding a ten-dollar bonus. When he got to Dillon, he said: 'Take it easy tonight, Rolly. Last year you wound up in jail.'

'Save your advice,' Dillon said. 'I'm quitting.'

Perrin straightened, tipping his hat back with a quick upthrust of his thumb. 'You won't find a better job than you've got on J Ranch.'

'I told you to save your advice, Perrin,' Dillon said.

Nobody said anything for a moment. We stood looking at them, Perrin's expression unchanged, Dillon's face sullen. I had never heard any of the crew call Perrin by his last name. It was Jim even with the Chinese cook.

185

Then slowly Perrin shoved four gold eagles along the bar to Dillon. He said, 'All right, Rolly, if that's the way you want it.'

'You God-damned tightwad,' Dillon shouted, 'you gave a bonus—'

'Loyalty is something that can't be bought,' Perrin said evenly, 'and it can't be paid for, but I've had it from every man in the outfit but you. I give a small bonus as a recognition of it. When your father—'

'You son of a bitch,' Dillon said softly, 'I've listened to your preaching all summer—'

I never saw a man move faster than Jim Perrin did, and I never saw a man hit harder. His right fist came up before Dillon knew it had started, catching him on his square chin, and the sound of the blow ran the full length of the room. Dillon went back and down, his head hitting the floor as his feet came up off it.

I thought he was knocked out, but he wasn't. He lifted himself on one elbow and looked at Perrin, then at me, and I wasn't sure which of us he hated more. He got to his feet and brushed the sawdust off his pants.

'If you've got a gun, nester,' he said to me, 'you'd best go get it. After I drill you, I'm coming after Perrin.'

He wheeled out of the saloon. Nobody said anything for a moment; they didn't move except to turn their heads enough to look at me, all but Jim Perrin. I could have ducked the fight, and I thought about doing it, for I

186

remembered Alec Brown telling me that Perrin was handy with a gun. I don't think he had his with him, but he could have borrowed one.

'Let's see now,' Perrin said as if nothing had happened. 'Who hasn't been paid? Ole, how about you?'

No, I couldn't duck it, not if I wanted to stay on J Ranch, but I couldn't risk going into the street. There was a back door and I headed for it. Lane said something. I didn't hear all of it, just, 'Let him go, Jim. He's got...' Then I was in the alley and walking toward the stable where I had left my buckskin.

I wasn't scared. Not then. I untied my slicker and buckled the gun belt around me. I tied the holster down. I checked the action of the .44, eased it back into the stiff leather, and went out through the archway.

A dozen thoughts raced through my mind. They weren't really thoughts, just mental images of my folks. Virgil Lang. The Fergusons. Debbie Allison. Cissy, who had joshed me about wearing a gun. Then I saw Dillon halfway down the block, and he saw me and started toward me, boots kicking up little puffs of dust.

Then, with a sort of wrench, my mind closed out the mental images and I thought about the lesson Lane had given me, and what he had said about some men who could hit a tin can in a street but couldn't get their guns out of leather when they faced a man who planned to kill them. He had said it was something he couldn't teach me. I had it, or I didn't.

The sun was low, my shadow long beside me on the street dust. Dillon was closer, walking easily, very confident. I flexed my right hand. It seemed stiff. I seemed stiff all over. I don't think I was scared even then, or if I was I didn't know it. All I could think of was that I had to get Dillon or he'd get me.

I had become accurate enough with my Sunday-afternoon practices. I could put five bullets into the same three-inch circle Lane had done that first day, but I knew I was slow, and I knew Dillon had been practicing, too.

Then he made his draw, and it seemed to me his gun sounded before mine was clear of leather. He fired again, and I felt the tug of a bullet as it ripped through my coat just above my left shoulder.

My gun was up, lined on Dillon. Another burst of flame from his Colt and my hat was lifted from my head. But something had happened. I'm sure it wasn't matter of thinking. Perhaps it was the result of years of Bible teaching of memorizing the Ten Commandments. I don't really know, but I'm sure I could have killed him. Instead I hit him in the shoulder and knocked him down.

I ran toward him. He had dropped his gun, but now he reached for it with his left hand and I shot him again and I saw the bloody mass that had been a hand a second before. He fell back

188

into the dust as men came into the street and someone yelled for a doctor. Dillon looked at me, hating me and cursing me, and then the men were all around us.

Lane grabbed my arms and shook me. 'You damned fool, why didn't you kill him?' I looked at him. He asked, 'You could have killed him, couldn't you?' and I nodded.

I wrenched free from his grip and ran for an alley. I got off the street and leaned against a building, and then I got sick. Somehow I got my gun back into leather. I was sweating and still retching when Lane got there. He said, 'You need a drink.'

That night I ate supper in a hotel dining room with Lane and Perrin. I mean, I sat at the table and pushed food around on my plate, but I didn't really eat. When Perrin was done, he glanced at his watch.

'I'm catching a train for San Francisco in fifteen minutes,' he said. 'Lane, see that the boys don't get into too much trouble. Start home in the morning. I don't care how big their heads are. Take them home.'

Lane grinned. 'I will if I can stick in the saddle.'

Perrin looked at me. 'You're staying in town for a week, Danny. I guess I can count on you keeping out of jail.'

'I guess you can,' I said.

'I'm getting married,' Perrin said, 'and I'll be back with Rocky in a week. I'll send you a

189

telegram so you'll know when to meet the train. I've bought a team of blacks and a rig. It's in the Red Front Livery. Every day you're here I want you to give that team a workout. You'll be driving us home and I don't want to poke along.' I nodded, and he said: 'Lane, you see the boys are slicked up when we get home. I want the house cleaned up. Pull Wang's pigtail if he doesn't do a good job.'

Lane leaned back in his chair. 'Jim, don't you worry none. It's gonna be fine, having a woman on J Ranch.'

Perrin rose and put on his hat. He looked at me and cleared his throat. He said: 'Danny, usually there's a way to avoid a killing, but when you get to a certain place you can't avoid it. Then you've just got to do it.' He nodded at us. 'So long,' he said, and walked out.

Lane brushed at his mustache. He said, 'That's Jim's way of saying the same thing I told you.' His eyes turned to the lobby door through which Perrin had gone, and I think he completely forgot about me and Rolly Dillon. He said, 'By God, I hope he's getting the right woman.'

I stayed in Malone's Bar until after midnight, just watching. Ole Larsen got so drunk he had to lean against the bar. José Otero had a fight with a sheepherder, took a knife away from him, and threw him into the street. Lane went upstairs to one of the rooms that opened onto the balcony and came back an hour later, walking slowly and half smiling as if he were satisfied with himself and the world. And Pedro García sat at a poker table, a fat cigar cocked in one corner of his mouth, a tall pile of chips in front of him that got taller as the hours passed.

I ate breakfast with them in the morning, breakfast that consisted of countless cups of black coffee for Ole Larsen. When we finished, Ole carefully put a hat on his head and insisted someone had stolen his. He swore that his head was too big for the hat.

'Your head's too big for the biggest hat Stetson ever made,' Lane said. 'That's what you get for trying to drink all of Malone's whisky, you damned Swede.'

'I ain't no Swede,' Ole yelled, and took a poke at Lane that missed by a foot. 'Don't nobody call me a Swede. I'll lick the next God-damned buckaroo who calls me a Swede.'

'Come on.' Lane started him for the door. 'Let's ride.'

I stood on the boardwalk and watched them leave town, the chuck wagon lumbering along behind them. I was alone in Winnemucca, alone with a team of blacks I was supposed to work out every day. And in a week I'd meet Rocky O'Toole who would be Mrs Jim Perrin.

That afternoon I asked the doctor about Dillon. 'He'll live,' the doctor said, 'but he won't ever use his left hand again. All I've got to say is that it's too bad it ain't his right.'

It turned cold that week and snowed a good six inches, then the sky cleared. After that, the weather warmed up and the snow went off, leaving the streets hock-deep in mud. The last day of the week was cold again, freezing the mud, and that night the telegram came. I was to have the team and rig at the depot at six o'clock in the morning.

CHAPTER FOURTEEN

The next morning I tied the team at the hitch pole on the street side of the depot before six. For a time I walked along the track, the collar of the sheepskin coat which I had bought earlier in the week pulled up around my ears. At that hour of the morning, the wind was wicked. Then I thought it was foolish to stand out there and get cold, so I went into the waiting room.

Several people were standing around the pot-bellied stove, one of them a querulous old woman who kept asking peevishly why trains were always late. A baby began to cry, excited by the old woman, I guess. The crying irritated a drummer, who slammed his sample case down on a seat and stared out of a window, getting as far away as he could from the baby.

I don't really know what I was thinking. Perhaps I wasn't thinking at all. You know how it is when you've been waiting for something which you know is going to happen, and when you finally reach the time for it to happen your emotions have been so blunted you just stand there, and noises like the crying of a baby are distant, neutral sounds. I was only sure of one thing. I didn't want to meet Mrs Jim Perrin.

Presently we heard the whistle, still far to the west. I left the waiting room, suddenly impatient, the others remaining inside. I paced back and forth on the cinders, the locomotive close now, its bell jingling, then it rolled past, snorting and banging and blowing out great clouds of smoke and steam like a dragon come to life out of some ancient legend.

I saw Perrin on the steps of a 'Silver Palace' car before the wheels stopped turning, and I walked rapidly toward him. I waved and he waved, then the train stopped and he stepped down. I had never seen him wear anything but his work clothes. Now he looked different in a black broadcloth suit, a heavy black overcoat with a fur collar, and a brand new, broad-brimmed black Stetson that must have cost him the price of a steer.

He was down on the cinders before I got there, his hand extended as he asked, 'Stay out of jail all right, Danny?'

'Sure did,' I said.

He turned and helped his wife down, then he swung back to me. 'Danny, meet Mrs Perrin.'

I took off my hat and looked at her, and I hoped she was thinking that my face was red because of the cold. Meeting her was the strangest, most uncanny experience I had ever had. It was as if the picture above the mantel in the big house at J Ranch had broken through the glass and come to life.

She seemed very tall, nearly as tall as Perrin, an illusion of height that was exaggerated by the long brown traveling coat that she wore. When she was close to me, I realized the picture did not do her justice. I had never been able to translate the black and white of the picture into color. But I saw her in color now, the blue eyes that were so very blue, the rich red lips, the hair that showed below her cap—auburn, I think it would be called. At least it was not the bright-toned red I had thought it would be.

I held out a hand to her, and she took it and leaned forward and kissed me on the cheek. I hadn't expected that. I almost broke and ran. Perrin laughed softly. 'You scared him, Rocky. He's not used to being kissed by the boss's wife.'

She laughed too. 'I might add that the boss is not used to being kissed by his wife, either.' She squeezed my hand and dropped it. 'Danny, it's nice meeting you. Jim's talked about you so much.'

I didn't have good sense right then. I mumbled something about hoping she would like it on J Ranch, and she said, her eyes

194

twinkling as if she knew I was embarrassed: 'I know I will, Danny. Jim tells me it's just one step short of Heaven. Sometimes I think even the step isn't there.'

Her luggage had been piled beside the tracks: suitcases, boxes, and a big trunk. Jim said, 'Bring the rig here, Danny. No use carrying all this stuff over there.'

'Stuff, is it?' she said. 'I suppose next you'll be telling me I don't need it and that you have everything on J Ranch a woman will need.'

'Almost,' he said, trying hard to be cheerful, and failing.

I had a vague feeling then that something was wrong, a feeling that stayed with me as we ate breakfast. There was nothing definite about it, just a faint uneasiness. Perrin had made a mistake, I decided, bringing her to his country at this time of year. Spring would have been better, or summer, and then she could have been prepared for winter.

We were nearly done eating when she asked suddenly, 'How old are you, Danny?'

'Nineteen,' I said. 'I had a birthday a couple of weeks after I started working on J Ranch last spring.'

Perrin looked up from his coffee. 'You didn't say anything about a birthday, Danny.'

'No need to say anything about it. We all have birthdays every year. Natural enough. Just like dying.'

'Danny,' Rocky said. 'What a morbid

thought!' She smiled. 'You know, we're almost the same age. 'I'm nineteen, too. My birthday was in July.'

So she was a month younger than I was. The thought startled me, for I had supposed she was older. She seemed very much a woman, with none of the girlishness that was so apparent in Debbie Allison or in Cissy Hammond. But she couldn't be compared to them. There was something about her, some quality that I couldn't quite identify, which set her apart from them. I suppose it was a sense of self-assurance, of complete confidence which came from her experience and background, a world that Debbie and Cissy would never know.

Perrin scooted back his chair. 'We'd better start. We've got a long way to go.'

Rocky finished her coffee and rose. 'Is he always this impatient, Danny?'

'No,' I said. 'Not always.'

'I just want to get home,' he said, giving her that quick grin of his; then it was gone, and his face was grave and a little concerned when he added, 'My home that is going to be our home.'

'"Where thou lodgest, I will lodge: thy people shall be my people, and thy God my God,"' Rocky said.

'What's that?' Perrin asked.

Rocky looked at me. 'You know, don't you, Danny?'

'Ruth,' I said, 'and her mother-in-law.'

196

Perrin gave me a quick look as if to remind me of what he had said about me being a bridge between her old life and the life she'd have to get used to on J Ranch. I nodded to let him know I remembered, then he helped Rocky into her coat and handed her the muff which matched the fur she wore around her neck.

We talked very little on the long ride home. The wind kept clawing at us all day, whipping the words out of our mouths as fast as we said them. And it required a shout to be heard above the racket of wheels and hoofs on the frozen ground. Rocky rode between me and Perrin, a buffalo robe across our laps, her hands inside her muff, her fur wrapped around her face so that only her forehead and her eyes and the pug tip of her nose were visible.

We crossed the Nevada-Oregon line in late afternoon and reached Ferrill's ranch before dark. Ferrill ran more of a hotel than a ranch. I doubt that he had fifty head of cattle under his Circle F iron, and he butchered them as fast as he needed them for his dining room, buying from his neighbors when he needed more meat.

Ferrill's place wasn't particularly clean, and he had little variety of food to offer. We ate beefsteak and biscuits and coffee for supper; we had the same for breakfast; and we were on our way again before the sun was up. We swung west a mile north of Ferrill's ranch, following a road that was not really a road over the shoulder of Garnet Mountain, wheeled down the west side, and by the middle of the afternoon we reached Giant Springs Ranch.

Rocky was terribly tired, but when Perrin said we could spend the night there she said she wanted to go on. Then Perrin began to talk. It was warmer in the valley, and the road was soft under wheels and hoofs so that he could talk without shouting. He told her about things that had happened when he had first come into the country more than six years ago; he told her how the valley had looked and how he had felt. He had not known what he would find, but the instant he had seen Thunder River and its valley, lying between the desert and the mountain, he had known it was the place he had been looking for.

I had never heard Perrin talk that way before. I think he was trying to tell Rocky something, but he wasn't able to put it into words. He was trying to share with her his feelings and his dream, wanting her to know that everything that he sought in this life was on Thunder River.

The seeds of tragedy were sowed on the cold fall afternoon that Jim Perrin brought Rocky to J Ranch. For him it was homecoming. He had been gone for nearly a month, and I suppose that every hour he had been away had seemed like a year to him. Now that he was back, the impatience was gone from him.

But the trouble was—and it was the thing that was always wrong between them—he did not understand her feelings. I suppose she was a little frightened at the prospect that faced her. Certainly it must have been a terrifying experience to be uprooted from one life and set down in another. Perrin had foreseen that, so he had asked me to help. But he was never able to sense her feeling at a particular time, and that was what was wrong now.

She was simply too worn out to match his mood and his enthusiasm. She tried, but she failed, and presently he stopped talking, his face quite grim. Perhaps even then, as tired as she was, she realized that with him the land came first and always would. It may have been then that jealousy was born in her. She was made to love with all her heart, and she was incapable of sharing that love with anyone or any thing.

We reached J Ranch in late afternoon, with the sun hanging low above the rimrock in the west. I stopped in front of the poplar trees, tall skeletons at that time of year, and Perrin stepped down and gave Rocky a hand. When she stood beside him, he asked, 'Do you like it?'

And she said, 'It's wonderful, Jim.'

'Put the horses up,' Perrin told me. 'Rocky will want to rest before she meets the boys.'

I drove on to the barn, and Lane Sears came out of the bunkhouse. Before I stepped down, he asked, 'What's she like, Dan?'

'Nice,' I said. 'And she's pretty.'

He helped me unhook, and then he

muttered, 'By God, I hope he's got the right woman.'

'That's the second time you've said that,' I told him. 'What are you worrying about?'

He didn't answer me until he had watered the horses and led them into the barn. Finally he said: 'Danny, most of us have known Jim a long time. There ain't nothing on this green earth we wouldn't do for him, not nothing; but I'd hate like hell for him to get hurt.'

'She's fine, Lane,' I said. 'She wouldn't hurt him for the world.'

'I reckon not,' he agreed. 'Not if she knowed she was hurting him. But this is a hell of a place to fetch a woman. Sure, he's got a fine house for her and she won't have to work much. She'll be comfortable and warm and she can eat her head off. Now and then he'll probably send her back to California, or to New York if that's where she wants to go.'

'Sounds pretty good to me,' I said.

He shook his head, his face more melancholy than I had ever seen it. 'No, it don't sound good to me. She won't have no women to talk to, no doctor to call in if she gets a mite bilious, and when she has her babies, she's gonna be mighty alone.' He shook his head again. 'Don't tell me your mother stood all them things and then some. That ain't the point. The proposition is whether Mrs Jim Perrin can stand 'em. I hope to God she can.'

I said nothing. There was nothing I could

say. I just didn't know.

We carried Rocky's heavy trunk to the front porch of the big house. Lane said, 'You go in and see how she's making out. I got the boys scrubbed up till their faces shine like they was kids about to give a Christmas program. All I hope is they stay scrubbed up.'

He stalked back to the bunkhouse and I went into the house. Rocky was standing in front of the fireplace, her back to it. She was wearing the same trim, almost severe, brown suit she had worn on the train.

'We'll fetch your things in now, Mrs Perrin, if you want them,' I said.

'No hurry.' She smiled at me. 'Danny, tell me something. What do you say when you're introduced to a bunch of buckaroos?'

Perrin came in from the dining room in time to hear the question. He laughed. 'Rocky, just remember one thing. The boys are more scared than you'll ever be.' He turned to me. 'Are they ready to come in?'

I nodded. 'Lane's got them all scrubbed up, he said.'

'I'll fetch them,' Perrin said, and left the house.

I walked across the room to the fireplace. 'Do you like the house?'

'Very much,' she said. 'It's unbelievable, finding things like this here.' She made a wide motion with her hand. 'I've got a big job ahead of me, Danny. Will you help me?'

There was nothing she could have said that would have surprised me more. Impulsively I said, 'Of course.'

She was silent then, her hands held behind her, palms toward the fire. I don't know why she asked that, unless she felt some common ground with me that she did not feel with Perrin. Or it may have been that suddenly she sensed her inadequacy, remembering what Perrin had said to her when we reached the valley, and knowing that she failed to comprehend what he had tried to tell her.

We heard boots on the porch, and she gave me a tight little smile. 'It's like a queen meeting her subjects, isn't it, Danny?'

'The queen of J Ranch,' I said, and stepped away from her as Perrin came in leading the procession.

I almost laughed aloud when I saw them. Every man was wearing a new shirt. Boots were polished. Hair was slicked down. All of them had shaved. But I was amused more by their red faces than by anything else. It just didn't seem possible that men with the leathery-brown skin these men had could turn red, but they did.

Perrin started with Lane Sears and went on down the line. They shook hands with her, and all of them tried to say something, a mumbled, 'Welcome to J Ranch,' or 'Howdy, Miz Perrin.' Ole Larsen tripped on the rug. Alec Brown had more trouble with his peg leg than

202

I'd ever seen him have before. Sam Boon, usually as crotchety as a sore-nosed bull, gave a sort of a giggle when he shook hands with her, and didn't say a word.

Pedro García was the last in line. He seemed to be all teeth when he grinned at her. Taking her hand, he bowed and kissed it. He said: 'Señora, the sun she will shine now. Señor Jim, he is lucky.'

'Thank you, Pedro,' she said. 'Thank you very much.' She stood straight and tall, her gaze moving from one to the other, then she turned to Perrin. 'They're nice, Jim. They're wonderfully nice. Why didn't you tell me?'

Perrin scratched his head. 'Well, to tell the truth, Rocky, I never saw them like this before. You must have hypnotized them.'

Lane cleared his throat. 'We've got a present for you, ma'am. Ole, go fetch it in.'

'Me?' Ole cried, his bald spot turning red. 'Pedro made it. He oughtta...' He swallowed, his Adam's apple bobbing up and down; then he walked out to the porch and came back with a new, four-strand reata coiled up in his right hand. He gave it to Rocky and backed away.

For a long moment Rocky held it in front of her, staring at it and not having the slightest idea what to do with it. I couldn't think of anything she needed less, but the gift itself was not important. The motive behind it was, and Rocky knew it.

'Thank you again,' she said. 'I feel like

203

crying. Isn't that crazy? This is the finest thing that's happened to me since Jim asked me to marry him.'

Perrin winked at her. 'They figure on you going out on spring roundup. I won't get a lick of work out of them. They'll all be trying to teach you how to rope a calf.'

'Let's carry Mrs Perrin's things upstairs,' Lane said briskly. 'Dan, give me a hand with the trunk.'

They went out of the room like a stampeding herd of steers. When Lane and I set the trunk down in Perrin's room, I asked, 'Why didn't you let Pedro give her the reata?'

He winked at me. 'Hell, I didn't want him kissing her hand again. He won't be worth a damn all winter. He'll think he's an Eyetalian count or something.'

A moment later they came banging up the stairs, dropped the suitcases and boxes in the hall outside the door of Perrin's room, and then fled to the sanctuary of the bunkhouse, Lane the first one out of the house. When I went back downstairs, Rocky was sitting in a chair, holding the reata on her lap.

Perrin grinned at me and pointed to the reata. 'Now isn't that like them?'

There were tears in her eyes when she looked up. She whispered, 'Jim, it's like coming home.'

CHAPTER FIFTEEN

I found out I had a new job the first day Rocky got to J Ranch. Perrin raised me to forty dollars a month and then began telling me what my duties were. I'd just sit around waiting for Rocky to give me something to do. Fetch in wood for the fireplace. Help her clean house. Move the furniture if she took the notion. Look after the brown mare Perrin was going to give Rocky. Put the sidesaddle on her if Rocky wanted to take a ride. And ride with her if she wanted company.

We were standing in front of the barn when he told me all this. I looked at the house. Rocky wasn't up yet. Then I looked at Perrin. 'I guess Mrs Perrin has been raised pretty fancy,' I said.

'Her family had money,' Perrin said, 'but most of it's gone. Her folks are both dead. I'm all the family she's got now, Danny.'

I looked at the house again. Perrin hadn't named the word, but I knew what I'd be. A servant! Rocky's personal servant. I'd stand around and wait for her to open her pretty mouth to tell me what to do. It would have been bad enough under any circumstances, but feeling about Rocky as I did it was intolerable.

How did I feel about Rocky? I didn't really know. Certainly not the way I felt about Debbie Allison, who wanted a husband. I had no illusions about Debbie's feeling for me. I was handy, I had reasonably good health, and I seemed steady, I suppose, to her.

And Cissy? She was different. Lane said once that Cissy's mother was three times more woman than any other female he'd ever seen. That described Cissy, too. It was exciting just to think about kissing her, but the excitement never lasted because I always started wondering what she'd thought the night I'd brought her back from the schoolhouse.

But Rocky was—well, first of all, Rocky had been a picture, and I suppose it's possible to fall in love with a picture. Or perhaps I was in love with the imaginary woman I had dreamed up. But she wasn't imaginary now. That was the trouble. She was here, attractive and very nice, and she was Jim Perrin's wife.

I said carefully, 'I guess she's used to having servants.'

'I guess so,' Perrin said, 'when her folks were alive.'

I started toward the corral that held my buckskin. It didn't occur to me that I was giving up the only job I'd ever wanted, that I was getting more pay than I'd get anywhere else, that I didn't have anywhere to go, and that with winter coming on I didn't have the slightest chance of getting on with any of the other outfits in the country. All I knew was that I had to get off J Ranch.

'Where the hell are you going?' Perrin asked.

'I don't know,' I said, 'but I'm getting out of here.'

'Danny.' He ran after me and grabbed my arm. 'Why, Danny? For God's sake, why?'

He was more upset than I had ever seen him. I said, 'I just can't be Mrs Perrin's servant.'

He took a long breath and let go of me. He said, 'I never aimed for you to be, Danny.'

He looked at me as if wondering what he could say that would change my mind. Again I had the feeling that he was a lonely man who seldom let anyone see or feel what he really was, and right now he was helpless.

'Danny,' he said finally, 'I never reminded a man before in my life that he owed me anything, but I am now. You owe me enough to stay here and give this job a try.'

What could I say to that? 'Yeah, I guess I do,' I said finally. 'All right, I'll give it a try.'

'Thanks, Danny. Now go and curry Bird down. I want Rocky to see her when she gets up.'

Rocky stayed in bed until noon that day, probably worn out by the long trip from Winnemucca. That afternoon she came out of the house wearing a white blouse and tan skirt, her dark red hair braided and pinned in a coronet on top of her head. Perrin and I stood in the big barn door, watching her walk to us in the lithe, graceful way she had.

'Good morning,' she said, smiling, 'and don't tell me it isn't morning. It is to me. I just

207

couldn't wake up.'

'I'm glad you did, finally,' Perrin said. 'We've got a present for you.' He nodded at me. 'Bring Bird out, Danny.'

I backed the mare out of her stall and led her through the barn door. Rocky just stood there, her eyes wide, and I knew then she was a good judge of horseflesh.

'Her name is Bird,' Perrin said proudly. 'Danny's going to take care of her for you. Any time you want to ride, just tell him.'

'She's beautiful, Jim,' Rocky said. 'Just beautiful.'

Perrin nodded, satisfied with the knowledge that he had done the right thing. 'You want to try her out today?'

She shook her head. 'I'm still kind of tired, Jim.'

The next day Perrin took her to the Valley Ranch in his two-wheeled cart. They stayed there that night, and I had nothing to do except work up some wood for the fireplace. Usually that was Manuel's and Harry Gillam's job, but they were still hauling from Garnet Mountain, and would until the snow stopped them.

Perrin and Rocky returned late the next afternoon, Rocky still exclaiming over Paradise Valley. After supper she said, 'Jim, I want to own the Rafter R.'

He stared at her, shocked, unable to say anything for a moment. It must have hit him hard, because he wasn't a man to let his feelings show on his face. Finally he laughed. 'You own J Ranch, Rocky. You own everything I do.'

She came to him and sat on the arm of his chair. 'Of course I do, honey, but this isn't quite the same. I mean, I'd like to own something myself. Look at it this way, Jim. You made J Ranch. It's still really yours and it always will be. I'd like to feel that way about the Rafter R. Don't you see?'

He didn't. His dark eyes were on the fire, his lips drawn tight against his teeth. On a matter that made no sense to him, he could be fiercely unyielding. Finally he said, 'You can't buy it if Joe Ryan won't sell it.'

'Maybe he will someday,' she said. 'Promise me one thing, Jim. If it ever can be bought, let me have it.'

From where I sat across the room, I could see his face grow darker and the hard bulge of muscles at the hinges of his jaw. I was sure he would say no. I had never known him to yield on any question that was really important to him, and nothing was more important to Jim Perrin than land.

I'm not sure what decided him. Maybe he thought the Rafter R would never be for sale. Or perhaps he hoped that Rocky would realize how great a concession he was making to her. But whatever the motive was that prompted him, he said, 'All right, Rocky, I promise.'

She leaned down and kissed him. 'Thank

you, Jim,' she said.

They were entirely unaware of my presence. I rose and went upstairs to my room, knowing that I shouldn't be in the house, particularly now when they were making their adjustments to each other. But it was Perrin's idea that I stay, and I was caught in a trap of obligation from which there was no escape.

I was in bed when they came upstairs. The partition between the rooms was thin enough so that I could hear the slightest sound on the other side. I had often heard the bedsprings squeak as Perrin turned over in his sleep, and I had heard him snore.

Now the murmur of their talk came to me. I heard Perrin's boots hit the floor, and then the springs squeaked as they got into bed. Silence for a long time after that, and I was almost asleep when I heard the bedsprings again. I lay motionless, sweating, and I thought of Cissy Hammond.

The next day was cold with a dark sky that threatened snow. After supper I had a feeling I could not go back into the big house. I stood beside the corral gate, the collar of my sheepskin pulled up around my neck, knowing what I wanted to do but unable to make the decision, held back, I suppose, by my strict raising, by the moral platitudes that had been said to me as long as I could remember.

Now, standing there with my hands rammed into my pockets, the reason occurred to me that my mother had said she would like me to marry Debbie Allison and settle down beside them. She hadn't mentioned it since I had tried to take Cissy to the dance. Thinking about it, it struck me, with a sudden, savage impact, that if I had the name I might as well have the game.

'Feels like snow,' Lane Sears said.

I hadn't heard him come up. It was so dark I could hardly make out his figure, standing not more than three feet from me. I said, 'Cold enough.' He was silent a moment, then he said casually, too casually: 'Thought I'd ride over to the Hammonds tonight. Want to go?'

'Might as well,' I said, and hoped I sounded as casual as he did.

Lane was always something of an enigma to me. Many times, just as he had tonight, he seemed to read my mind. I pondered it as we rode toward the Hammond place, the cold wind knifing at us as it ran across the flat. It helped keep my mind off what was ahead.

I didn't want Cissy's mother. I wanted Cissy, and I had a terrible fear that I'd be received the way Rolly Dillon had been. Lane didn't give me the slightest clue about what he thought, if he gave it any thought at all. Presently I forgot about Lane's mind-reading talent because my thoughts were fastened on Cissy.

When we tied at the hitch pole in front of the house, I asked, 'How much does it cost?'

'Five dollars,' he said. 'In advance.'

We crossed the porch and Lane knocked.

Cissy opened the door. She said, 'Come in before you let all the cold air...' Then she saw me. She just stood there, lips parted, staring at me.

'Come on, Dan,' Lane said. 'That cold air froze her right where she's standing, I reckon.'

I followed him into the room and Cissy closed the door. Mrs Hammond rose from where she had been reading beside the little mahogany table with the carved legs. She said, 'Good evening, Lane,' and her eyes came to me, studying me. Then she said, 'Sit down, both of you,' her voice low.

'I ought to put the horses in the barn,' I said. 'It's pretty cold to leave them outside.'

'I'll get a lantern for you,' Cissy said, and went into the kitchen.

Mrs Hammond looked at me and licked her lips. She cleared her throat, but she didn't say anything. She sat down again at the table, and when Cissy returned with the lantern Mrs Hammond said, 'I suppose Jim is happily married by now.'

'Seems to be,' Lane said. 'Fetched back a real pretty wife. Redheaded, too.'

I took the lantern from Cissy and went outside. When I came back after putting the horses in the barn, Mrs Hammond and Lane had disappeared. Cissy stood where I had left her, her eyes on me, waiting. I blew out the lantern and put it down. I took off my sheepskin and threw it across a chair.

I looked at her, and then because a kind of wildness had been building up in me, I said in a shaking voice: 'You lied to me that night after we came back from the schoolhouse. About you and your mother.'

She lowered her gaze. 'You didn't want the truth, Dan.'

I went to her and, taking one of her hands, put a gold piece into it.

She stared at the coin for a moment, then threw it across the room as hard as she could. She lifted her eyes to mine and cried, 'Dan, oh, Dan, why did you have to come *this* way?'

* * *

After that, a long time after that, while I was riding back to J Ranch with Lane, the swirling snow all around us, he asked, 'Well?'

'I'll never go back,' I said. 'For that.'

I never did.

CHAPTER SIXTEEN

I went into the house one morning in the middle of December to ask Rocky if she wanted to go riding. The sky had cleared after a week of cloudy weather, and although the day was chilly there was little wind, so that it didn't seem as cold as it actually was.

The evening before, Rocky had been more restless than I had ever seen her. Even Perrin, who usually spent the evenings upstairs in his office or sitting in front of the fireplace absorbed in thought, was concerned about her and wanted to know what the trouble was.

Rocky dropped into a chair and thrust her feet out toward the fire. 'I guess I'm bored, Jim. I've read everything in the house, and a bad cold along with the disagreeable weather has kept me inside for a week. I think I'll start spring house cleaning in the morning.'

'I could ride to the lake and get some of my father's books,' I said. 'Do you like Seneca?'

'Seneca?' She put a finger to the side of her nose and looked thoughtfully at Perrin. 'Wasn't he the man who discovered America?'

She often needled him that way. He could talk with Lane Sears by the hour, but he did well to talk to Rocky for five minutes at a time. When he got away from land or cattle as topics of conversation, he was lost, and of course Rocky couldn't talk intelligently about either.

I don't know what Rocky had in mind when she said things like that. Perhaps she had a futile hope that she could get him to read some of her books, or maybe she wanted to belittle Perrin's knowledge and talents. I'm inclined to think that the latter was the answer because her education was of little value to her in the valley, and from indirect things she said now and then I knew she felt utterly useless. I suspect she

214

wanted Perrin to realize that there was another world outside J Ranch where he would be as out of place as she was in his.

He gave her a sour look and rose. 'I know Seneca didn't discover America,' he said.

She giggled, and then, remembering my question, said: 'No, I don't like Seneca. Thanks just the same, Danny.'

Perrin stood there, waiting for her to go upstairs with him, but she remained where she was. He said: 'I'm taking the boys to Giant Springs in the morning. We'll be gone a couple of days. Lane's got a bad knee, so he'll stay here, and Pedro's working with a sick horse.' He looked at me. 'Better get Rocky outside in the morning. She's like any thoroughbred. She needs exercise.'

'I guess I do,' she said.

She went upstairs with him then. Although Rocky had been there only a few weeks, I was beginning to understand why Lane worried about her. Even Perrin may have been wondering if he had the right woman.

I was still thinking about it as I stood at the foot of the stairs that morning waiting for Rocky to come down. When I called to her, she said she was putting on her riding skirt and would be down in a minute.

The minute doubled and tripled, and then I heard someone on the porch and turned to the door just as Lane came in, limping on his injured knee. Frank Allison was with him. One look at Allison's face told me something had happened. He said, 'Morning, Daniel,' and stood there holding his hat in his hand, twisting the battered brim nervously.

A number of things crowded through my mind: my mother had fallen and injured herself; my father had finally quarreled with Matt Cartwright; they'd told him he wasn't to preach any more. But for some reason the thing I had worried about most didn't occur to me.

'Tell him, Allison,' Lane said, not looking at me, his face as melancholy as his droopy mustache.

'Ben died yesterday,' Allison blurted. 'The funeral's today. Your pa thought you'd want to come.'

I just stood there, looking at him, not getting the full import of what he said for a moment. Then Rocky was beside me, asking softly, 'What happened, Danny?'

'My little brother died yesterday,' I said, and my mind reached back across the years he had been alive. I could see him chasing a butterfly on his poor thin little legs, or digging with a stick in the yard. Mining, he had called it.

Rocky's hand fell lightly on my arm. 'I'm sorry, Danny. I'm terribly sorry.'

When I looked at her, something happened to me. It was as if I had never seen her before, as if she was a real woman and not a strange and unreal creature who had walked out of the picture above the mantel. For the first time I fully realized what a fine person she was, possessing a great capacity for genuine sympathy and understanding.

'How did it happen?' I asked Allison.

'Nobody seems to rightly know,' he said. 'Ben had a cold, and your ma was keeping him in bed. Then he got worse, sudden-like, and just died. Pneumonia, maybe. He wasn't strong.'

'I'll saddle up and ride back with you,' I said.

Rocky's hand dropped from my arm. 'When is the funeral?'

'This afternoon at three,' Allison said.

'We'll be there, Danny,' Rocky said. 'I'll send Pedro after Jim right away.'

But Perrin wouldn't come. That was my first thought, and I didn't intend to condemn Perrin by it. The explanation was simple. He had work to do, and he couldn't change anything by making the long ride to the lake.

Lane swallowed and started to say something. I shook my head at him. I said: 'Don't send for Jim, Rocky. He wouldn't have time to get there.'

Then I went out with Allison and saddled up and rode north with him. Neither of us felt like talking. We just rode, and my thoughts were on my mother, not Ben. I had known Ben's death was coming, and it was better than if he had grown up. I don't believe I was callous or heartless. It just seemed to me he was happy

217

now. But my mother wouldn't feel that way, and I didn't know of anything I could say that would help her get through the lonely days that lay ahead.

When we reached our place, Allison said: 'Go on in, Daniel. I'll put your horse up.'

I went into the cabin. Mrs Allison was getting dinner, working as silently as she could. My mother sat in the rocking chair, her hands folded on her lap, the room filled with the creak of the chair. My father was sitting in one of the cane-bottom chairs beside the door, his open Bible on his lap.

'I'm glad you came, Daniel,' my father said, nodding at my mother.

I went over to her and knelt beside her, and she put a hand on my shoulder and kept on rocking. She wasn't crying. I don't think she had cried. She seemed stunned, as if unable to comprehend what had happened. We were that way a long time, and then her hand fell away.

I got up and pulled the curtain aside at the other end of the room. Ben's body was in a little coffin. I heard later the Ferguson boys had made it; and someone, Mrs Cartwright, I think, had lined it with white satin. I don't know where she got it. Perhaps it was a piece she had saved for years.

As I stood there looking down at Ben, a strange feeling came to me. He had not been changed by death, and I thought that all I had to do was to ask, 'How are you, Ben?' and he'd say, 'Fine.' Death was not new to me. My father had preached many funerals, and I had helped prepare the bodies for burial. But the stiff, clay-like change that comes when life leaves had not come to Ben. His thin, waxlike face looked exactly as it had the last time I had seen him. His little hands were folded across his chest. I touched them, and they were cold. I turned and dropped the curtain and sat down beside my father. Then the tears came. But they were for my mother, not for Ben. No one could help her; no one could reach her. Through the days ahead she would be asking, 'Why, Lord, why?' and no one could answer.

Outside, Allison and Morris and some others were digging the grave on the ridge south of the cabin where Ben had chased butterflies last summer and where the milk cow had grazed. Presently Mrs Allison said, 'I've got something to eat, folks.' But we didn't move. We didn't say anything. Then she said: 'I know how you feel. I lost three and raised just one. But the living have to eat.'

My mother didn't even look up. My father said, 'Thank you kindly, Mrs Allison, but we can't eat just now.'

She left the plates on the table, and the food dried in the pans she had on the stove. I don't know how we lived through the next hours, but somehow we did, wearing them out minute by minute. Outside, people were gathering, standing in little groups and talking as they shivered in the cold, but none came to intrude upon our privacy.

Then it was three, and Frank Allison knocked on the door. We got up and I helped my mother put on her coat. My father went out first, wearing his old black suit and carrying his Bible.

We stood beside the grave, the three of us. Everyone who lived along the lake shore was there, even the Ferguson boys. Then I saw Rocky and Lane and Alec Brown.

The pallbearers carried the little coffin out of the house and set it beside the open grave. A women's quartet began to sing. I didn't notice who they were, except that Debbie was one. My father stepped forward when they were done, and read the Thirteenth Chapter of First Corinthians. He had picked the right text for my mother, I thought. Love was not something to talk about, not her kind of love anyway; it must be lived, and she had lived it as long as I could remember.

And then my father closed the Bible and looked at these people who were his friends. At that moment even Ernie and Carl Ferguson could be called friends, I think. My father said, 'At a time like this when the good Lord...' He stopped, and tears ran down his cheeks and were lost in his great beard. He bowed his head and stood there, a strong, helpless figure.

Frank Allison stepped forward and raised his hand and prayed. It was a good, honest prayer coming from an honest heart, simple, homely words, but the right words. Then the coffin was lowered into the grave, and for the first time since I had come that morning my mother cried.

They came to him then, these people who loved my father as no group of people had ever loved him before. If love can transform a man, their love had transformed him. They shook our hands, not saying much, just a few words, but letting us know of their sympathy. Even the Fergusons came, cleaner than I had ever seen them. I thought about it often after that, how the evil that was in them had been for the moment changed to goodness by the death of a little boy.

Lane was there, just shaking my hand and saying nothing. And Alec, hobbling over the hard ground on his peg leg, and Rocky, crying a little. She put her arms around me and hugged me. She went on to my mother, and she was the only woman who kissed her. She said very softly: 'I'm Mrs Perrin. I want you to know that—that we love Daniel very much.' And she went on and got into the rig beside Lane, and Alec climbed in and they drove away.

The grave was filled, the mound rounded up, and Debbie came and left a bouquet of artificial pink flowers upon it. I don't know where she found the material for them, but they made a tiny bit of color in the surrounding somberness of winter. My mother whirled and ran into the cabin and shut the door. No one followed.

My father remained outside until everyone had gone, then he handed his Bible to me and walked in long strides toward the barn and came back with a shovel. Without a word he began digging a hole about ten feet from the grave.

'What are you going to do?' I asked.

'Build a fence,' he said, and kept on digging. 'Cattle and horses come here to graze, but they will never tromp on Ben's grave.'

'I'll help you.'

He stopped and looked at me. He said, 'This is something I must do, Daniel.' He tipped his head toward the cabin. 'She blames me for Ben's death.'

'She can't...' I saw the tears in his eyes again, and a lump was in my throat so that I couldn't swallow.

'We have never been very close, Daniel, you and I,' my father said. 'The answer is not hard to find. Somehow, by the grace of God, I sired a son who is a man, but I have never been. I've been shiftless and lazy and futile, and we would have starved if it had not been for you.' He shook his head at me when I started to say something. 'I owe one thing to Jim Perrin. It was what he said to me that morning when you rode away with him, when I said your wages should come to us. I saw myself after that as I

222

never had before. I'd always been able to hide behind something, but not since then. I've asked God for strength and just a little ability to do what must be done in a new country, and He has given it to me; but if I lose your mother ...'

Then he began to dig again. I turned from him and went into the cabin. My mother was sitting in the rocking chair again. She looked at me and turned her head away. It was cold, so I went outside and brought in an armful of wood and loaded the range with as much as I could put into the fire box. I was not really aware that there were only a few more sticks of wood behind the cabin.

My mother said, 'We'll be warm tonight, Daniel. Tomorrow he can freeze.'

I pulled up one of the cane-bottom chairs and sat beside her. I said, 'You can't blame him.'

She began to rock with feverish energy. She said: 'He knew we were short of wood. He could have taken the team and gone after some, but no, he sat there and read for hours at a time, and prayed as if the Lord would dump a load of wood behind our house the way He gave manna to the Children of Israel. Even when I knew Ben was terribly sick, he said not to waste the wood. Just keep Ben covered, he said. He killed Ben, Daniel. Don't you see?'

'No,' I said. 'I don't see.'

She looked at me. 'Do you know how many

babies I've lost? Born dead, or just lived a few hours or a few days and then died. Just you and Ben. You were too strong to die, and Ben...' She swallowed. 'I think Ben was God's gift to us in our old age, and then He took His gift from us.' She stopped rocking. 'Do you remember that time in Colorado when Ben was a baby and you climbed up on the tongue of the wagon with the rifle?' She shook her head. 'You've been right about so many things, about your father. I've never been a wife to him since.'

I didn't say anything. All I could feel was shame for what I had done, so certain in my boyish wisdom that I was doing right, hating my father and having so much love and sympathy for my mother. But I knew better now, for I understood what a man needed. If the Lord in His infinite wisdom had made men the way He had, then there was a reason for it, a reason for which I had not had the slightest understanding six years ago.

'We have never talked to you about our families,' she said. 'When you were born, Bartram made me promise not to tell you or any of our children, but I'm breaking that promise because you have a right to know. I'm going away, Daniel. I don't know where. I've got to go away. I'm not good for your father. I never have been. If I hadn't married him, he would have been one of the great preachers of our country. In Boston. Or New York.'

'You never said a more foolish thing in your life,' I told her. 'Your love has been the best thing—'

'The worst thing,' she interrupted. 'Let me tell you. He came from a rich family. He was the only child. His parents centered everything upon him. He wanted to be a preacher, so that was what they wanted. When I met him he was going to college. He was young and very handsome, and he'd always been given anything he wanted.' She shook her head. 'But when he wanted me, it was too much. They had picked out another girl for him. My parents were dead and I was teaching. I don't think Bartram's folks had anything against me. It was just that I had nothing to offer him. The other girl did. Her social position would have helped him get the kind of church they wanted him to have.'

She put a hand over mine and squeezed, a hard, bony hand that would not have been that way if she had not married my father. She would have been in the East, living in relative comfort, maybe an old maid, still teaching. I wondered if she had thought of that, and if she had, would she have exchanged her present life for that of a spinster teacher in some small, proper New England town.

She was silent a moment, reliving, I suppose, that exalted moment long ago when love had been so fine, and undemanding. Then she said: 'Bartram courted me and asked me to marry

225

him. Of course, we had no idea what would happen. He bought me a ring and he was going to take me to his home to meet his folks, but a storm came up and we couldn't go. We thought we couldn't wait, so we got married. Then the girl his folks wanted him to marry came to his college town to visit him and found out. She got back to his people before we did. When we got there...' She stopped, still hurt by the memory. 'It wasn't any use. They wouldn't even let me in the house. His father gave him a draft for a thousand dollars and told him never to come back.'

My mother spread her hands. 'You can't understand, Daniel. No one could understand who didn't know his parents. Of course, they hoped to break us up. But Bartram took the money and quit college. He wanted to come West. You were born nine months and three days after we were married. We lived as long as we could on that thousand dollars. After it was gone I don't know how we lived. We just drifted. Bartram preached wherever he could, but he wasn't ordained, so all he could find were places like this, and he was never satisfied to stay anywhere until we came here. After you left, he had to stay.'

She began rocking again, staring across the room at nothing. 'All he had was his books and he wouldn't give them up. I don't know to this day whether he couldn't work, or just wouldn't. After you got big enough to earn a

226

little money, we got along better, but you know how it's been. Because he realized he had failed so miserably, or it might have been because he'd had such fine dreams when he was younger, he started all that posing and pretending you hated so much.'

She got up and walked to the window, and when she saw my father working at the grave she whirled and came back to her chair. 'I've tried, Daniel, I've tried awfully hard, but I just haven't been able to do anything for him. I know you've wondered why I haven't left him a long time ago. There was just one reason. I felt I was to blame for what happened to him, but now I don't care. I just don't care.'

'You will,' I said, 'after it's too late. I think he would kill himself if you left him.' I watched her face to see if that touched her, but I didn't think it did. 'He has a chance now, Ma. Don't take it from him.'

I got up and dropped some gold pieces in her lap, all that I had been able to save since I had been there the last time. I left then. I couldn't say anything more. When I rode away, my father was still working at the grave.

Perrin was not at J Ranch when I got back, so I asked Lane if I could haul a load of wood to my folks. I said I'd pay for it. 'Go ahead,' Lane said. 'It's little enough for Jim to do.'

I took a load to my folks the next day. When I got to the cabin, I saw that the fence was in place around the grave. My father was gone.

My mother cooked dinner for me, not saying anything about the wood, but when I was ready to go she said: 'I'm going to stay, Daniel. I've thought about what you said.'

She looked at me, smiling gently. 'You know, we're not really old. I think I'd like to have a baby. He'd have a home. It wouldn't be like the others, in a wagon. Since Ben's gone, my arms have felt so empty.'

It was dark when I got back to J Ranch, and Perrin had returned with the crew. I went into the big house, wanting to tell him about the wood, but he and Rocky had gone to bed. I took off my boots and tiptoed up the stairs, thinking they might be asleep, but as soon as I went into my room I knew they weren't.

'You could have come,' Rocky was saying in an angry voice. 'I sent Pedro to tell you.'

'We didn't have time,' Perrin said, as angry as she was. 'We were working. I couldn't have done any good anyhow. Besides, we lost a horse. If Pedro had stayed, he'd have pulled him through.'

'A horse,' Rocky said cuttingly. 'You think about the loss of a horse when you have more horses than you need. What's the matter with you, Jim? Don't you know what you're doing to yourself? And me? All you think about is more land. More cows. More horses. Your crazy greed is going to destroy you, Jim, burn you up, consume you. Can't you see that?'

'No,' he said. 'All I can see is that you're my

wife and still you're a stranger to me. You don't know me, Rocky. You don't know me at all.'

I sat on the edge of the bed, a boot in my hand. I raised it and dropped it, and the noise silenced them. I did not sleep much that night. All this trouble between them after only a few weeks of marriage. And Rocky deserved so much.

CHAPTER SEVENTEEN

Winter on J Ranch was, in many ways, a season of waiting, a period of suspended animation when life waited for spring. But, suspended or not, the old pattern was continued.

I visited my folks every Sunday afternoon unless the weather was so bad that traveling was hazardous. There was not a single Sunday morning when my father failed to hold service, although it was often so stormy that only a handful of people were there.

My mother never again complained about not having enough wood, and although I did not haul any more from J Ranch the pile behind the cabin steadily grew so that in March, when Frank Allison was sick in bed, it was possible for my father to load up his wagon and take enough fuel to the Allisons to keep them supplied until Frank was able to get his own wood.

I never heard my mother say anything more about leaving my father, or about blaming him for Ben's death. I was sure that she hadn't meant any of it, and that her bitterness had been purged during the period of loneliness into which she had fallen after my brother died. Because she had questioned and been given no answers, because she had despaired and been given no comfort, she had turned against my father at a time when all of his past failures had been reborn in her mind. But it was not in her nature to keep on blaming him, and after a while Ben's death brought her closer to my father than she had been at any previous time within my memory. Though she did not mention any of those things to me again, and never said anything about having a baby, I was convinced she was being a wife to him for the first time since Ben was born.

I suppose that tragedy has its compensation, if one wants to rationalize about it, but it is not always so. As far as Rocky and Perrin were concerned, the pattern of their life was fixed on the night they quarreled because he hadn't come to Ben's funeral. There was nothing anyone could do for them; nothing they could or would do for themselves.

I, who loved them both, couldn't help them. It was the same with Lane Sears, although he had neither understanding nor sympathy for

Rocky. He had distrusted her from the first, and now I think he hated her. But I don't think he said anything to Perrin about it, for Jim Perrin was not a man to talk about his troubles.

I rode with Rocky a good deal during the winter, sometimes when the weather was so bad she should have stayed in the house. But because she had reached the point where she was almost hysterical when she had to stay inside for a long period of time, I never argued with her when she told me to saddle the horses.

Perrin made only one attempt to break the monotony of her life. That was during a warm spell in February when he took her to visit the Pritchards on the other side of Garnet Mountain. They were gone for two weeks, getting back barely ahead of a storm that lasted three days and laid two feet of snow upon the valley. Rocky said little to me about the trip, but I sensed it had been more of a trial than a pleasure for her. Mrs Pritchard, it seemed, could talk cattle and land with her husband and Perrin, and Rocky could not.

For the rest of the time, Jim left Rocky's recreation up to me. I knew it was a mistake, but it wasn't my place to tell Perrin so. And I didn't want to, for I was afraid something would happen which would keep me away from Rocky. I knew it was a situation which could not go on indefinitely. Still, I didn't want to be the one who brought it to an end.

Only once did Rocky talk to me about

Perrin. It was well into spring, when live green was replacing the dead tawny tone of winter which had gripped the valley for so long, and when the snow on Garnet Mountain had backed far up on the west slope.

We left J Ranch early that morning, Rocky and I, with lunch tied in a flour sack behind my saddle. We rode north. Rocky hadn't told me where she intended to go, but I knew that she wanted to look down into Paradise Valley again.

She said very little until we reached the rim. We ate our lunch, her eyes on the valley below us. Joe Ryan's buildings looked like toy structures, and riders coming down through a break in the east side of the valley were so small that I couldn't recognize them, but I had an uncomfortable feeling that one of them rode like Rolly Dillon. They stopped at the ranch, talked briefly to someone, and went on. It was my imagination, I thought, for I worried a good deal about Dillon, convinced that someday he would return. Rocky said, 'I've got to own that ranch, Danny; I've just got to,' and I forgot about Dillon. She looked at me, laughing a little, as if half ashamed of herself.

I asked, 'Don't you own enough?'

She shook her head. 'I own nothing, Danny.' She was sitting very near the edge of the rim, her legs under her. 'I don't understand it myself, so I can't expect you to. But then I don't understand Jim. Do you?' A lock of auburn hair that the wind was playing with seemed to annoy her. She brushed at it, her eyes meeting mine.

I said: 'Yes, I think I understand Jim. Some things about him, anyway. I guess nobody understands everything about anyone else.'

'You seem older than you really are, Danny,' she said unexpectedly. 'I keep thinking of you as a man.' She laughed, a little embarrassed when she realized how it sounded. 'I don't mean you aren't, but you're really just a month older than I am. What I meant was, you act like you're twenty-five. Maybe it's because you're bigger than when I first saw you last fall.'

I had gained thirty pounds in the year I had been on J Ranch most of it since Jim had brought Rocky home. I looked away from her, my mind turning to Cissy Hammond and then back again to Rocky, wondering what she thought. But it didn't matter. There were various standards for measuring manhood, and I wasn't sure what Rocky's were. All I knew was that I was afraid of what was happening between us, afraid to touch Rocky, afraid of the way we were talking.

She picked up a rock and threw it over the rim. 'Tell me about Jim, if you think you understand him.'

'He's lonely,' I said. 'He was lonely before you came, and he's still lonely.'

She gave me a sharp look, as if wondering

whether I was serious. 'How can he be lonely when he has all his cows and a million acres of land to keep him company?'

'You think cows and land keep a man from being lonely?' I asked.

'They should keep Jim from being lonely,' she cried. 'They're all he cares for. They're all he needs.'

'No,' I said. 'They're not all he needs. He . . .'

I stopped. I couldn't tell her that she had failed him, that he had done a great thing in coming to the valley and building J Ranch, something for which he could rightly be proud and which she did not properly evaluate.

She lay flat on her back, her riding skirt covering her long straight legs, her brown blouse pulled tightly across her breasts. She seemed tall, even lying down, and I wondered how much that had to do with her and Perrin's trouble. A wife, I thought, should always be shorter than her husband.

For a long time Rocky didn't say anything, her eyes on the woolly-white clouds that raced across the bright sky before the wind. Finally she said: 'I could like this country, Danny; I could love it if it were my friend. But I hate it because it's come between me and Jim. I want to be first with him, but I'm always second.' She raised herself up on one elbow and looked at me. 'How did he get so far in such a short time, Danny?'

'He bought the swampland along the river

from the state,' I said. 'He got it for a dollar and a quarter an acre. Of course, he uses a lot of land he doesn't own, but someday he'll get that, too.'

'I've heard them talk about the marginal lake land. What does that mean?'

So I told her about it, and how the settlers hated Perrin because they were afraid he would take their homes. She was sitting up now, listening closely, and when I finished she said bitterly: 'That's exactly what I mean, Danny. He doesn't need that land, but he'll take it no matter what it does to the settlers. Why? Tell me why.'

I shook my head. I had asked myself the same question many times. It was easy for Cartwright and Allison, and perhaps my father, to hate Perrin. To them he was all black, a devil who walked like a man; but I knew him. I liked Jim Perrin, and I respected him, but there was one side of him that neither God nor devil could change. If the court decided that he owned the marginal land, he would take it, even if it meant using force, a thing he would not do under other circumstances.

Rocky lay back again. 'I met him in San Francisco more than two years ago,' she said. 'Even as young as he was, everyone seemed to know him. They called him a miracle man. They said the day would come when he'd own all of this part of Oregon. I should have known then, I guess; but he was nice, and I suppose I

235

built him up in my mind into something he wasn't.' She was silent for a time, thinking about their courtship, I suppose.

I said: 'I saw your picture the first day I came to J Ranch, and I knew he was in love with you. He told me that he'd been putting off marrying you because of the Indian scares and all, but that he was going to marry you in the fall regardless.'

'And he broke his neck getting back. I wanted to come, but I wanted a honeymoon, too, and I never had it.' She sat up, pulling her knees under her chin, and stared morosely at me. 'I know I've failed, Danny, but why? As soon as he brought me here, I became part of the ranch, like a horse or a cow or—or just a clod.'

It would have been different, I thought, if she could have shared his dream. Whether it was her fault or his was a question in my mind. He had tried to tell her how it was that first day after we had crossed Garnet Mountain. I don't think he had tried since. Perhaps he never would again; and Rocky, who needed time as much as she needed his love, had been given neither.

'I have some money of my own,' she said, her eyes on the valley below us. 'Maybe if I could buy Ryan's ranch, and show Jim I can be independent of him, he'd feel differently about me.' She rose, suddenly restless and impatient. 'Let's go home, Danny.'

236

I felt guilty as we rode down the slope toward the Valley Ranch. I had had my chance to help her understand Perrin, and I had failed. Perhaps it was because I did not understand him; perhaps I had a selfish hope that someday I would have her myself. I tried to put the thought out of my mind, but I couldn't. Once more I made a decision. Either I would go on spring roundup, or I'd ride away from J Ranch. Which I did would be up to Perrin, but he wouldn't know why. I'd lie to him. How could I tell him I loved his wife? And how could I tell him he had brought it on by his neglect, by thinking I could fill a place in Rocky's life he couldn't and still remain indifferent to her?

Suddenly Rocky looked at me. She said: 'Danny, I know how much you think of Jim. He has so many good qualities. Sometimes I hate myself because I'm indifferent to them. It's just that the one thing I want to find in him isn't there.' She stared ahead at the buildings of the Valley Ranch.

'He told me how you saved his life that time at Lang's. He told me you were the kind of person he could trust with anything. Even me.' She laughed softly. 'Not that I'm a woman who would make a man forget himself. It's just that of all the men he has on J Ranch, you're the one he picked out to look after me because he could trust you.'

I wanted to tell her that Perrin was wrong, that I was made of man flesh and man desire, and that if we went on the way we were, the day would come when Jim Perrin would put on his gun and try to kill me, or I would kill him.

'I think the whole trouble is that Jim's a man's man,' she went on thoughtfully. 'I've tried so hard to understand it. That's the only explanation I have. You'd die for him if it came to that. So would Lane Sears and the others. The truth is, I suppose, that I keep expecting something from him he just can't give.'

I heard someone shout. Turning, I saw José Otero coming down the slope toward us. I waved at him and we angled toward him. When we met he took off his sombrero and bowed to Rocky, but the wide, friendly grin that was usually on his lips was not there today.

'Rolly Dillon is back,' José said. 'He's at the Ferguson place.'

So it had not been my imagination. I *had* seen him at the Ryan place. José had been staying alone at the Valley Ranch, and I sensed he was afraid. He wanted Perrin to send someone to stay with him, but he couldn't come right out and say it.

'Thanks, José,' I said. 'I'll tell Jim.'

But Jim was staying at Giant Springs. After supper I drew Lane Sears aside and told him, adding: 'Don't say I should have killed him last fall. I know it without you telling me again.'

Lane was silent a long time. He rolled a smoke and lighted it. Finally he said, 'Well it's a mistake you'll never make again.'

'José ought to have a man with him,' I said.

He nodded. 'I'll send Manuel over there tonight.'

'You reckon Dillon came back to get me?'

'Or Jim. Don't forget, Jim knocked him down. He didn't give the bastard a bonus, either.' He pulled on his cigarette, the smoke filtering from his nostrils. Then he said: 'Maybe he came back for Cissy. She caused the whole thing.'

'It wasn't her fault,' I said.

'No, but she caused it.' He shook his head. 'Damn it, Dan, I wish Jim was here. No, come to think of it, I don't. He'd say to wait. I figure we'd better go after Rolly. No good will come of waiting. Get your gun.'

I went upstairs to my room and buckled my gun around me, wishing I hadn't quit practicing. When I came back into the living room, Rocky saw the gun. She cried, 'What are you going to do?'

I didn't want to tell her. Though she knew about Dillon, this wasn't a thing she would understand. Besides, it was Lane's decision to go after Dillon, and I had no idea of what Perrin would say or do when it was over.

'Lane said to get my gun,' I told Rocky. 'I guess we're going coyote hunting.'

I went out quickly before she figured out what I meant. A few minutes later we rode north, four of us, Lane, Pedro, Manuel, who was to stay with José, and me. Lane didn't tell

239

me why I was along. He didn't need to. I knew. He was giving me a chance to make up for what I hadn't done in Winnemucca.

We left Manuel at the Valley Ranch and went on toward the eastern ridge line. Lane didn't say how he intended to work it, and neither Pedro nor I asked, but I'm sure he knew as well as I did what we would be up against if we found Dillon at the Ferguson place. We'd have to fight all three of them.

When the lamplight in the Ferguson shack was visible to us, Lane said, 'What do you think, Pedro?'

'We go in, easy,' Pedro said. 'If Rolly's there, we get him.'

'If he ain't, maybe there won't be any trouble,' Lane said. 'Well, we'll see.'

We rode on across the grass. José had told us he had seen Dillon the day before with the Fergusons, and as far as he knew Dillon had just reached the valley. Whether it was true or not, there was no reason to think the Fergusons would have a guard out.

We dismounted fifty yards from the cabin and walked in, slowly, our guns in our hands. It was easy, far easier than we had any right to expect. There was no cover. If the Fergusons had been watching, they could have cut us down in the moonlight before we reached the front door. As it was, Lane simply jammed the door open and went in fast. I was one jump behind him, Pedro staying outside.

Both the Fergusons were sitting at the table playing cards. They just looked at us, too surprised to move for a moment, then Carl began, 'What the hell do you think—'

'Where's Rolly?' Lane cut him off fast.

'He ain't here,' Ernie said.

Lane motioned to me. 'You and Pedro take a look around.'

I was back within a minute or two. There was no place to hide except in the shed, and it was empty. Carl was furious. He sat there, glaring at Lane and cursing him steadily.

'No one around,' I said.

'Shut up,' Lane snapped at Carl. 'Ernie, where's Rolly?'

'Dunno,' Ernie said. 'He rode out two, three hours ago.'

'Which way?'

'Didn't see.'

He was lying, but I knew where Dillon had gone, and Lane knew. He said, 'Get their guns, Dan.' I obeyed, then took their Winchesters down from the wall. Lane said: 'We'll leave these outside. We didn't come here to have trouble with you boys.'

We backed out and ran to our horses. I dropped the guns in the grass, and we mounted and rode west. When we reached the Allison place, I saw that it was dark, but I knocked and got Frank out of bed.

He nodded when I asked about Dillon. 'Yeah, he rode past here just about dusk.

Headed west.'

Dillon had come back for Cissy. If he had any thought of getting me or Perrin, he had decided it would wait.

CHAPTER EIGHTEEN

I'm not sure which is worse, actually to know that a tragedy has taken place, or to have the terrible cold-sweat fear which comes from the uncertainty of not knowing.

I knew that Cissy had not changed in her feelings about Rolly Dillon, and that Mrs Hammond would not change in her attitude toward Cissy. The only question was what Dillon would do, and that wasn't really a question, not after he'd had a winter to brood over what had happened. The only doubt in my mind was whether it would be Cissy or her mother, or both.

To our right the cabins along the lake shore were dark, vague shapes in the moonlight. Then we saw a pinpoint of light ahead of us in the Hammond house. Afterward it occurred to me, and probably to Lane and Pedro, that we were taking a great risk by coming in the way we did, putting our horses into a run and splashing across the river and riding up the slope. If Dillon was there, he could have shot the three of us before we had a chance to reach cover or fire back. But we would probably have done as we did even if we had thought of danger.

The moment we pulled up, I heard Cissy crying. She was sitting on the porch, lamplight from the open door falling upon her, and her crying was the most terrible sound I had ever heard. I was the first to reach her. I said, 'Cissy,' but I don't think she heard me, or even knew we were there. I would have picked her up and carried her inside if Lane hadn't said, 'Wait.' So I sat down beside her and, putting an arm around her, drew her head down against my chest. She continued to moan hysterically.

Lane and Pedro went into the house. They were there only a moment, and when they came out Lane's face was granite. I looked up at him, and I knew I didn't want to go inside.

Pedro said, 'Rolly, he is riding.'

'We'll hitch up their buggy,' Lane said. 'Pedro, you'll have to take Cissy to J Ranch. Send a wagon back for the body.'

They walked around the house to the barn and returned in a few minutes with the Hammond rig. Lane got out and tied Pedro's horse behind the buggy, then I picked Cissy up and carried her to the buggy. I placed her in the seat, but she would have fallen forward if Pedro hadn't put his arm around her.

'Don't tell Miz Perrin anything about her,' Lane said. 'Just say Cissy and her mother were settlers.'

243

'Rolly, he—' Pedro began.

'We'll get him,' Lane said. 'By God, we'll get him if we have to chase him to the moon, but I've got a hunch it won't be that far.'

Lane swung around and went into the house. He blew out the lamp and pulled the door shut. By the time we mounted, Pedro had crossed the river and the sound of wheels and hoofs on the grass was lost to us.

We rode west, the moon far over in the sky toward the horizon. It would not be long until morning. Finally, when I couldn't stand it any longer, I asked, 'How do you figure it, Lane?'

'He'll head for O'Hara's Box O.' Lane's voice was normal enough, but something had happened to him, something that made him a different man. 'It's the only ranch out here, and he knows O'Hara. Probably get a change of horses and keep going if we don't get there first.'

But that wasn't what I wanted to know. I asked, 'I mean, how do you figure what happened back there?'

'I don't figure; I *know*,' Lane said. 'Mighty close, anyhow. She had her nightgown on and a robe over it. She was lying on her back, the side of her head caved in. That little .32 she had was lying on the floor beside her. Might be she plugged him. She'd fired a couple of shots. But she didn't hit him hard enough to keep him from slugging her with a gun barrel. There were a few drops of blood between her and the

244

door. That's why I think she hit him. Might be we'll find him out here.'

'Where do you suppose Cissy was when it happened?'

'In her room, maybe. Or she might have got out through the back door. Maybe she'd been out riding. She had her riding clothes on. She liked to go at night when there was a moon.'

We were silent then. I thought of Cissy and wondered what would happen now. She couldn't stay in the house alone. I wished I had my money. I would have given it to Cissy. I didn't suppose her mother had saved much. Then I wondered what Perrin would do for her, and how he would feel about her being on J Ranch with Rocky. But I didn't say anything to Lane about it.

We reached the rimrock as the sun was coming up, climbed to the top by way of a narrow gap, and went on across the desert. There was grass among the sagebrush and junipers, and the land ran on and on toward the sky, with here and there a butte breaking a monotony that seemed more level than it was.

Occasionally we dropped into a dry wash and climbed out, and then, in mid-morning, rode down into a dry lake bed with a white patch of alkali in the middle. There was no vegetation of any kind. A coyote streaked out across the alkali and disappeared among the rocks to the south. Ahead of us a buzzard made a slow, sweeping turn in the sky. I wondered about it, and then I saw that Lane was watching it, too.

We didn't stop until we were close to the western rim of the lake bed. Lane pulled up suddenly and stepped out of the saddle. It wasn't until he knelt and began studying the ground that I saw the horse tracks angling south. He rose and scratched his nose, eyes on the rim.

'He's there,' I said. 'He didn't get to O'Hara's ranch.'

Lane came back to his horse. 'He's there, all right. But what shape is he in?'

'Bad,' I said, 'if he's not traveling.'

He scratched his nose again, still studying the rim, his lips squeezed flat against his teeth. His face was bleak, without mercy, without the slightest trace of doubt or weakness. Rolly Dillon did not have long to live. I wondered if Lane blamed me for what had happened.

Suddenly Sears mounted and jabbed a finger toward the rim. 'You can make it to the top through that break yonder. Just keep your eyes peeled.'

I nodded and started off across the lake bottom toward the break he had indicated. When I looked back I saw that he was headed directly toward the spot where Dillon must have gone. Then I reached the talus slope and lost sight of Lane.

The break must have been cut through the rim by some prehistoric stream that had emptied into the lake. It was narrow, the bottom covered with boulders, and in several places it was so steep that I didn't think my buckskin could make it. But he did, heaving and grunting, his muscles standing out under the strain of the climb, hoofs dislodging rocks that rolled down the ravine with a great clatter.

If Dillon was alive and close enough to hear the racket, I'd get a slug the instant I came into sight. At the moment it did not occur to me that Lane was counting on that very thing happening, that I was the one man Dillon would take a shot at, even if it meant giving his position away.

The last fifty feet of the climb tapered off, and I was on top in a clump of junipers. It may have been that the junipers saved my life, or it was possible that Dillon was hit too hard to be accurate in his shooting. Maybe he was panicky, just as he had been when I'd faced him on Winnemucca's Main Street.

In any case, I heard the shot to my right, but I wasn't hit. My horse stumbled, and I thought the bullet had tagged him, but he regained his footing and lunged on toward a tall rock ahead of us. The second shot was closer, close enough for me to hear the *zing* of lead as it passed within inches of my head; then the buckskin reached the rock and I pulled him to a stop and slid off.

I drew my gun and climbed up on a ledge so that I could look over the top of the rock. I saw

Dillon's horse tied to a juniper. The sandy ground was flat, but the sagebrush was waist-high and there were a few rocks big enough to hide a man. I considered what I should do, thinking that Lane must be somewhere between Dillon and the rim. He was a dead man if we could get him in a cross fire. But I had to spot him first.

I suppose I remained there five minutes, my eyes searching the sagebrush, and finally I caught a hint of movement between the rim and Dillon's horse. I cocked my gun, then eased the hammer down when I realized it could be Lane. The possibility that Lane might get shot jarred me into action. If either of us had to be killed, it should be me because it was my fault that Dillon was still alive.

It took a moment to get down from the ledge, then I moved to the edge of the rock and started on a dead run toward the spot where I had seen someone move. I must have covered fifty feet when the gun cracked again and I felt the sudden pain of the bullet as it laid a gash open under my left arm.

I fell instinctively, the sagebrush covering me; then I heard two more shots, farther to my right. They must have come from the rim. Lane, I thought. I lay there a moment before he called: 'All right, Dan. I got him.'

I stood up and holstered my gun, feeling the warm flow of blood down my side. I wadded up my bandanna, opened up my undershirt, and slid the bandanna under it.

Lane called, 'Did he get you?'

'Not bad,' I said.

'Fetch your rope,' he commanded.

I went back to my horse and got the rope. When I reached him, I saw that he was looking down at Dillon, who was on his back, staring at the sky with wide, blank eyes. Lane had shot him through the head. Another bullet hole was in his left arm, just above the elbow, where Mrs Hammond had wounded him. Lane looked at me, his face expressionless; then, without a word, he reached out and took the rope.

Hanging a dead man seemed a futile gesture to me, but I said nothing and Lane made no explanation. He simply put a loop around Dillon's neck, drew it tight, and dragged him through the sagebrush to a big juniper. He threw the end of the rope over a limb, pulled on it until Dillon's boots were off the ground, then tied the rope and turned away.

'I left my horse at the base of the rim,' he said. 'I'll meet you east of the lake.' He swung around and walked away.

I stood there a moment, staring at Dillon's grotesque body, which was swaying a little, the mouth open, eyes protruding from the head. I walked unsteadily to my horse.

I got into the saddle and rode around the rim, thinking of Cissy, and then of her mother, who had been kind to me, and understanding. My father would have said she had drawn her wages of sin, but he knew nothing about her.

I waited for Lane when I reached the east end of the lake bed and we rode back the way we had come. When we got to the Hammond place, we saw that a wagon had been there. We stopped and Lane went in. He returned a moment later, carrying a sack heavy with gold.

'Liz had a hunch,' he said. 'She showed me where she kept this and made me promise to give it to Cissy if anything happened to her.' He stepped into the saddle, his hard eyes on me, and I wondered if I had ever really known him. 'You going to marry Cissy?' he asked.

'No.' I said it quickly, surprised that he would even ask; and then, meeting his eyes, I sensed that he knew how I felt about Rocky. He leaned forward and spat into the grass in front of my horse.

'You're like the rest of 'em,' he said. 'Jim won't be no different.'

We rode back to J Ranch, neither of us speaking. He hadn't asked me about my wound, which hurt with a nagging ache; he didn't care. He hated me, I thought. Perhaps he hated everybody except Cissy. When we reached J Ranch, Perrin was waiting at the corrals. It was dark, but he held a lantern in his hand, tilting it so that he could see Lane's face.

'Why did you tell Pedro to bring Cissy here?' Perrin asked coldly.

Lane didn't put his horse up. He stepped down and looked at Perrin, very tall beside the shorter man, and said, 'Jim, you're gonna do something for Cissy.'

I was on the ground now, not fully understanding, but for the first time I had some idea of what Lane had been when he was a younger man.

'I'll take care of Cissy,' Perrin said, and even though he had to look up he still had that startling, big-man appearance I had seen so many times. 'But if you figure you have any reason to kill me, make it plain. My gun is in the house.'

Lane took a long breath, then shook his head. 'I've got no cause to blame you, I guess, or Dan, here. But if either one of you had done what you should, Liz would be alive now.' He took another deep breath. 'I want my time, Jim.'

I could see that Perrin was hard hit, but he didn't question Lane's decision. He said, 'Come into the house.'

I put my buckskin away and got a dressing for my arm. When I reached the house I saw that Lane had given the gold to Cissy. She sat on the couch, her face pale, her eyes red, and although the shock had passed she was still not herself. She looked at me and tried to smile, but she could not, and she turned her head away.

Rocky wasn't in the room. Perrin stood in front of the fireplace, unsmiling and grim. Lane, holding his hat in his hand, made a slow turn to face Perrin.

'Jim, I reckon Cissy will be leaving the valley. Nobody else would buy her place but you. I'd say it's worth a thousand dollars.'

Perrin nodded. 'I'll give it to her.'

Lane looked at me, and then at Cissy. 'I ain't staying for the funeral. I reckon Liz would know how it was with me.'

Cissy nodded. 'She loved you, Lane. I guess most people didn't think she could love a man, but she could.'

'She had more love to give than any woman I ever knew,' Lane said. 'She would have married me if it hadn't been for Jim.'

He clapped his hat on his head and walked out. We didn't move or speak until we heard him ride away, headed south. Then Perrin said, 'We'll have the funeral in the morning, and then Dan will take you to Winnemucca.'

'All right,' Cissy said, and got up. 'Thank you, Jim, for all you've done.'

She went upstairs. I looked at Perrin; for a moment our eyes met, then he gave me his back. I went upstairs to my room, bone-tired, and so drained of all emotion I couldn't sleep for a long time.

*   *   *

The funeral was very short. Some of the men had dug a grave within the fenced inclosure on the ridge above J Ranch where three buckaroos were buried who had died in the seven years Perrin had been here. Ole Larsen and Harry Gillam had made a coffin, and Rocky had lined it with some white satin she had had in her trunk.

I did not ask Cissy if she wanted me to go after my father. I knew she wouldn't, and I was glad because I didn't think he'd come if I did ask him. Rocky asked me if I'd say what I could. Cissy wanted me to, Rocky said, but she wasn't sure I would. I couldn't say no, but it was the hardest thing I had ever been called on to do.

I recited the Twenty-third Psalm and I said the Lord's Prayer, and then I looked around at the men, bare-headed, several of them openly crying and unashamed of it. Rocky was crying too, but Cissy wasn't. She just stared at the coffin as if she could not yet quite believe what had happened. Then I glanced at Perrin, and I wondered what he was thinking and what he was feeling.

I tried to think of some of the fine phrases I had heard my father use, often for men who didn't merit them, but they escaped me. I looked up at the wind-swept sky, so very blue, and I said, my voice trembling: 'Lord God, Thou knowest better than any of us the goodness that was in Mrs Hammond, and how it overshadowed all the human weakness that was in her as it is in all of us. We commit her soul to Thee. Amen.'

I turned away as Ole Larsen and Harry

Gillam picked up the shovels and began to fill the grave. Cissy and Rocky walked down the slope together, Rocky's arm around Cissy. We followed them, Alec Brown hobbling along on his wooden leg, Perrin keeping step with me. When I looked at him, he seemed lonelier and more withdrawn than I had ever seen him.

When we reached the house, Perrin asked me to harness up a team and take a buckboard and go after Cissy's things. I told him she'd have to go too. When I brought the buckboard to the front door, she was waiting for me.

We didn't talk. I felt she didn't want to. I waited outside while she packed, and then she called to me and I carried her valises and an old cowhide trunk out to the buckboard. She shut the door and stood staring at it a long moment, and then came and got into the seat beside me.

'I'd like to thank you, Dan,' she said, 'but I can't say the right words. Not words that could tell how I feel.'

'Don't try,' I said, and took her hand. I held it all the way back to J Ranch.

That night Perrin gave her a thousand dollars in exchange for the release of her squatter's right on the piece of land and buildings beside Thunder River. We ate breakfast by lamplight in the big house the next morning, Rocky and Perrin eating with us. It was barely dawn when I drove the buckboard to the front door.

Rocky and Perrin walked with Cissy to the

rig. Perrin shook hands with her and Rocky kissed her and for a moment they clung to each other, woman-like, and again I wondered how much Rocky knew about Cissy and her mother.

We wheeled south toward Giant Springs Ranch, the sun brightening the sky above Garnet Mountain. I asked, 'Did you want to stay here?'

'Yes, but Jim wouldn't let me,' she answered. 'You know why.' I nodded, and then she leaned close to me, peering at my face in the thin light. 'She's nice, Dan. I wish I could have known her better.' She leaned back and was silent a moment. Then she said: 'She shouldn't have married Jim. She knows it, but he doesn't. I guess all men are blind, but he's blinder than most of them. I never understood why my mother loved him the way she did. She was so much older, and he always seemed so cold.' She sighed. 'You'll marry her someday, Dan. You'll see.'

So she knew.

We stayed the night at Ferrill's place and went on again before the sun was up. It was evening when we reached Winnemucca. We went first to the depot and asked about the next east-bound. We had barely made the only through train that night. The next one was not due until early morning.

Cissy bought a ticket for Cheyenne. She didn't tell me why she picked Cheyenne and I didn't ask. I brought her luggage to the depot, and we stood there until we heard the train whistle. There were others waiting, but Cissy looked at me as if unaware of the others. She asked, 'Will you kiss me, Dan?'

I took her into my arms and kissed her, and when I let her go, she said, 'Dan, Dan, I wish it wasn't like it was.'

As she turned away, I saw Lane Sears coming toward us. I don't know whether he had seen us kissing or not, but his face was still as dark as when I had seen it at J Ranch. He said, 'Where are we going, Cissy?'

'Cheyenne,' she said.

'Well, that's as good as any,' he remarked curtly, and went inside for his ticket.

He came out a moment later, took Cissy's arm, led her to a coach, and followed her inside. He hadn't said a word to me, but presently he stepped from the coach and walked directly to me.

'Dan, I'm man enough to say I might have been wrong about you,' he said. 'Leastwise she says you've been good to her. But I want to say this. You'll have a hell of a rough time before...' He stopped. 'So long, kid,' he said, and held out his hand.

I shook hands with him. 'Thanks for—'

'Don't thank me,' he said. 'Not for anything.'

He wheeled and strode toward the coach, and it was then that I noticed he was wearing

256

his gun. I wondered why he had it, but I could think of only one answer. He had made his living once with his gun and now he was going back to it.

The train started just as he swung up the steps. As the coach rolled by that held Cissy, I saw her face pressed against the glass. I waved to her and she waved back. I stood there for a long, long time beside the deserted wind-swept depot, staring down the empty track. I thought, I'll never see or hear of her again.

CHAPTER NINETEEN

When I returned to J Ranch, I discovered that Pedro García was the new foreman. There was no better cowman in the country than Pedro, but he couldn't take Lane Sears's place. Lane had hurt Perrin more ways than one when he left. Not that Perrin showed it, or said anything about it. But I knew. Perrin was bound to his men by a rare kind of loyalty that was almost fanatical, and he demanded the same kind of loyalty from them.

When I got back from Winnemucca, I told Perrin I wanted to go on spring roundup. For weeks he drove us with frantic urgency, as if time was running out. I believed he had only one thing in mind: to work so hard and become so tired that he could forget Lane Sears and,

257

for the moment, the steadily widening gap between himself and his wife.

We had heard whispers of impending Indian trouble for a long time. That spring the whispers became reality, although it was like Perrin to ignore them. The Bannocks went on the warpath and fled into Oregon from Idaho. Buffalo Horn, their leader, was killed. They were joined by some of the Piutes, and Egan, the Piute war chief, led both tribes.

The story came to us in fragments, of isolated ranches attacked by the Indians, of settlers to the east of us who fled to the army post for protection, and of Pete French's heroic rear-guard defense that saved the life of all his men except the Chinese cook. Still Perrin kept us on roundup, making no concession to the fear that touched all of us.

Then, after we finished roundup, we heard the unbelievable. The Indians were fleeing into central Oregon, but somehow a small party of them had circled back, murdered Joe Ryan and his boys, and run off most of their stock. Mrs Ryan, who had been visiting the Allisons, was safe.

It may have happened that way, although all of us on J Ranch believed it was the Ferguson boys who had done the killing because it was inconceivable that the Indians, already beaten, would return to kill the Ryans and steal their cattle.

Later another story was started, probably by

Virgil Lang or the Fergusons themselves, that some of us from J Ranch had done the killing. About that time one of O'Hara's riders west of us found Rolly Dillon's body, or what was left of it, hanging from a juniper limb. The Fergusons claimed we had done the killing, and Frank Allison admitted I had stopped at his house and asked if Dillon had gone by.

Apparently none of the settlers knew that Dillon had murdered Mrs Hammond, or if they did, they probably said it was good riddance. Someone—I always suspected Matt Cartwright—burned the Hammond house a few days after Cissy and I were there to get her things.

All the charges and countercharges and gossip that raced across the valley did not worry Jim Perrin. He never asked me about Rolly Dillon, but I was convinced that if a lawman came after me Perrin would not have surrendered me.

Then, one day after visiting my folks, I met Frank Allison on the road. He said directly: 'There's a lot of talk about you killing Rolly Dillon, Daniel. I'm afraid you're in for trouble.'

'It's Ferguson talk,' I said. 'They're the only friends Dillon had around here.'

'Sure. Just smoke screen to make folks forget the Ryans. But you know how it is. The whole thing goes back to Perrin.'

'Anybody going to work for him this summer?'

Allison laughed shortly. 'It's a funny thing. Everybody but me and your pa claims they're going to kill Perrin if the court gives him the marginal land, but they like his gold. He'll have a hay crew all right.' He started to ride on, then stopped. 'Mrs Ryan says Perrin wanted to buy the Rafter R a while back. Reckon he still wants it?'

'He wants it, all right.'

'Tell him to go see her. She can't stay there alone. Debbie's with her now, but she's got to come home.' Allison licked his lips. 'She's talking about marrying Jed Cartwright, come fall.'

'You can't let her ...'

I didn't finish the sentence. It wasn't any of my business, but I knew Frank Allison didn't like Jed and Debbie didn't like Mrs Cartwright. It was wrong, but the Fergusons still lived beside the Allisons, so I suppose Jed was the lesser of two evils.

'I can't stop her,' Allison said. 'She's scared of being an old maid.'

He gave me a straight look. I thought he was going to say I was the one who could keep Debbie from marrying Jed, but he didn't. He reined his horse around and went on, a good man who was not strong enough for a violent land.

A man will be a certain kind of man in one country and quite a different man in another. I

260

thought of my father, transformed in a way I would not have believed possible a year ago. And there was Frank Allison, who lacked some quality he should have had, and because he lacked it the land was sucking him dry until he couldn't even keep his daughter from marrying Jed Cartwright.

It was easy to say that in a wild new country the weak perish and the strong make their own destiny. But it was only a half-truth. There was nothing weak about Jim Perrin, yet I had the feeling he was perishing. I remembered how it had been on the day he brought me to J Ranch when he looked at Rocky's picture. He had everything then; he had much less now, not even the anticipation of a happy marriage.

When I reached J Ranch I told Perrin what Allison had said about Mrs Ryan. He gave me that quick boyish grin I hadn't seen for a long time. He said, 'Let's go into the house.'

I went with him, wondering what he wanted. Rocky was sitting in a chair, the late afternoon sun falling across her auburn hair and making it more red than it really was. She smiled at Perrin, ignoring me.

Perrin handed her a piece of paper. 'You wanted to own the Rafter R. Now you do. I bought it this afternoon from Mrs Ryan.' He turned to me. 'I've been to see her three times, but we couldn't get together on price until today.'

Rocky looked at the paper, then slipped it

into the pocket of her apron. She said, without any real feeling, 'Thank you, Jim.' She was being cruel, I thought, denying him the rightful pleasure he should have received.

I backed toward the door, feeling like an intruder. Perrin walked past Rocky to the fireplace and dropped into his chair in front of it. Then I stopped and stood rooted there by the door, for Rocky had held up the cloth she was embroidering. It was a baby's shirt.

'It's time you knew about this, Jim,' she said.

He got up from his chair, and it was one of the few occasions when I ever saw him allow his feeling to show in his face. He started to say something, then closed his mouth and just stood there, swaying back and forth like a cattail when a wind sweeps across the marsh.

'If it's a girl, you can name her,' Rocky said nervously. 'If it's a boy, he'll be James Perrin the Second.'

He walked to her and knelt beside her. She turned her head to see if I was still in the room. 'I wanted you to know, too, Danny. I was wondering if your mother would come and stay with me.'

Perrin frowned. 'Has she ever—'

'She knows what to do,' I said. 'She'll be glad to come.'

I edged toward the door, wanting to run, but still Rocky would not let me go. I had a feeling that at such times she shrank from being alone with Perrin. That was her mistake, a mistake they had both made over and over: holding up the barrier that had grown between them.

'Danny, I'd like to have you work for the Rafter R,' Rocky said, 'if Jim can get along without you.'

'You can have him,' Perrin said, and looked at me. 'But you can't stay there alone. How about José?'

Suddenly I rebelled. 'Am I being ordered to go to the Rafter R, or asked?'

'I'll pay fifty dollars a month,' Rocky said.

'To hell with it,' I said, and walked out.

Outside, after supper that night, Perrin remarked, 'I guess you don't want to go to the Rafter R after there's been so much talk about Rolly Dillon.'

I was standing in front of the house, my back against a poplar trunk, my eyes on the rim across the river. It had been a hot day, and the heat still held, even with the sun down and the purple haze of twilight deepening along the rim.

'No,' I said. 'I just don't like the idea of being taken so damned much for granted.'

Perrin didn't say anything for a while. He got out his pipe and filled it. I saw the match flare, the flame raveling up briefly to touch his dark face. I could tell nothing from it.

'I don't take you for granted, Danny,' he said finally. 'Rocky doesn't, either. It's just that sometimes we're careless about telling another person that he's kind of special. You

263

were a boy when you came here. None of us can say for sure when we become men. With me I think it was the day I left California to come here. Maybe someday you can decide when it was with you, like the night you and Pedro and Lane went after Rolly.' He hesitated, then said carefully, 'I think you should go, Danny.'

I said, 'All right, Jim. I'll go.'

I left J Ranch the next day with José, leading a packhorse loaded with our clothes, two Winchesters, and enough shells to hold the Rafter R against the attack that I was convinced would come.

CHAPTER TWENTY

Mrs Ryan and Debbie had cleaned up the Rafter R ranch house so that there was not a particle of dust anywhere. It was comfortable enough, containing a sitting room, a kitchen, and two bedrooms. Mrs Ryan left everything except her personal belongings, even food on the pantry shelves.

I had a strange feeling of kinship with the Ryans when I stood in the sitting room that July afternoon, my eyes on the worn furniture that was as scarred by miles of travel as the furniture my folks had in the cabin south of the lake. The Ryans had been wanderers too, I thought, until they had seen Paradise Valley.

I had never met Joe Ryan, but he must have been a tough-minded, courageous man to have settled between Perrin and Pritchard, two range giants who could have crushed him like an acorn between the jaws of a hog. But he had settled, and he'd stayed until he was murdered.

I went outside. Paradise Valley seemed very different than it had been from the rim. From up there it had been as beautiful as a small, perfect emerald, a sort of fairyland far removed from reality. Perhaps that was why it had appealed to both Rocky and Perrin.

Now, as I gazed at the high, steep walls surrounding the valley, it did not seem a fairyland. Rather it was a world set apart from the lake and the valley, from Thunder River and Garnet Mountain, for I could see nothing of them. Here was peace, a silence stirred only by the murmur of the creek and the song of a meadow lark from the grass that was ready to be cut for hay.

That night I asked José a question that had been in my mind for days. 'The Piutes were supposed to have killed the Ryans, but we think it was the Fergusons, and they claim it was us. Why hasn't somebody figured out who did it?'

José had the same gift of laughter that Pedro García had, and the same soft voice. But he shook his head at me, his swarthy face very grave. 'Who would do that, Señor Dan? We have no law.'

265

That was true, of course. No one along the lake who could read sign would take the responsibility even if they had the authority. And the soldiers were still pursuing the Indians. We needed a county of our own. Then we would have a sheriff to look into such crimes.

We started haying the next day. After it was finished there were fences to fix in the breaks of the rimrock that surrounded the valley. Later Perrin and Pedro drove in a small herd of cows and two bulls, all branded with the Rafter R iron. Several weeks after that Billy Ralls drove a heavily loaded wagon through the gap in the north rim. When he left, we had supplies for the winter.

Ducks and geese fled south from the lake. It snowed on the rim, but winter came slowly in the valley. I visited my folks almost every week. They told me that Debbie Allison and Jed Cartwright were married, that settlers were pouring into the northern half of the valley now that the Indian scare was over, and that Virgil Lang was getting rich selling lots. It was the harvest he had hoped to reap, but one thing disappointed him. The new people changed the name of his town to Ivanhoe.

'Too many Howards this and that already,' my father said.

'You wouldn't know the place,' my mother said. 'Another store. A hotel. Livery stable. Blacksmith shop.'

My father shook his head, troubled. 'I don't know, Daniel. They're building a church in town and they've asked me to preach every other Sunday. But the people here have done so much for us I hate to leave them.'

'You'll still preach here on the Sundays you aren't in town, Bartram,' my mother said. 'You have to accept.'

'I suppose so,' he said heavily. 'But it's been good, even with all our troubles. I hate to see the changes come.'

So did I. It had been good, except for Ben's death. I had never seen my mother look better or happier. She had gained weight, her face filling out so that it had lost that pinched look the years of wandering and privation had given her. I had asked her if she would go to J Ranch when it was time for Rocky's baby, and she had said she'd be glad to. I think she was pleased that Rocky wanted her.

The following week it snowed; then it turned cold and the sky cleared and at night the stars glittered above a white valley. We had to feed the cattle, but there was little else to do. Mrs Ryan had left some books, and I read every evening while José braided a reata.

We didn't have a calendar, and I hadn't given a thought to Christmas, largely, I suppose, because it was not a day of gift giving in our family. We had thought of it as a religious day, and now that I wasn't going to church I had not been reminded of it until one noon Ole Larsen rode in.

He came into the house, stomping snow from his boots. He slammed the door, yanked off his gloves, and held his hands out over the fire. 'By God, boys, it's cold,' he said, and rubbed his face. 'The sun shines like hell, but it ain't doing no good. Reminds me of when I was riding for an outfit in New Mexico and we had a big dry. No grass at all, and everybody was hollering for rain. We'd see them big clouds boil up and head toward us, and the boss, he'd stand outside and watch 'em. After they'd gone over, he'd cuss for an hour. "Just another empty," he'd say.'

José laughed. 'Did she ever rain?'

'Hell, no. The wind came up and blew our land into Texas. You know what them Texicans done? Well, sir, they just turned the wind around and blowed New Mexico back across the line. Had enough dust in Texas already, they said.'

Ole didn't tell me what had brought him to the Rafter R until after dinner. Then he said: 'Well, got to get back. You're riding with me, Dan. Miz Perrin, she sent for you. Gonna have a big Christmas dinner. Then you're coming back and José comes over and gets his belly full.'

I took my sheepskin down from a nail on the wall, wrapped a scarf around my ears, and put on my hat. I went outside and saddled my buckskin. I wasn't sure of my feelings. I wanted

268

to see Rocky and I didn't want to, but I had to go.

I was concerned about José. We'd had no trouble, but I had expected it when we first came to the Rafter R, and I still did. But as I rode away with Ole, I reassured myself with the thought that trouble wouldn't come with a foot of snow on the ground and the temperature standing below zero. The Fergusons would wait until spring or later, when it would be easier to drive cattle.

It was almost dark when we reached the Valley Ranch, and getting colder by the minute. We stayed the night there, and went on in the morning, a wind coming up now and beginning to drift the snow. Because we had slow going, fighting our way through the piled-up snow, it was nearly noon when we got to J Ranch.

Pedro came out of the bunkhouse and took our horses. We stumbled inside, rubbing our hands and faces, and stood by the fire thawing out. The crew joshed us about hugging the fire so close we were putting it out, and Ole joshed back, but all the time I had a feeling I was an outsider, a visitor from another ranch.

I heard the door open and shut. Turning, I saw that Perrin had come in. He shook hands with me and asked about José and how we were making out, from a sense of duty, I thought, as if it were expected of him. The Rafter R was Rocky's spread, not his.

269

He held his hands out over the stove, silent a moment, then said, 'Rocky wants to see you.'

I put on my sheepskin and went out, the snow crunching under my boots. I wondered what they'd say, Ole and Manuel and Harry Gillam and the rest. Probably nothing as long as Perrin was there, but they'd talk after he left, and it wouldn't be nice. Or was it my imagination again?

Rocky was standing in front of the fireplace when I went into the big house. She cried, 'Danny, it's wonderful to see you again,' and came to me, holding out her hand and walking in the awkward way a woman does when she is near her time.

I took her hand and dropped it quickly, telling myself I shouldn't have come. I didn't want to see her so, but there was something else, too, a fear that was a deep, terrible ache in me. She wasn't well. Her face was pale, not just white, but gray, as if she had suffered a great deal.

'Come over to the fire, Danny,' she said. 'I can't seem to stay warm today.'

So I walked beside her to the fireplace, our footsteps muted by the thick rug. I had almost forgotten how it was, but I remembered now. It was still Jim Perrin's room, Jim Perrin's house, beautifully furnished, and as devoid of human warmth as the bitter December day.

'You've never been over to see your ranch,' I said.

'I knew it was being well taken care of. I never thanked you for going. You didn't want to, but you did, and I'll always be grateful to you.'

For a moment our eyes met, and then I started toward the door. I belonged in the bunkhouse, not here, for if I stayed I'd tell her why I'd gone to the Rafter R. I'd ask her why she was torturing herself, why she insisted on living here in the ash heap of what could have been happiness.

'Danny.'

I turned. 'I don't belong here. I should have stayed on the Rafter R.'

She shook her head. 'No, I couldn't go to you, so I sent Ole to bring you here. You see, the mail is terribly slow and I wouldn't ask Jim for money to pay you. But my money finally came. Now you get your wages.' She held up her fingers and counted off the months from July through December. 'Six months, and six times fifty is three hundred dollars.'

She picked up a canvas bag and held it out to me. 'José gets the same. We're having Christmas dinner today.' She smiled. 'No presents because there's no place to buy them, but we'll have a little Christmas spirit—'

The door slammed open and Perrin came in. He didn't say a word, but I glimpsed his face, tight and dark and furious. He ran up the stairs, taking them three at a time, without answering Rocky's hurried, 'What's happened, Jim?'

He was going to have it out with me, I thought. Maybe the men had said something... No, he wouldn't hear what they said. A moment later he came back down the stairs, buckling his gun belt around his slim waist. I had never seen him wear a gun before.

'Jim, what is it?' Rocky cried.

'Billy Ralls just got in from Giant Springs. Some toughs raided the ranch and shot Ike Bellew. He's dead. They ran off with our horses, fifty head of the best I had.'

'You can't go, Jim! This is our Christmas. Danny's here.'

'Ike's dead,' Perrin said. 'Can't you understand? I'm going to get those horses back if I have to chase them clear across Nevada.'

She put a hand to her swollen belly and leaned forward. 'Jim, you ought to be here when the baby comes. You owe him that much.'

'It's two weeks yet,' he said. 'I'll be back a long time before that.'

He went out. I walked to the window. I should go with him, I thought, when I saw that the crew was at the corral, saddling up. He was taking everybody but Alec Brown and Wang, and he'd have taken them if they'd been of any value to him. I stood there until they left, riding south, snow flying around them, kicked up by the hoofs of a dozen horses, and then I knew there was no reason for me to go. I didn't belong to J Ranch now. I belonged to the Rafter R.

I heard Rocky groan. I whirled. She had dropped down onto the leather couch, her face paler than ever, and I saw fear in her eyes, fear that came from pain, and fear of the unknown travail through which she must pass.

'It's started, Danny,' she whispered, 'and he isn't here.'

I had a crazy idea she had started the pains by her own will to punish Perrin for going off and leaving her, then the thought was gone. I helped her upstairs to her room. The pains were real enough, whatever had started them. 'I'll get my mother,' I said. 'Stay here. It may be a long time.'

I ran downstairs and back to the kitchen. 'Put water on the stove,' I yelled at Wang. 'A lot of it, and keep it hot!'

I grabbed up my sheepskin and scarf and hat and left the house on the run. I found Alec Brown in the store hugging the stove. 'You ever have a baby?' I asked.

He grinned. 'I never did. I guess I ain't made right—'

'You get into the house. Mrs Perrin is having hers.'

He got up, his face white. 'Hell, boy, I've helped plenty of mares, but a woman ...'

'It's you and Wang,' I said. 'Jim's gone.'

I went to the barn, running through the snow and sucking the frigid air into my lungs. I

273

harnessed Jim's best team and hooked the horses up to his sleigh. I punished them all the way to the lake, where I hurried my mother into her coat and headed back, fighting a way through drifts belly deep on the horses.

I almost killed them, but I didn't care; I didn't even care what Jim Perrin said. When we pulled up in front of the house, my mother ran through the darkness to the front door and I went on to the barn. I put the horses up and rubbed them down, knowing they would never be much good again, but I had made a trip that was little short of miraculous and I was proud of it. I lingered in the big barn, afraid to go into the house, afraid of what I would learn. But I couldn't stay outside. I had to know.

Alec sat in front of the fireplace, tired and worried and as pale as I had ever seen him. He said, 'She's having a wicked time, Dan; a hell of a wicked time.'

The baby came that night, a boy. He was born dead.

CHAPTER TWENTY-ONE

My mother said it had been a hard delivery, that Rocky had fought against it. I suppose she wanted to wait until Perrin got back, but even her strong will was not enough to postpone birth.

At noon the next day my mother told me Rocky wanted to see me. I asked, 'Will she be all right?'

'She's young and strong and she'll probably have many more babies.' Then my mother shook her head, and the anger that had been smoldering in her broke out in bitter words, 'What kind of man is this Jim Perrin who would go off and leave her at such a time?'

I couldn't answer her. As I went upstairs to Rocky's room, I wondered if the baby would have lived if Perrin had been there to help Rocky through her hours of agony. It was a question that could not be answered, but I was sure that Rocky would always be convinced that Perrin had killed his baby by leaving. And Perrin would always be plagued by doubts.

Rocky lay on her back, motionless, her auburn hair very dark against the pillow. I drew up a chair and she held out a hand to me. She couldn't smile; she didn't even try. She just looked at me, her blue eyes bright and a little feverish. She seemed more ghost than woman, and even her lips, that had been so richly red, were colorless.

Sitting there, holding her cold hand in mine, I felt a great pity for her. I should, I suppose, have hated Jim Perrin, but I couldn't. No one could make an honest and objective judgment of her and Perrin, indicting one or the other for the failure of a marriage that might have been successful. But I was sure that Perrin was not

275

entirely to blame.

'I want you to do some things for me, Danny,' she said, her voice very low. 'I don't have any right to ask you, and I wouldn't except that there isn't anyone else.'

'You have every right,' I said.

She squeezed my hand, and then hers went slack again. 'I want you to bury the baby tomorrow. Have Alec make a coffin. There's some white silk in the top drawer of the bureau. It was left from my wedding dress. I think there's enough to line the coffin.'

She turned her face from me, and I was glad. It wasn't like the day we had buried Ben. I had never known the baby, and I couldn't love someone I hadn't known; but the irony of using a part of her wedding dress to line the baby's coffin shocked me. I knew she wasn't seeing it the way I was. She was just trying to do something nice for the baby she had never heard cry, that she had never nursed or held in her arms.

'Dig the grave today,' she said. 'Get your father in the morning. I want him to preach the funeral.'

I managed to say, 'All right, Rocky,' and, releasing her hand, stood up. I couldn't argue with her, but there were two sides to everything, even this, so I made myself say, 'You ought to wait until Jim gets back.'

Without turning her head to look at me, she said coldly, 'I'll never wait for Jim for anything.' I started toward the door, but before I reached it she said: 'Have Alec carve a headboard, Danny. Tell him to put James Perrin, Junior, on it.'

I took the piece of cloth to Alec and told him what to do. To dig the little grave took most of the afternoon, for the ground had been frozen before the snow fell. Early the next morning I left for the lake. On the way back I told my father about Perrin leaving and how Rocky felt, but I couldn't tell him so he'd understand because he didn't really know either of them. And, like everyone else along the lake, he had listened to Virgil Lang too long.

'The Lord will punish Jim Perrin,' he said. 'I don't know how or when, but He will.'

There was nothing I could say to my father, who thought that Perrin was a devil who walked like a man, so I didn't say anything. But I didn't believe that the Lord punished anyone. Jim Perrin had punished himself.

My father had a talk with Rocky before the funeral. I wasn't with them, so I don't know what he said, but all of his sympathy was with her. I'm sure he comforted her.

The funeral was short and not much of a funeral, as we judge such occasions. My father read from the Bible and prayed. Then he said a few words about the glories of Heaven and the blamelessness of a child's soul, and prayed again. That was all. There wasn't even an artificial flower to lay on the grave.

Alec and I filled the grave, which was beside Mrs Hammond's and the J Ranch buckaroos who had died working for Jim Perrin. We slipped the headboard into place and walked down the slope to the house, leaving the small dark spot of earth on the white hillside.

My father talked with Rocky again, and then I took him home. He said very little on the cold ride back to the lake, but when we reached the cabin he said, 'Your mother will stay with Mrs Perrin as long as she's needed.' He got out of the sleigh and stood there, giving me a long, searching look. Then he said: 'I feel sorry for her, Daniel. She will have only unhappiness as long as she stays there.'

It was late when I got back, and bitterly cold. I found my mother waiting for me in the living room, and as I stood with my hands extended over the fire I asked about Perrin. 'He isn't back yet,' she said. 'But it doesn't make any difference as far as Mrs Perrin is concerned. He's lost her.'

He had lost her a long time ago, I thought. She'd leave him now and go back to California, and I thought of my father saying she would never be happy as long as she stayed here. I wondered if she would ever be happy, anywhere.

'I've heard so much talk about Jim Perrin,' my mother said, 'even before we saw him that day at Lang's store. When our neighbors run out of anything else to talk about, they can always start on Perrin. They think he has everything, but he doesn't, Daniel. He has very little.'

I went to bed that night in the room that had been mine from the first night I had come to J Ranch. In the morning I would go back to the Rafter R. But I didn't. I was so worn out that I slept until noon. After I had breakfast, my mother said Rocky wanted to see me again.

I found her looking better, much better than I had expected. I pulled a chair to the side of her bed and sat down. She smiled at me, and I saw there was some color in her face. She held her hand out, and I took it just as I had two days ago, but now it wasn't cold.

'What would I have done without you, Danny?' she asked.

I didn't answer for a moment, afraid my voice would betray me, then I said, 'It will be different now.'

'Yes, it will be a great deal different because I'm leaving J Ranch.' She closed her eyes and was silent for a time, then she said: 'It's the season of death. I don't mean just the baby. It started with your brother. Then Mrs Hammond and the Ryans. Danny...' She stopped, and then went on. 'Danny, I understand you so much better now that I know your father and mother. You can't help being exactly what you are.'

I thought of how much we had been together, but always talking about impersonal things. I suppose we had been afraid to talk about anything else.

'Your father is a wonderful man,' she went on. 'He said something that made me feel differently about the future. I didn't even want to live. But he said all of us must walk in the deep shadow for a time, some longer than others. He said that it had been years with him, but that if we have any faith, sooner or later we come out of the shadow and find the sunshine all around us.'

She was silent again, and I remembered with a sense of guilt that I used to think I owed nothing to my father.

'Sometimes I wonder why I ever married Jim,' she went on; 'but I know, if I can be honest enough to admit it. He had money, and I wanted that. He was respected and wonderfully successful, and I liked that. But the real thing was never there. I know it now, so I can't blame him entirely. I keep telling myself I hate him, but I don't really. I just never want to see him or talk to him again.'

She opened her eyes and looked at me. 'It's been a terrible Christmas, Danny. It could not have been more terrible, and I had hoped to give you something good to remember when you were back on the Rafter R. Now I understand something I didn't before. It wasn't the fifty dollars a month that made you go there. It was something else I should have known about, but I didn't, and I'm sorry. I've been thinking of myself too much, and fighting Jim.'

I heard my mother coming and I released Rocky's hand and stood up. When my mother reached the door, she said, 'Mr Perrin's back.'

He came in a moment later, his spurs jingling, his gun still buckled around him. He was cold and grim-faced, and I knew he had been told what had happened. He walked directly to the bed, tried to say something, and couldn't. Rocky looked at him, and then she turned her face to the wall. My mother and I slipped out of the room. I waited downstairs for a long time. Presently Perrin came down. He had taken off his gun belt.

He said: 'You'll sleep in the bunkhouse tonight. I'm moving into your room.'

Later, in the bunkhouse, I heard what had happened. Perrin had caught the horse thieves far south of Giant Springs Ranch. He hanged them and recovered the horses. He and his men had been in the saddle almost all the time since they had left J Ranch. Only Pedro and Ole Larsen had returned with him. The rest had stayed at Giant Springs Ranch to thaw out and catch up on their sleep. He must have been thinking of Rocky, or he wouldn't have driven himself through the cold, as tired as he was.

I left early the next morning, carrying a second bag of gold coins that my mother brought from the big house to me. It was José's wages. There would be no Christmas on J

281

Ranch for him or anyone.

CHAPTER TWENTY-TWO

A blizzard struck the day after I got back to the Rafter R, the worst storm I had seen since I had come to the country. We were marooned in Paradise Valley for weeks, then in early February a chinook melted the snow and for days after that the ground was a bog. It dried out and the weather stayed warm, strangely warm for the time of year, and José shook his head, deeply worried. We'd have a second winter, he said, and grass would be slow coming in the spring.

Ole Larsen rode in again about the middle of February. Rocky was leaving and I was to take her to Winnemucca. I was surprised, and yet I shouldn't have been. I had known she wouldn't stay, and because she wouldn't let Perrin drive her to the railroad it was natural enough to send for me.

I thought about Perrin as I rode south with Ole, and worried about what he would think, but I don't know why I did. His feelings were locked in his heart. There had been a time when he'd been able to talk to me. If Lane Sears had been on J Ranch, Perrin might have been able to talk to him. But as far as I knew, Lane was a thousand miles away, and in spirit I was fully as far. I would never, I was sure, come back to J Ranch to live.

Not once during the time I was there did Perrin show any temper or displeasure. As far as appearances were concerned, Rocky was merely taking a vacation. It may have been that no one but the three of us knew she would never return as Jim Perrin's wife.

When I went into the big house, Rocky smiled and asked how we made out during the storm. When I told her everything was fine, Perrin said she'd have to look a long ways to find a better pair of buckaroos than José Otero and Danny Nathan.

We left early the next morning, the day not yet born. Everybody was there to tell her goodbye, even Wang. She shook hands with all of them, looking as if she wanted to cry, but when she came to Perrin she hesitated, not knowing quite what to do. But Perrin said, 'Take care of yourself,' and put his arms around her and kissed her.

I don't think there was the slightest spark of love left between them, but still she thought enough of him to keep up a front. She said, 'You take care of yourself, Jim,' and then got into the buggy and we drove south. A moment later the big white house and the poplars and Perrin and his men were out of sight, lost in the misty dawn light.

It was cold, but she was bundled up, a fur wrapped around her neck and her hands in a muff. We had a buffalo robe over our laps. She seemed lost in thought, and quite distant, her body stiff and tense beside me. Though she was very thin, she seemed strong enough, and there was color in her face again.

An hour or more passed before she said anything. The sun was up, slowly cutting away the night chill. When she looked at me, I saw that she had been crying. She wiped her eyes and gave me a small smile.

'I'm sorry, Danny,' she said. 'I was just thinking of the time you drove us to J Ranch. I was so young, and it seems so long ago.' She was silent, staring ahead, then she added: 'I don't really know why I was crying. It wasn't because of the baby, and it certainly wasn't because I'm leaving Jim. And it's not because I'm leaving this miserable country, either.'

I didn't look at her. I couldn't. The truth came to me then, and it killed something in me. All the while I had hoped that some day, when she got over the loss of her baby, she would come back to the valley, and me. Now I knew she never would, that I had been dreaming a foolish boy's dream that had no basis in reality.

This was my country just as it was Jim Perrin's country, and I couldn't leave it any more than he could. For the first time I understood why her marriage with Jim had failed. It was the land that had beaten them, its violence and distance, its isolation and loneliness.

284

We rode on in silence, my eyes on the long trough of the valley that ran for miles, on Garnet Mountain with its deep covering of snow on one side of us, and the rimrock on the other, bleak and gray, for the wind had blown the snow off the sheer, unbroken rock.

I was glad I had never told her I loved her, or thought I did. I was sure she felt kindly toward me, and trusted me, or she wouldn't have wanted me to drive her to the railroad. But that was not enough. Even if by some miracle she had loved me, it would not have been enough. She belonged in one kind of country and I belonged in another. The more I thought about it, the better I understood the brutal finality of it.

The miles fell behind with the hours. Once she broke one of the long silences to ask, 'Danny, would you like to buy the Rafter R?'

I looked at her in shocked surprise. 'Why did you want it in the first place?'

'I've asked myself that question many times,' she said moodily. 'I think it was because Jim wanted it. I was trying to make him do something for me he didn't want to do. I had to find out whether he loved me as much as he loved a piece of land.' She turned her face to look at me. 'There's no reason to keep it now. I have some money of my own, and Jim made a generous settlement. I'd like to be rid of it and I'd rather have you have it than anyone else.'

'I don't have any money,' I said.

'Well, let's leave it this way. I'll go on paying you fifty dollars a month. You can save part of that, or maybe you can borrow some money.' She gave me a small smile. 'It would be all right if you could make just a little payment.'

'I'd like to have it,' I said, and let it go at that.

We stayed the night at Ferrill's. We went on the next morning, the good weather holding, and reached Winnemucca late that afternoon. We asked at the depot about trains, and when we were told that the next west-bound was due shortly after nine Rocky bought a ticket for San Francisco.

I left her luggage at the depot and drove to the hotel for supper. Several men were lounging in front of the hotel, most of them buckaroos who were spending the winter in town, idle men who had nothing to do but gossip. One of them recognized Rocky. I don't know who he was or when he had seen her. Perhaps he had been in town when she'd got off the train with Perrin. Or it might have been someone who had stopped at J Ranch for a meal and had seen her there.

As I stepped up on the boardwalk after trying the team, the man said: 'Say, that's Jim Perrin's woman. He must wear the hell out of 'em. She's the second one that hombre's fetched to town.'

Rocky was going into the lobby as he spoke. At the moment it didn't occur to me that she might not have heard it, that it would be better

286

to overlook it. The same fury was in me that I had felt on the evening I'd fought Rolly Dillon and on the night Matt Cartwright had stopped Cissy and me when we were going to the dance.

I reached the men in three strides. 'Who said that?'

They snickered, sensing a little excitement to break the monotony of idleness. One of them asked, 'Ain't you a mite proddy, mister?'

It wasn't the right voice. Then I saw the one at the end edge away from the pool of light that came through a lobby window, a fat man who wasn't a cowhand and probably never had been. Just a moocher trying to entertain the others in the hope of getting a free drink. I lunged toward him.

One of the others yelled, 'Look out, Slim!' The fat man was backtracking, scared now.

He shouted, 'I didn't mean nothing—' stumbled over a loose board, and fell on his back.

I wasn't wearing my gun. If they had jumped me, I'd have been in for a beating, but they let me play it out, probably because they knew he had it coming. He rolled over on his hands and knees, then I had him by the coat collar and yanked him to his feet. He struck at me, cursing and straining to break free, but he was more lard than muscle. Still holding to his coat collar, I dragged him off the walk to the horse trough and rammed his head into the water.

I would have drowned him, I think, and I

287

don't suppose anyone would have missed him. The men along the wall were laughing too hard to stop me, but the town marshal, hearing the commotion, ran along the walk, yelling, 'What the hell are you doing?'

The fat man had almost stopped struggling. The marshal, seeing it, cracked me across the face with a back-handed blow that sent me reeling and pulled the fellow's head out of the water. He lay on the ground, gurgling for breath, and the marshal whirled to face me.

'You a stranger in town?' he demanded.

'Just got in,' I answered.

He recognized me then, and asked, 'You're one of Jim Perrin's boys, ain't you?'

'I was,' I said. 'I'm working for the Rafter R now.'

'I'll throw you into the cooler until you—'

'Let him go, Luke,' one of the men said. 'Slim made a remark.'

'I'm leaving town in the morning,' I said.

The marshal glanced at my hip and saw I wasn't wearing a gun. He shrugged. 'All right, see that you do.'

Rocky was waiting for me in the lobby, her face very pale. She said, 'Danny, I never saw you like that before.'

I was breathing hard, a little ashamed now that my anger was dying down. I said, 'You never will again.'

After we were seated at a table in the dining room and had given our order, Rocky leaned forward. 'Jim told me you were that way sometimes. Like a wild man, but I never believed it. You've always been so kind.' She sat back, suddenly embarrassed. 'But you would with me. It's just that I don't understand men, or why they fight.'

'Men fight for different things,' I said. 'I guess I've got a bad temper.'

She shook her head. 'It's the country. It takes you and molds you into something different than you were. Look at Jim.'

'It can't put something into you that wasn't there in the first place,' I said.

Then I thought of my father, and I wasn't sure I was right. But as far as Jim Perrin was concerned, I knew he hadn't been changed. Rocky hadn't, either. Our food came and we began to eat. Presently she put her fork down and leaned back, asking, 'What kind of girl is Cissy Hammond?'

'A good girl,' I said quickly. 'She's what she is and she doesn't pretend to be anything else.'

'I liked her,' Rocky said. 'I didn't know about her mother and Jim until Cissy told me. I could overlook that because Jim was faithful to me after we were married, but I couldn't forgive him for being so furious about Cissy coming to J Ranch. The only time he ever said a mean thing to me was when I asked him to let her stay.'

When we finished eating it was almost train time, so I took Rocky back to the depot and we stood waiting beside the track, the chill night wind hurrying past us. I thought of Cissy, and of how I had brought her to Winnemucca just as I had brought Rocky. But there was all the difference in the world between them. In one respect Rocky was better off. At least she was going back to her kind of people, but Cissy was an exile from the only home she had.

We heard the plaintive cry of the train whistle far to the east, and suddenly it came to me what it meant. I would never see Rocky again. I took her by the arms, roughly, more roughly than I intended, and looked down at her, and then I let her go. I'd had my boy's dream and it was over and I was awake.

'I know how you feel about me,' she said softly. 'Why did you never tell me?'

'I couldn't,' I said. 'Jim's my friend.'

'Are you sure Jim's your friend? Is he anyone's friend but his own? Does he ever do anything for anyone unless he thinks he can profit by it? Think back, Danny. Think back to the time he hired you. He didn't want trouble with the settlers and he needed their help with the haying. Don't you see?'

The train was close now, its headlight boring a white expanding tunnel into the darkness, its bell clanging. Rocky was bitter, and maybe she had a right to be, but she was being unfair to Perrin, so I said nothing.

'Goodbye, Danny,' she said.

She reached up and put her hands around

the back of my neck and kissed me. Then she let go, whirled, and walked toward the train.

I turned and stumbled around the depot toward the buggy. I had never had a sister, but if I had I suppose she would have kissed me the way Rocky had. And this I knew. It was nothing at all like the way in which Cissy had kissed me. I thought: I haven't lost Rocky. I couldn't lose something I never had. Then, for some reason I didn't understand at all, I remembered that I had lost Cissy.

I got back to J Ranch in two days, reaching it just before dark. They had seen me coming. Perrin stood waiting by the corral, his dark face as expressionless as ever. He did not ask me to stay the night.

Ole Larsen took the team, and Pedro García led my saddled horse toward me. I knew now what Perrin thought. His attitude told me as plainly as words that he hadn't trusted either of us. For the first time I questioned my judgment of him, and I wondered if Rocky was right.

When I stepped into the saddle, Perrin said, 'Send José back. He belongs on J Ranch, not the Rafter R.' He didn't ask about Rocky. He didn't care. I looked down at him, uncertain, and then the uncertainty was gone, for he added, 'You will not be welcome on J Ranch after tonight.'

I couldn't bring myself to tell him the truth. He wouldn't have believed it anyhow. I rode home through the cold night to the Rafter R, the only home I had, and the next morning I gave José Perrin's message and he left. Two days later another blizzard struck, and I was alone, with a herd to feed.

CHAPTER TWENTY-THREE

The days became weeks and the weeks months. There was no trouble with the Fergusons, and for that I was thankful. Ivanhoe had its boom, saloons and hotels and more stores and a bank, and Virgil Lang became fatter than ever and smoked the most expensive cigars he could buy and wore the best clothes of any man in the valley. The Fergusons stayed in town, working as carpenters, which may have been the reason that they left me alone.

The legislature carved out a new county for us, and Ivanhoe became the county seat. The settlers were everywhere, filling in the empty places wherever there was water. Howard Valley had been an island around which the human current had passed, but now it was filled and bulging.

I was a spectator to all this, yet hardly even that, for I actually saw very little that was happening. I heard about it from Allison, who helped me with haying, and from my folks when I had time to visit them. My father preached in Ivanhoe every other Sunday, and conducted evening services for a little settlement called Branby up in the foothills of the mountains.

The most surprising thing to me was my father's election to the legislature. Perrin fought him, throwing his weight behind O'Hara, who was snowed under as was everyone who ran on the cattlemen's ticket. Almost as surprising was the way in which my father helped me buy the Rafter R.

From the day that Rocky left, I found that she was in my mind less and less, and as my memory of her became indistinct I discovered that my mental image of Cissy became sharper, that she was filling the void in my thinking. I hated myself for letting her go as I had. I could at least have asked her to write to me. Now I had no idea where she was or how I could trace her.

I finally reached the point where I wondered why I had ever fallen in love with Rocky. She mailed me a check the first of every month. No letter. Not even a note. Then, in late summer, she did write. She was buying a house in San Francisco and she needed money. She had no desire to keep the Rafter R. Would I buy it for three thousand dollars?

I didn't know what Perrin had paid Mrs Ryan. I don't suppose Rocky knew. But certainly the Rafter R was a bargain at that price. The trouble was, I had only a small fraction of it. When I told my folks about

Rocky's offer, my mother brought me more than two hundred dollars that she had saved out of my wages. With my savings we could raise five hundred. But it wouldn't do. I suppose Rocky had forgotten what she'd said when she left Winnemucca, about my making a small payment. In her letter she made it clear that she wanted cash.

My father said, 'Let's go to town. It's possible we can borrow what you need.'

I had no faith, but we went. I had still less faith when we sat down at the banker's desk and my father explained why we were there. The banker's name was John Stanley. He had hollow cheeks and a spade beard, and zealous black eyes that were fixed on me from the time I shook hands with him.

'Yes, we'll lend you the money,' Stanley said the instant my father had finished talking.

It was as easy as that. When we left town, I couldn't help glancing at Virgil Lang's store and thinking about the first day that we were in the valley, when my father made his bargain with Lang, posing as something he wasn't and not giving a damn whether the debt was ever paid back. When I tried to thank him, he shook his head at me, smiling.

'It is a small thing for me to do for you, Daniel,' he said. 'And I might add I'm glad you're not working for Perrin any more.'

I instinctively opened my mouth to defend Perrin, but closed it without saying anything. I could expect trouble from him just as I could expect it from Pritchard and the Fergusons. No, I decided, it was not for me to defend Jim Perrin.

After that I had a different feeling about the Rafter R. It was mine, not Rocky's. But my trouble was still loneliness, and buying the Rafter R couldn't cure that. I brooded too much, my thoughts turning inward, and Frank Allison, who was helping me with haying, said I'd be as loco as a sheepherder if I didn't change my way of living.

My mother must have had the same feeling. One day in early fall she said: 'You ought to get married, Daniel. There are lots of nice girls living in Ivanhoe. If you'd go to church in town with your father ...'

'I don't want a "nice" girl,' I said.

My mother and father looked at each other, remembering Cissy, I suppose. As I rode home, I thought about it, my imagination building up the talk that must be going around. Sleeping with Cissy. Killing Rolly Dillon. Breaking up Jim Perrin and his wife. They'd believe that, I thought, now that Rocky had almost given me the Rafter R. They were probably saying she'd divorce Perrin and come back and marry me. I didn't give a damn what they said about me, I told myself. That night I wrote to Cissy, asking her to write to me. I addressed the letter to her at Cheyenne, General Delivery, not having the slightest idea she'd get it, but it was the best I could do.

I rode into town the next day to mail the letter. While I was there, I hired a buckaroo named Sol Craig, a small, silent man who wore his gun the way a man does who knows how to use it. I couldn't afford to hire a hand, but I couldn't face a winter of living alone.

Craig's coming to the Rafter R helped. He was a strange, reticent man with pale blue eyes and a preoccupied manner as if he were listening to the wind or a coyote call or maybe the hoofbeats of someone coming for him. I was convinced he was a wanted man, but I never once regretted hiring him.

Through all these months I had the weird feeling that I was marking time, waiting for something I couldn't identify, a vague something that was bound up with the land and Perrin's hunger for land. It was like waiting for the climax of a play, a climax that could not be hurried but was as inevitable as death.

When it did come, the manner of it was both unexpected and surprising. Sol and I were eating dinner on a cold day in early December. Sol got up and went to the stove for the coffee pot. As he looked out of the window, he said, in a dry, expressionless voice, 'We've got company.'

I went to the window. The Fergusons were dismounting in front of the house. I said, 'I'll talk to them.'

I wasn't surprised they were there, for the boom in Ivanhoe was over, and it was natural for them to return to their place on the lake since there was no more carpentry work in town. But I was surprised when I opened the door and Ernie said in a friendly voice: 'Howdy, Nathan. We rode over for a little palaver.'

They waited for me to invite them in. I hesitated, trying to think of some reason for them to be so friendly instead of acting proddy as they habitually did when I happened to run into them.

'It's God-damned cold out here,' Carl said in an aggrieved tone.

'Come in,' I said, and backed into the room.

Sol remained by the stove. When the Fergusons were inside and had closed the door, I said, 'You boys know Sol Craig?'

'Sure we know him,' Ernie said. 'A good man to have on our side and a bad man to have on the other.' He nodded at me. 'You heard?'

They were as swarthy-skinned and ugly as ever, and as dirty and stinking as ever. The instant they closed the door, the stench of their bodies came to me. I moved back to stand beside Sol, asking, 'Heard what?'

'The court finally got around to deciding the marginal-land business,' Ernie said. 'It's Perrin's. You know what he'll do now.'

I knew, all right. He'd told me often enough. I thought first of my folks, and then of the

Allisons and the Cartwrights and all of them. Sure, Perrin had warned them, but that didn't help now. All their work was for nothing. I thought of the heartbreak and despair, the resentment and bitterness, that would follow.

'He'll move you out,' I said. 'I'm sorry, but that's what he'll do.'

'You mean he'll try,' Ernie said. 'That's why we're here. There's a meeting at the schoolhouse tonight to decide what to do. You be there?'

I shook my head, for I had long realized that my position was an anomaly. I was neither fish nor fowl. I said: 'I don't have any land on the lake. Besides, there's nothing you can do if the law says the land is his.'

'We'll do something, all right,' Carl said hotly. 'Don't forget, your folks will lose their place if we don't.' He waggled a finger at me. 'You ain't sitting so good, neither, bucko. Where'll you be if we don't stop that son of a bitch, and stop him now?'

He was right. If it came to open war, I'd better fight when I had someone to fight with. But my case was different. The Rafter R belonged to me; the marginal land belonged to Perrin. If the settlers fought, they'd put themselves outside the law. Then I knew I had to go, to keep my father and Frank Allison out of trouble, if for nothing else.

'All right,' I said. 'I'll be there.'

After they had gone, Sol sniffed

distastefully. 'Never smelled nothing like it, not even with a sheepherder in the room.' He scratched an ear, looking at me intently. 'I'll go along, just for fun.'

'Thanks, Sol,' I said.

That was loyalty, the kind of loyalty that makes you feel good because you don't ask for it. It was different from the loyalty Jim Perrin gave and demanded from those who worked for him.

That night Sol and I stopped at the Allison place to see if Frank wanted to ride with us, but Mrs Allison said he had gone on with my father. Then she asked: 'What can we do, Daniel? Have we got to go?'

I saw no reason to avoid the truth. I said bluntly: 'You'll have to go. If they fight, there's a good chance Frank will get killed, or have a U.S. Marshal arrest him.'

I wheeled away from the door, mounted, and rode on through the cold darkness. I didn't stop to see my mother. I couldn't. She would have asked the same question Mrs Allison had, and I would have had to give her the same answer.

'Looks like you've got your tail in a crack, Dan,' Sol said.

'Something like that,' I said.

'The Rafter R ain't in on this,' he said slowly. 'Not yet, so it's up to the others whether they're gonna die and get it over with, or run and hate themselves. I hit a deal like this once. I

299

plugged a man and then I ran, and I've been running ever since. If I had it to do over, I'd have stayed and finished it.'

I didn't say anything. I saw no sense in telling him he was wrong; but it seemed to me that fighting for something which is yours is one thing, but fighting for something which the law says is not yours is quite another.

By the time we reached the schoolhouse, the crowd had already gathered. We tied and went in. Every man and half-grown boy on the lake shore was there, all of them armed except my father. He nodded at me, his face very grave. So did Allison. The others just looked at me and Sol, no warmth of friendship on their faces. They didn't want me there, I thought, but they wouldn't send me away. They might need my gun. Sol's, too.

Cartwright said briskly, 'Better call the meeting to order, Brother Nathan,' and my father nodded and walked up the aisle between the seats to the teacher's desk. I couldn't help marveling. He was accepted as a leader, and no one questioned it.

He tapped his fist against the desk for order, and there was immediate silence. He said: 'I won't go into this situation because we are all familiar with it, and we know what we face, but I do want to say one thing. When the legislature meets, I will do everything I can to straighten up this marginal-land question and see that justice is done. The truth is that Jim

300

Perrin is a greedy, powerful man. He has the money to hire the best counsel, so it's possible I can do nothing to change the court's decision.'

I didn't know Virgil Lang was there until he got up and folded his hands across his vast belly. 'Brother Nathan,' he said, his voice sounding as if he had dipped his tongue in syrup, 'I know Jim Perrin better than any man here unless it's your son who worked for him. Only one thing can stop Perrin. Force! Men with guns in their hands.'

I hadn't intended to say anything, but I couldn't stay out of it. I jumped up, shouting, 'Lang, will you be one of the men who holds a gun?'

He made a slow, ponderous turn to look at me over the heads of the men who sat between us. He said, 'I don't believe I need answer a man who worked for Jim Perrin and made love to his—'

'Come outside, Lang,' I yelled. 'If you don't have a gun, borrow one!'

There was a lot of shouting then, and it was a full minute before my father restored order. But I couldn't sit down. I said: 'All of us have a stake in this except Lang. I question his right to speak. I question his honesty and courage. He's here for just one thing. He hates Perrin and he sees a chance to get even for something Perrin did to him years ago.'

'I don't deny anything you say except your aspersion on my honesty,' Lang flung at me, his face red. 'I don't pretend to be a fighting man, but there is not one of you in this room, except you and the gunslinger who walked in here with you, who has not been helped by me. Now I will pay one thousand dollars to the man who shoots and kills Jim Perrin. I am not ashamed to make that offer because the life of Jim Perrin stands between you and your homes. If the law is wrong, and I say it is, then you have but one course. Take the law into your hands!'

They cheered him, every man but my father, Frank Allison, Sol Craig, and myself. They were in a killing mood. The issue had run on too long, and the right or wrong of murder was not a moral question in their minds.

Matt Cartwright was on his feet, yelling, 'Hooray, for Mr Lang!'

And Carl Ferguson, as pleased as a hungry coyote with a chicken in his mouth, shouted, 'I'll take that thousand dollars, Virgil.'

My father pounded for order, his face flushed. When they were quiet, he said: 'Gentlemen, there is no use of continuing this meeting. You came here to decide a great issue, but as your legislator and your pastor I will have no part in a plan for murder. Meeting adjourned.'

He stalked down the aisle and went out through the door, Frank Allison following. I rose, meeting Carl Ferguson's bold eyes, and then left with Sol Craig. I hurried to my father, who was getting into Allison's wagon. I said, 'That was a brave thing to do.'

He laid a hand on my shoulder. 'Daniel, I never dreamed I would see the day when you'd say a thing like that to me.'

Then Allison was in the seat, the lines in his hands, and I stepped back and he drove away.

CHAPTER TWENTY-FOUR

By morning I had reached a decision. I had to warn Perrin, although I knew he wouldn't welcome my warning. By every principle of cold logic, I should have stayed out of it. But I couldn't. There had been a time when I had come as close to worshiping Jim Perrin as a boy could worship a grown man, and although we would never be friends again enough of the old feeling remained to make me go to him.

Without telling Sol where I was going, I rode up the trail that followed a steep, narrow break in the rimrock, forcing my buckskin through belly-deep snow that remained from the last storm. I did not take my gun. I didn't want Perrin to misunderstand my reason for coming.

I asked at the Valley Ranch for Perrin. José and Harry Gillam were there, both eyeing me with frank suspicion. Harry said, 'He's at J Ranch.'

303

Then José, caught between conflicting loyalties, said, 'Don't go, Señor Dan. Ride back.'

He liked me and I liked him. We had got along well in the time we had been on the Rafter R together, and I had some idea of the friendship he felt for me. Harry scowled at him. 'Let him go, José. What the hell!'

'I've got to go,' I said, and rode on.

Someone saw me coming, I suppose, and told Perrin, for when I reached J Ranch Perrin stood alone in front of the poplars, his cold black eyes holding no trace of the old warm friendship that had once been there. Some of his men were standing in front of the barn, others had come out of the bunkhouse, and even Alec Brown hobbled out of the store, all watching me. I had the feeling that none of them, not even Pedro García or old Alec, was my friend.

'If you're here to talk me out of taking my land,' Perrin said evenly, 'save your wind.'

I shook my head. 'I came here to warn you. The settlers had a meeting last night. I don't know what they decided because I left, and so did my father and Frank Allison, but they were talking about killing you.'

He smiled, not the quick boyish smile I used to see and like. It was cold, and a little skeptical, as if he were trying to find a motive that was not evident. He said: 'I thought you knew me better than that. I'm not afraid of any man, let alone a bunch of hay-rakers like your people on the lake.' He stroked his mustache, frowning. 'I don't savvy. What *did* you come here for?'

'For the sake of a memory, I guess,' I said. 'There was a time when I would have done more than warn you.'

'Yes,' he said. 'That was before you took my wife away from me. You know she's divorcing me, and you know you're responsible for it.'

I could only stare at him, stunned. I wanted to deny that I had taken Rocky from him, but it would have been of no use. He was too proud and self-centered a man to admit even to himself that it was his own fault he had lost Rocky, and it was natural enough for him to blame me because I was the only one he could blame.

I started to rein around when he said, 'Wait!' and walked toward me, his head tipped up to stare at me, and for the first time since I had met him at Lang's I did not have the feeling that he was a big man. He said: 'Now that you're here, warning me, I'll return the favor. If Rocky comes back to marry you, I'll kill you.'

In that moment I pitied him. 'She'll never come back to marry me,' I said quietly. 'She'll never come back.'

For a moment we were silent, our eyes meeting, his upturned face dark and bleak. It may have been that he hated me. I don't know. I do know I couldn't hate him.

I rode away then, without looking back. The thought occurred to me that Perrin might not do anything about the settlers. Perhaps he would wait for them to make a move, knowing that they were frantic with fear, and knowing, too, that Lang would work on their fear. If they resorted to violence, then public opinion as well as the law would be on his side, and his case would be absolute.

I rode past the Valley Ranch, not wanting to see either José or Harry Gillam. Rocky had been right in saying that Perrin's appetite for land would consume him. But I couldn't help feeling that he had good reason to feel bitter. He had lost much in the time I had known him. Lane Sears. And me, for I still believed he had been fond of me. Rocky. And a son. He had his land, and he would soon have more if he drove the settlers from their homes, but how could that balance his losses? It couldn't, by any standards I had; but my standards were not his, and maybe there was something in his sense of values that made the land worth all it had cost him.

When I got back to the Rafter R, Lane Sears was waiting for me. I was never more surprised in my life than I was when I saw him come out of the house and stride across the yard to me. I dismounted, the reins dangling, and stood there, staring at Lane, who had not changed at all, unless his droopy mustache was a little droopier, the usual melancholy expression a

306

little more melancholy.

'You don't look real happy to see me, Dan,' he said.

Then the shock passed, and I let out a squall of pure joy. Lane reminded me of Cissy, and although there was only one strange horse in the corral I couldn't help hoping that Cissy was in the house.

'You bet I'm happy, Lane,' I said. 'I was just surprised. Is Cissy here?'

We shook hands, Lane's eyes searching my face, and then he said: 'No, she's in town. Will you go in to see her?'

'Of course I will, but why didn't she—'

'Now wait a minute. She doesn't know I'm here. I lied like a son of a bitch. I told her I was going to get a job with Pritchard.' He cleared his throat, still looking at me, not quite sure of my feelings then he blurted, 'Cheyenne wasn't no good for either one of us. Then she got your letter . . .' He cleared his throat again. 'Damn it, Dan, she's in love with you, and she always has been.'

I stared at him for a long moment, and then, for some perverse reason which I didn't understand myself at the moment, I said bitterly: 'Maybe you're the one who ought to marry her. You've been—'

'Dan!' The one word silenced me. 'You damned-fool pup, I ought to beat hell out of you. I was in love with her mother. You know that. I didn't care what she was. I'd have married her if she'd had me. As far as Cissy's concerned, I passed her off as my daughter, and I was proud to do it.' He stared at the ground, and then he looked straight at me. 'I know one thing now I didn't when her mother was alive. Liz protected her. She wouldn't let Cissy be a part of the business. It's the reason she died. *That* ought to mean something to you if what I say don't!'

He strode past me toward the corral to get his horse. I called, 'Lane!'

Without looking back, he said, 'Tell Cissy I've gone to Pritchard's.'

I had a feeling that he didn't intend to do anything of the sort, that he was riding out of the country and leaving Cissy to me. I went into the house and wrote a note to Sol Craig, and when I came out Lane was gone.

On the way to town, I remembered how much Cissy had been in my mind during the last months. I remembered how she had attracted me, even the first time I had talked to her. Then, as the miles fell behind, the reason I had flared up at Lane became clear to me. I had been jealous of Lane ever since I had last seen Cissy and him on the train at Winnemucca. I was in love with Cissy. I had been in love with her all the time, but I had been blinded by the moral veil that the 'respectable' people of the valley had drawn between themselves and Mrs Hammond. Smug, self-righteous, I had been afraid of what my family and neighbors would think if I married Cissy. So I had turned to Rocky, thinking I loved her, sympathizing with her because Perrin didn't understand her. Yet—and I felt now that I could make a fair comparison—I knew that Cissy was the better of the two, the more compassionate and understanding, the one who would fit into the hard life of the country. 'You fool!' I said to myself, and spurred the horse mercilessly, but it was myself I was roweling.

I reached Ivanhoe in the late afternoon, and the closer I got to town, the more the desire to see Cissy became a wild hunger in me. I tied at the rail and ran into the hotel, stopping only long enough at the desk to get Cissy's room number. I went up the stairs two at a time and knocked on her door. She opened it at once and then stepped back, her eyes wide, her lips slightly parted.

'Dan,' she breathed. 'Dan.'

I went into the room without waiting to be asked and, closing the door, leaned against it. For a long moment I stood looking at her. She had changed. Her yellow hair was no longer curled as it had been, but pinned in a sort of coronet on the top of her head, and she was wearing a plain dark blue suit. But there was something else that was less evident, and it took a little while for me to realize that the intervening months had brought maturity to her, and a dignity she had not possessed before. I must have frightened her, for she began backing away. Perhaps it was the way I was looking at her.

She said: 'I told Lane not to see you. He said he was going—'

'I'm glad he did see me.' I crossed the room to her and took her hands. 'Listen, Cissy. I haven't got much to offer you but a little spread with a mortgage on it. A lot of hard work. Maybe trouble with Perrin or Pritchard. But I love you and I want you to marry me. Will you, knowing all that?'

She stared at me, slowly drawing both of her hands free and lifting them to her cheeks, which had gone first white, then red. At last she said, almost in a whisper: 'I can't, Dan. I don't know why I came back. I thought I could live down our reputation. I—I just wanted to live where I could see you once in a while.'

I followed her until she backed against the wall. 'Will you marry me, Cissy?'

'I tell you I can't!' she cried. 'Your folks would never speak to you again. And all those people along the lake ...'

I laughed aloud. I felt like a free man again—free of fear, free of prejudice—and Cissy was going to share my freedom. I told her that, and then I said:

'We're mavericks, both of us. We haven't anyone else, but we've got each other. Look at me, Cissy! Can you tell me you're not in love with me?'

'But Rocky—you were in love with her, Dan.'

'I thought I was.'

There was no use denying it. But I knew that my real difficulty was to convince Cissy that I loved her, and I didn't know what I could say or do to make her believe me. I turned away from her and walked to the window.

She said: 'Dan, I can't tell you I'm not in love with you. It's what brought me back. I'd be a liar to say anything else. But don't you see? I can't marry you and then wonder all the time if you were thinking you had made a mistake.'

I looked at her and saw misery in her eyes, and I think she must have seen it in mine. There we were, two people in love with each other and yet miles apart, and for no good reason. *I had* to bridge the gap between us.

She stood there, very still, waiting, and suddenly I became angry. I wasn't going to get down on my knees and beg. I went back to her and put my hands on her shoulders and shook her. 'I'm not going to let you get away from me this time. You're going to marry me. You've *got* to. Tonight, if there's still time.'

I put my arms around her and pulled her to me and kissed her, hard, and it was only then that I understood what she had been waiting for. Her arms came up to my shoulders and around my neck, and her lips were hungry for mine. Always before, our lovemaking had been that of a boy and girl; now we were man and

311

woman. She held me with all the fierce strength of her young body, and I knew she wanted me as much as I wanted her.

We reached the courthouse before the offices were closed, and Judge Hendryx married us, with Sheriff Olney and George Beam, the country clerk, acting as witnesses. I slept very little that night. Why should a man sleep when he's in Heaven? I didn't think I would ever be closer than I was then.

Cissy slept on my shoulder, and some time before dawn she woke and her lips came to mine again. She whispered, 'It's been so hard to wait, Dan.'

I told her what had happened since she had left, about buying the Rafter R and not having enough cattle and how hard it was going to be to pay off the bank unless I had a bigger herd.

She said: 'I still have the thousand dollars Jim gave me. You've got to take it, Dan.'

So the Rafter R became hers as much as mine. We might not have a friend in the valley, but we had each other; and, the Lord willing, we'd make a go of the Rafter R.

CHAPTER TWENTY-FIVE

I hired a rig at the livery stable the next morning, and carried Cissy's luggage downstairs from our room. Just two suitcases. Quite a contrast, I thought, to the pile of boxes

312

and valises and the trunk Rocky had had when I'd met her and Perrin at Winnemucca. But then, there was quite a contrast between Cissy and Rocky. And between their marriages, too. Rocky had married a rich man, Cissy a poor one; but Cissy's marriage would not end as Rocky's had. I was determined about that. My poverty, I thought, was an advantage. Whatever we made, we would make together.

I gave Cissy a hand up, then sat down beside her and spread the buffalo robe over our laps. We left town, my buckskin tied behind the rig. Cissy, glancing back, said: 'It's quite a town now. I didn't think it would ever amount to a hill of beans.'

'Lang claimed people would come after the Indians were whipped,' I said. 'I guess he's made a fortune out of his town-site.'

We were silent then, Cissy sitting close to me, a wool cap pulled down over her ears, a fur wrapped around her face. Once, when she looked at me, a smile on her full lips, I asked, 'Happy?' A foolish question, I suppose, our marriage less than twenty-four hours old, but I didn't intend to be foolish. I just wanted to hear her say she was. She didn't disappoint me.

'I was never so happy in my life.' She looked away, blinking. 'You've done more for me than you'll ever know, Dan. It's more than being with the man you love. You don't have any idea what it's like to want to be respectable and be so sure you never will.'

They were words she had to say to me, I thought. Perhaps she would never mention it again, but it had to be said once for all. All of a sudden I was choked up for no good reason except that I was happy, so happy I was about to pop. I put my arm around her and hugged her, and she laid her head against my shoulder and was content to leave it there.

The day was bitterly cold, a strange day, the sky overcast and gradually taking a leaden hue. When we reached the east side of the lake, and could look out past the tule to the water, I saw that it was not blue, but a sullen gray, and there was no wind, not even enough to stir the tule.

I whipped up the team, and we clattered loudly over the frozen ground. I knew we were in for it. On such a day you can hear sound from a great distance. It seems to hang suspended in the cold air as if frozen there.

I wondered about Sol Craig. If Lane Sears had seen him as he left the valley, he might have told Sol why I was going to town. I don't think Lane had any doubt in his mind about my bringing Cissy back as my wife. If he told Sol, I was sure Sol would not stay on the Rafter R. He'd know that we needed a few days alone, and so I was not surprised to meet Sol on the road.

I introduced him to Cissy, who smiled at him, saying: 'I'm glad to meet you, Sol. Are you leaving because Lane told you I was a terrible cook?'

314

He lifted his hat, grinning self-consciously. 'No, he didn't tell me that. I just got to thinking, ma'am. I ain't got drunk for a long time and I figured this was a good time to take care of it.' He looked at me. 'Well, Dan, I didn't think you had it in you. How'd a man with a mug as ugly as yours ever rope a pretty wife like her?' He grinned again and went on, and we turned toward the notch in the hills which the road followed to Paradise Valley.

Cissy said: 'I tried to write to you after I got your letter in Cheyenne, but I couldn't. I didn't know what to say. Seemed like you just wanted to know where I was.'

'That's right,' I said. 'I did. Now I know where you are.'

She laughed. 'I thought you might be wondering why I didn't answer your letter.' Her face turned grave. 'Dan, I heard in town that the courts had given the marginal land to Jim.'

'He's got it, all right, but the farmers haven't moved.'

'Will there be trouble?'

I nodded. 'Plenty of trouble, but I don't intend to be in it.'

She squeezed my hand. 'I'm glad to hear that, Dan. A person can stand so much trouble and then he's full of it. We've had our share, both of us.'

I was silent then. She had changed a great deal. She'd had trouble, all right, more trouble than I knew. But there would come a day, I told myself, when she'd be her old self, filling our house with gay laughter.

An hour later we were through the ravine that led into the valley. When we reached the house, I tied the lines around the whipstock and carried her suitcases into the house. I left them in the bedroom, and then I followed her through the house as she explored each room. I wondered if she had the same feeling I had had when I walked through the house for the first time: that it had been built for living and loving, a house to raise a family in, a small house that was first of all a home.

Suddenly she whirled and ran to me. 'Hold me, Dan,' she whispered. 'Kiss me and love me and never leave me.' I held her in my arms, and I kissed her, and then I saw that she was crying, and she put her face against my chest. 'Isn't it funny a woman has to cry when she's so happy? Can you understand, Dan? I belong to you and this is ours and you belong to me.' I kissed her again and tasted the tears that were on her lips.

I started a fire in both stoves and put the horses away. When I came back she had exchanged her blue suit for a house dress and had tied a frilly white apron around her waist. She had started dinner, and for a time I stood in the doorway between the sitting room and the kitchen, content to watch her. She was thinner than when she had left the valley, and she was better looking because of it.

She glanced at me over her shoulder. 'Get me some wood, Dan?'

I went out through the back door, and when I straightened up, holding an armful of stove wood, I saw Perrin riding across the valley toward the house. I stood motionless, unable to understand why he would come to the Rafter R.

I hurried into the house, dropped the load into the wood box, and then went into the sitting room. I checked my gun, impelled by an instinctive sense of caution, and I wondered what Cissy would say to him. She had every reason to hate him. In that instant I think I hated him for intruding, for destroying what was to me an idyllic happiness that might never again be quite what it was now.

I stood at the window watching him ride into the yard. He wouldn't come on a friendly errand, or to make a neighborly call. I didn't believe he knew about my marriage; but whether he did or not he certainly had no reason to come as my enemy. Then I was aware that Cissy stood beside me, a hand clutching my arm.

'Jim!' she said. 'What's he doing here?'

'I wish I knew.'

Perrin reined up and dismounted, and as he stepped away from his horse I saw that his gun belt was buckled around the outside of his heavy coat. It was the second time since I had first met him that I had seen him carrying a gun. I knew then. He had come to kill me. But why? I moved to the door. I knew only that I couldn't kill him, and I certainly wasn't going to stand there and let him murder me.

I had never been so thoroughly trapped by indecision as I was during the short interval of time that it took me to move from the window to the door. If I knew why he had come ... Suddenly an idea born in the desperate helplessness of the moment came to me. He wouldn't force a fight if he knew a woman was here.

I threw the door open, shouting: 'Come in and meet Cissy, Jim. We got married last night!'

He wasn't more than thirty feet from the front door, a dark-faced, bitter man, his cheeks red with the cold, when he stopped as if he had been hit. The next instant he was an entirely different person. I saw the bitterness drain from his face, leaving only an expression of shocked incomprehensibility there.

Cissy stood beside me in the open doorway, the chill air flowing around us. She called: 'Come in, Jim. I was just starting dinner.'

He shook his head and dragged a hand across his face as if to wipe an idea by force out of his mind; then he stumbled toward us. We stepped out of the doorway as he came in, and I shut the door behind him.

He held out his hand to me. He had regained his composure, and for one brief moment I saw a quick upturn at the corners of his mouth that reminded me of the boyish smile I used to see so often on his lips.

'Congratulations, Danny,' Perrin said, and I was sure he meant it. 'You couldn't have found a better wife, or a prettier one.' He turned to Cissy, digging into his pocket. 'I came to give you a wedding present. It's too cold to have a chivaree, but we'll see you get one in the spring.' He glanced at me, probably to see if I knew he was lying. He turned his gaze back to Cissy and held out his hand. 'I didn't have anything to give you—I mean, anything that was fitting—so I want you to buy something.' She held out her hand, puzzled, and he laid a dozen gold eagles in her palm. 'For your house. Or yourself. I don't care.'

Cissy looked at the money, biting her lower lip as her eyes turned uncertainly to me. I shook my head, hoping she would understand that the game had to be played out. She did.

'Thank you, Jim,' she said, and kissed him on the cheek. 'I'll go shopping as soon as I can get Dan to take me into town.'

He turned to the door. 'I just wanted to pay my respects. You come to J Ranch as soon as it warms up.'

'Stay the night with us, Jim,' I said. 'We're in for a hell of a storm.'

He shook his head. 'I'm not afraid of a storm, Danny. You ought to know that.'

He opened the door and went out. No, he

isn't afraid of anything, I thought, unless it's losing a piece of land that he believes is his. I followed him to his horse, Cissy staying in the house.

Perrin said nothing until he swung into the saddle and looked down at me. He said, 'How does a man like me go about telling a man like you that he's made a fool of himself.' He swallowed. 'I was paying a man in Ivanhoe to get word to me as soon as you were married. I thought it was—Rocky.'

So that was it! I should have guessed. I looked up at him, realizing how much he had blamed me, and I saw misery in his face, and self-contempt. I said, 'I'd like to be neighbors, Jim.'

'So would I,' he said quickly. 'I need you here between me and Pritchard. If I can do anything for you, let me know. And tell your people not to worry about losing their home.'

He nodded at me, wonderfully relieved, I think, and rode away. I went back into the house, shivering with the cold, and stood with Cissy at the window watching him. Before he reached the rim, it had started to snow.

'Why did he come, Dan?' Cissy asked.

I couldn't tell her. I answered, 'You heard what he said.'

She shook her head, staring through the window until he was hidden by the snow, and I knew she wasn't satisfied. 'I never saw him wear a gun before. I think he came to make trouble. Why is he that way, Dan?'

I didn't attempt to answer. How could anyone explain why Jim Perrin was the way he was?

CHAPTER TWENTY-SIX

The blizzard lasted for two days, piling snow against the house as high as the eaves, one of the worst storms I had ever seen. I was sure Sol Craig had reached town safely, but I was doubtful about Perrin.

The storm blew itself out by the morning of the third day, and the sun came up in a clear sky to shine on a white earth and dazzle our eyes. That afternoon Ole Larsen, Pedro García, and Harry Gillam rode into our yard and came into the house.

When they saw Cissy, they were as startled as Perrin had been. They were uneasy in her presence, even after they had recovered from the first shock of seeing her, and I sensed part of what had happened even before they told me. It was in their faces, a sort of stunned grief, as if they could not quite comprehend what had happened.

They stood in the middle of our sitting room, shifting their weight uneasily from one foot to the other, their hats in their hands, melted snow from their boots making little wet spots on the carpet. Finally Ole demanded, 'When did you see Jim last?'

'The day the storm started,' I said.

'What is it?' Cissy cried. 'What happened?'

'The storm,' Pedro said. 'She got him. We found his body 'bout fifty yards from the Valley Ranch.'

Cissy cried out and backed away to stand against the wall, a hand coming up to her throat, but the men were watching me, not her. Ole said, 'Dan, we want you to come with us.'

I had a hunch, looking at their bitter faces. Something else had happened, but I couldn't guess what it was. Cissy said, 'I'll be all right, Dan, if you need to go.'

I knew she would, and I was sure Sol Craig would be along, but there was no need for me to go. I couldn't do anything. But I'd have trouble if I refused, and I didn't want to bring it into the house for Cissy to share. I couldn't tell her what I thought was coming, for I remembered her saying: 'Hold me, Dan. Kiss me and love me and never leave me.' And she had said, 'A person can stand so much trouble and then he's full of it. We've had our share, both of us.' Now I was to have more, and I couldn't tell her.

'Sure, I'll go,' I said. 'Go saddle my horse, Harry.'

He was the toughest of the three. If any of them forced the issue, he would be the one. He hesitated, chewing on a mouthful of tobacco,

322

then Ole jerked his head toward the door and Gillam left.

I put on my coat and buckled my gun belt around it, depressed by the feeling that they blamed me for Perrin's death, although the reason wasn't clear to me. I kissed Cissy, told her that Sol would be there soon, and left the house, hoping that she didn't suspect the truth. But I wasn't sure I was doing what was right. If I didn't come back, it might be harder on her than if she was prepared. We mounted and rode away. I waved at Cissy, then turned and did not look back again. Right or wrong, I simply didn't have the courage to tell her what I faced.

'What's this all about?' I asked.

'As if you didn't know,' Gillam said jeeringly, 'you God-damned—'

'I'll tell him,' Ole said. 'Jim's horse was shot. That was why he froze to death.'

Murder, any way you looked at it. I said, 'You figure you've got a rope that'll fit my neck. That it?'

'You're damned right,' Gillam said.

'I didn't do it,' I said. 'I had no reason to kill Jim.'

I wasn't sure how much they knew. It was possible they didn't even know Perrin had left J Ranch with the intention of killing me. They were surprised to find Cissy at the Rafter R, but whether they were surprised to find Cissy instead of Rocky was something else I didn't know.

I saw that my denial hadn't touched them, and I felt my anger begin to rise. 'I tell you I didn't shoot Jim's horse. Why in God's name should I?'

Gillam began to curse again, but Ole broke in wearily: 'Shut up, Harry. You can save your wind, Dan. We know Jim was packing a gun when he left J Ranch, and we know he was headed for your place. That's good enough for us.'

He was right about saving my wind. They had made up their minds that I was guilty. I remember how it had been when Lane and I went after Rolly Dillon. We had no doubt about his guilt, and no amount of talking on his part would have changed our intentions if we had caught him alive. Jim Perrin couldn't be brought back to life, but by hanging me these men would satisfy something inside themselves. Tomorrow they would regret it, but not today.

We fought our way through deep drifts, and when we came out of the ravine to the flat valley it was easier going because much of the ground had been swept clear of snow by the wind. I looked north toward town, but Sol was nowhere in sight. I would have no help. Though I was scared, as scared as I had been for a long time, I knew that as long as I had my gun I had a chance, and I began to consider who had done it.

I hadn't heard what had happened at the schoolhouse after I'd left, but Frank Allison would know. It seemed to me that though one of the Fergusons might have shot Perrin's horse, I couldn't overlook Matt Cartwright, or Jed—or any of them, as far as that was concerned. Even a mild, decent man like Morris or Longley could be capable of murder under the circumstances.

'Have you boys forgotten there's a sheriff in Ivanhoe?' I asked finally.

Gillam snorted. 'You think we're letting a hayraker jury let you go?'

'You didn't look for no sheriff when you was after Rolly,' Ole said.

We were on hard, frozen ground then, and I suddenly whirled my horse to face them, my hand on my gun. I said: 'I tell you I didn't shoot Jim's horse! If you boys are so damned sure that I did it, pull your guns and we'll finish it now!'

I'm not sure why they hadn't taken my gun unless it was the lack of leadership among them. Lane Sears would have disarmed me long before. Or Perrin. But Pedro, who was foreman of J Ranch, was not a leader, and Harry Gillam wasn't overly bright. I suppose Ole just hadn't thought of it. Or it may have been they thought I'd make a play and they'd have an excuse to shoot me. If that was so, they hadn't expected me to make my try when I did. Now they were silent, staring at me.

'All right,' I said. 'I'll tell you what I'm going to do. I'll get the man who killed Jim. If I don't, I'll still be around for that rope.'

Gillam began to say something, but Ole threw out a hand to silence him. 'Shut up, Harry.' He squinted at me, a gloved hand gripping the saddle horn. 'Now, why would you go after the man who killed Jim?'

I looked across the flat, and even at that distance I could see the Ferguson cabin. I thought back to when I had first known Jim, a great cattleman who had been kind to a kid who had no home but a worn-out old wagon. I looked at Ole when I said: 'I owed Jim a lot. The least I can do is to get the man who killed him.'

Ole looked at Pedro, who nodded, and then Ole brought his gaze back to my face. 'I wasn't never real sure you done it. Didn't seem like your way of killing a man. If you figure you can get the right gent, go ahead.'

'Who you starting on?' Gillam demanded.

'The Fergusons,' I said.

Ole shook his head. 'Don't seem like their way, neither. They might cut him down from the rimrock, but shooting a horse so a man would die in a blizzard is too low down even for them. Looks more like that weasel of a Matt Cartwright.'

'I hadn't forgotten him,' I said.

I wheeled my horse and headed north, knowing I was taking a risk, but I was reasonably certain that neither Pedro nor Ole would let Gillam shoot me in the back. I wouldn't have given him the chance if he had been alone.

I settled my gun in the holster and angled toward the Allison place, taking a zigzag course to stay on the higher land that had been blown clear of snow. The more I thought about it, the more I was convinced one of the Fergusons, or both, were the men I wanted. I didn't agree with Ole that it wasn't their way of killing a man. I knew them better than anyone on J Ranch, and I had sensed their animal cunning from the first. No, it was exactly their way, but I had to have more than a hunch to go on.

Dusk caught me before I reached the Allison place. There was a light in the cabin, and then, when I was closer, I saw that there was one in the barn, too, and I was glad. I didn't want to talk to Frank in front of his wife, so I circled the cabin and rode on to the barn.

Dismounting, I waded through the snow and pulled the door open. Allison was sitting on a sawhorse working on a bridle. He glanced up when he heard the door creak, and when he saw me he let out a long breath of relief. He said, 'Howdy, Daniel.'

I said, 'Howdy, Frank,' and closed the door. He was jumpy. He made no pretense of being a hero, but it wasn't like him to be as nervous as he was. He knows something, I thought, and he's afraid I'm going to ask some questions.

He tossed the bridle into the corner. 'What fetches you out on a cold night, Daniel?'

'You know something I need to know,' I said. 'Let's have it.'

He looked away, the corners of his mouth working. 'All I know is, we just had a mean storm.'

'What happened at the meeting after we left?'

'Oh, that what you're talking about? Morris told me. They agreed Perrin had to be rubbed out, so they drew for it. Had little pieces of paper. Whoever got the marked one was to hang around J Ranch or the Valley Ranch and plug Perrin before he ran us off our places.' He swallowed, glancing at me briefly. 'Matt Cartwright got the marked paper.'

I was startled. So Ole was right. Matt had killed Perrin. I didn't want to go after Matt and make a widow out of his wife and leave her to support all those children. Then I wasn't sure. The Fergusons would know Matt had drawn the marked slip, and suspicion would fall on him.

'Have you seen Matt since then?' I asked.

'No. Why?'

'Jim Perrin's dead.'

He got up, his face turning gray. 'You're joshing.'

I told him what had happened, and added: 'I'll need help to go after Matt. May have to bring Jed in, too.'

He sat down again. 'You don't know what you're asking, Daniel. Jed's my son-in-law, and Matt's his father.' He rubbed his chin with a big-knuckled, calloused hand. 'I didn't think any of them would really do it. I figured they was just relieving their feelings with all the talk and cussing around, and in the end they'd pull up stakes like me and your dad are gonna do.'

I studied him a moment before I said, 'Frank, I'm going to get the man who killed Jim Perrin, and you're going to help me.'

He shook his head. 'We've got a sheriff. Let him do it.'

'We'll take him to the sheriff, but we're doing the job and we're doing it tonight. I don't think Matt or Jed did it, but I said I did because I wanted you to look at it the way the sheriff will if he has to take a hand. There's another thing. If Perrin's men hear about that meeting, they'll clean everybody off the lake shore. They thought a lot of him.'

I didn't think they would, but I needed Allison's help, and I couldn't think of any other way to get it. He looked at me a long time, his face still gray. Finally he said: 'All right, Daniel, I'll tell you what I know. I figured it had happened, although I didn't think Perrin froze to death. I'm pretty sure it was Carl Ferguson.'

He seemed to run out of breath. I waited, and presently he went on. 'The day of the

329

blizzard I saw Carl riding south. I didn't think of it at the time, but that evening he landed up here. He just stumbled onto our place, or he'd have froze like Perrin did. We had him in the house all during the storm. His nose was frost-bit and so were his fingers. We had a hell of a time with him, and I ain't sure now but what he'll lose his fingers. I took him home this morning.'

Allison got up and started walking around the barn. 'Carl mumbled a lot. I couldn't make sense out of it, but he kept repeating Perrin's name over and over.' Allison swallowed. 'When I got him home, Virgil Lang was still over there. He didn't thank me for saving Carl's life. Neither did Ernie. They said they'd kill me if I told anybody about it and they'd burn my cabin.' He threw out a hand, as if hoping the gesture would make me understand. 'Don't you see, Daniel? They'll do it. I've got to think of my wife. And myself.'

There was a good chance, I thought, that Lang had rigged the drawing so that Matt Cartwright would pick up the marked slip, or at least fixed it so that Carl wouldn't get it. Carl had probably ridden out that morning on the off chance he'd have an opportunity to dry gulch Perrin, and it had been sheer luck that he'd seen him ride into Paradise Valley. By the time Perrin climbed back to the rim, the blizzard had started. Carl shot his horse, counting on the storm to kill him. I don't know why he did it that way unless he thought people would say, as Ole had, that it was like Cartwright.

'That's good enough for me,' I said, 'and I'm sure it'll be enough for a jury. Go get your gun.'

'I can't,' he pleaded. 'I'll go to town for the sheriff—'

'No, you'll help me take them to the sheriff, and then we'll know they're where they belong.' But I saw that he was still frightened, so I said deliberately: 'If we don't get them, they'll do something worse. You know what happened to Mrs Hammond. The Fergusons could do the same thing to your wife, or Debbie if they caught her here.'

He stared at me, trembling, and then, without a word, left the barn. He was back in a minute with his rifle. I had thrown gear on one of his horses. He blew out the lantern and we rode away.

As we passed the cabin the door was flung open and Mrs Allison screamed, 'Frank! Frank!' but we went on.

CHAPTER TWENTY-SEVEN

Darkness had replaced the twilight. There was no moon, but the sky was full of stars, and with snow upon the ground there was more light than there would ordinarily have been. As we rode, I considered what lay before us, and I realized at once that it wouldn't do just to ride up to the Ferguson cabin and dismount. They knew they wouldn't be safe until Matt Cartwright had been lynched.

I was sure they'd be a little nervous, jittery enough to be on their guard. If Virgil Lang was still there, we'd have three to handle, and I couldn't count on Allison when the shooting started. Though I preferred to take them to town to stand trial, I realized it might be impossible.

Even when the lights of the Ferguson cabin were directly ahead of us, I was still not sure of what to do. There were too many imponderables for one thing. The condition of Carl's hands was one. If he could handle a gun, I'd have to kill him. He was the man who had been directly responsible for Perrin's death, and he was the most certain to hang.

'How do you figure it, Frank?' I asked.

'I don't know,' he said hoarsely. 'This isn't my kind of game.'

'I've been thinking about it,' I said. 'There's no window on the west side of their cabin. We'd better leave our horses out here and walk in. Lang won't be outside getting cold. Neither will Carl if his hands are frost-bitten. But we may have to watch out for Ernie.'

Allison was silent, but now, having put it in words, I could see our course more clearly. Ernie's location was another imponderable, even more important than the condition of his brother's hands. If Ernie was outside, and we were forced to fire even one shot to get him, Carl and Lang would be warned. They'd blow out the light and bar the door, and we'd be faced with a stalemate that might last for hours.

Finally Allison asked: 'Suppose all three of 'em are inside? We can't go in after 'em.'

'I figure we can,' I said. 'That's how I'm hoping it'll be. Let's work it this way. You knock on the door. Lang or Ernie will open it, probably Ernie. Make a little talk. Any kind of talk. Tell them the J Ranch crew are coming after them.'

It was the best I could think of. If Allison could lull them into believing there was no immediate danger, I'd have a chance to cover the man in the doorway. I made up my mind to handle the play from then on because Allison wouldn't think fast enough or be decisive enough when the blow-up came. If I could immobilize Ernie, and if Carl couldn't handle a gun, there would be only Lang, and I wasn't worried much about him. But if *I* opened the door, there'd be hell to pay, especially if Ernie had a gun in his hand, as I judged he would.

But I had overestimated Allison. He said in a low tone: 'I can't do it, Daniel. I tell you I can't do it.'

I said, 'All right, Frank,' and wondered why he had come this far if he wasn't going to play it out.

I stepped down and started toward the dark side of the cabin. There wasn't much snow on the ground, but when I had to wade through a drift it seemed that the cold chilled me all the way up to my chest. But maybe it wasn't the snow. Maybe I was afraid. I thought of the lonely months I had spent on the Rafter R, and then I thought of Cissy and how everything was changed for me by her return. I remembered again her saying: 'Hold me, Dan. Kiss me and love me and never leave me.'

For a little while I thought of turning back, of sending Allison to town for the sheriff while I watched. I had something to live for now. Cissy had given my life purpose which I had lacked from the moment I had known that my dreams about Rocky were those of a foolish adolescent. I needed Cissy and she needed me, and in my moment of indecision I told myself that my duty to her came first, that it would kill her if I lost my life doing something that it wasn't my job to do.

Then I thought of Perrin, who had been more man for his size than anyone else I had ever known. I don't believe Carl Ferguson or Rolly Dillon or anyone could have faced Perrin and shot him. And I thought of Perrin striving so desperately to reach the Valley Ranch, probably traveling in circles, and knowing all the time he wasn't going to make it, but still trying, his great heart driving him until he fell and could go on no longer. After that, there was no indecision in me.

I reached the shed where they kept their horses, and stopped, my heart jolting. A man stepped out of the cabin and circled it; he came to the shed and stopped within twenty feet of me, looking around. If he had come a few seconds sooner, he would have seen me, but now I hugged the wall, my gun in my hand. Presently I heard him grunt something under his breath, and go back to the cabin. It must have been Ernie, I thought, although it was too dark for me to be sure.

When I heard the front door slam shut, I went on to the cabin, my boots crunching in the snow, a sound that was alarmingly loud to my ears. I stood motionless for a moment leaning against the dark side of the cabin, a sense of impending failure haunting me. I mentally condemned Allison for what seemed to me to be cowardice, and then I heard someone behind me and I wheeled, my back against the side of the cabin.

I was jumpy, and my finger tightened on the trigger before I realized Allison had overcome his fear enough to follow me. He stood there, breathing hard, his rifle in his hands. I whispered: 'You damned fool. I almost shot you.' He didn't act as if he heard me. He said, 'I'll do what you wanted me to,' and his voice seemed like a shout in the cold silence.

'All right,' I whispered, thinking we'd better

get it over with before he lost his courage. 'Go on. I'll follow.'

He slipped around the corner. I kept two steps behind him. We ducked under the window, and then he was in front of the door and pounding on it. I pressed against the wall. The door swung open, lamplight spilling out upon the snow, and Allison said: 'It's me, Ernie. I came to warn you.'

I had hoped Ernie would come outside, but he didn't. He said, 'Nothing to warn me about.'

'The J Ranch bunch is after you,' Allison said. 'I mean, they're after Carl.'

'He told 'em,' I heard Carl yell. 'The God-damned double-crosser. Kill him, Ernie, kill the bastard! We'll tell the sheriff he did it himself. The son of a bitch of a sheriff will think Allison got Perrin.'

It wasn't working the way I had hoped, and now I saw that I couldn't wait. Allison stumbled back into the snow, trying to swing his Winchester into line. I saw Ernie's right hand come up with a gun. Carl's panicky words had set the ruckus off. I did the only thing I could, and for one terrible moment I was afraid I'd be too slow. I lunged toward the door, reaching out and bringing my gun barrel down across Ernie's right wrist.

'Hold it, Frank,' I yelled.

Ernie let out a scared squall. I must have broken his wrist, for he dropped his gun and his hand drooped grotesquely as he raised his right arm. I gave him a hard shove, sending him stumbling back into the room.

Then I was in the doorway; I saw Carl over by the stove, both hands bandaged, and I was surprised at the stark terror which showed so plainly in his face. It proved something I had always known: men like the Fergusons, or any man who would kill someone as Carl had killed Perrin, are really cowards. Carl could not use his hands, but he could use his voice, and he began to yell at me not to kill him.

Ernie was standing on the other side of the room, his left hand holding his right arm just above the wrist. Of the three it was Lang who surprised me. Too fat a man to be fast, he was facing my gun and Allison's rifle, and still he tried to fight. He spun toward the wall and grabbed a shotgun from the pegs that held it.

'Don't make me shoot you, Lang!' I shouted.

But Lang could not be stopped by words. If I hadn't shot him, he would have shot me, but because I didn't want to kill him I took a chance on stopping him. I let go with a shot that sliced through the fat just under his right arm. Even that didn't stop him. He kept turning in his ponderous way, fumbling awkwardly with the hammer, and I would have been forced to kill him if Carl hadn't batted Lang's shotgun down as he screamed: 'Don't kill us, Nathan! Don't kill us!'

Lang looked at me, blood staining his shirt,

and he must have realized that another hostile move on his part would end it. He licked his thick lips. 'Brave men, the Fergusons, mighty brave.' He licked his lips again. 'Looks like Perrin wins, after all. He has to reach from the grave, but he wins.'

'Frank, get their horses,' I said. 'Lang, wad up a bandanna or something and hold it against that bullet gash. Ernie, you'd better rig up a sling for your arm.'

Carl, knowing, I guess, that he wasn't going to be shot, let out a virulent string of oaths. He shouted: 'You can't take us to town tonight. My hands are frost-bitten. I'll lose both of 'em.'

'You won't need hands where you're going,' I said. 'Now let me make one thing plain, Carl. There's a chance a jury might free you, so when I start thinking about Jim Perrin I wonder how big a fool I am to take a chance. I guess it'd be safer if I shot you now.' He began to beg again, so I said, 'Shut up.' After that none of them gave us any trouble.

We delivered them to Sheriff Olney in Ivanhoe. He locked them up and called a doctor; then we sat down in his office and Allison and I told him what had happened.

'Carl will hang,' he said. 'No doubt about it. And Lang will get a stretch in the pen if you can prove that he offered a thousand dollars to the man who shot Jim Perrin. But don't look to me like you got anything against Ernie.'

I stood up, wanting only to get away and go

home. It was up to the law now. But Allison said, 'He threatened me when I took Carl to their cabin, and tonight he tried to kill me.'

Olney nodded. 'We'll sure give it a try. I hope we can put Ernie away for fifty years. The country will be better off if he's in jail. Well, you boys done right bringing 'em in. Not that I'd blame you for shooting 'em—you had excuse enough—but with a new county government like we got here, we've got to get folks into the habit of letting it keep order.'

'See that it does,' I said curtly.

I turned toward the door and would have left if Olney hadn't said, 'How's married life by now, Nathan?'

'You married?' Allison demanded.

It hadn't even occurred to me that he hadn't heard. I said, 'Yes. To Cissy Hammond.'

I saw the color go out of his face as he shook his head at me. You could have had Debbie, but you turned her down for a prostitute's daughter. No, he didn't say it, but I knew what he was thinking. He walked past me and got on his horse and started home.

'What's the matter with him?' Olney asked.

'Hard to tell,' I said.

I mounted and caught up with Allison, but neither of us said a word until we reached the fork in the road. I said, 'Thanks for the help, Frank,' but he rode on without answering, and a moment later he was lost in the thin dawn light.

That's the way it will go, I thought. I didn't care, I told myself; but I did, for it would be hard on Cissy. Then I remembered that my folks hadn't heard, either, and I knew it would be hard on me. Still, knowing that, I had no regret for what I had done.

CHAPTER TWENTY-EIGHT

I was bone-tired by the time I reached the Rafter R. I suppose I went to sleep in the saddle, for part of the ride I couldn't remember. I realized with a start that the sun was up and the Rafter R buildings were just ahead of me.

Sol Craig was there waiting. I dismounted stiffly. Sol looked at my face. He didn't ask any questions. He just said, 'Your wife's worried about you.'

I stumbled into the house, weaving like a drunken man. Cissy saw me before I reached the porch. She threw the front door open and ran out, calling, 'Dan, I didn't think you'd be gone—' Then she stopped, her mouth open, the tip of her pink tongue showing between her lips. She said: 'I've got coffee on the stove. I'll get your breakfast right away.'

She waited just long enough to hug me, then whirled and ran into the house. I plodded after her and shut the door. I took off my hat and

340

coat and gun belt, and followed her into the kitchen. I was cold and tired and I wanted to sleep, but I let her give me a cup of coffee and I drank it while she dipped mush into a dish and brought it to the table. Then she put a pan of biscuits into the oven to warm and began slicing bacon.

With my eyes on her trim back, I thought how different she was from most women, who would have scolded me for being gone so long and then fired a dozen questions at me. But not Cissy. I said, 'I love you and I'm glad you're my wife and I'm the luckiest man in the state.' The words flowed out of me in that order, without any thought on my part and certainly with no intention of making Cissy feel good. I simply wanted to say them.

She turned and looked at me, and I thought she was going to cry. She laid the knife down and came to me and knelt beside me, her head on my lap. I kissed her head and patted her shoulder, and after a while she got up and went back to the stove.

As I ate breakfast, I told her what had happened, and when I was done, she said: 'Then it's over. I'm glad.'

'J Ranch will go to Rocky,' I said. 'She'll let the farmers have the marginal land. She didn't agree with Jim about it.'

I almost went to sleep in my chair, and Cissy said, 'Go on to bed, Dan.'

I did, but for a time I found it hard to relax

enough to go to sleep. I tried to recall Perrin as I had first known him, a man who had liked me and whom I had worshiped. I remembered the good things he had done. Bringing a quarter of beef to my folks the morning of the house raising. Taking me into the big house at J Ranch to keep me and Rolly Dillon apart. And many more.

There were the other things, too, things I would rather forget. Coming to kill me was one. But again that memory was diluted by others that were good. I remembered him looking down at me as he said, 'Tell your people not to worry about losing their home.' I have no way of knowing what memories had warmed his mind when he had said it, but one may have been that of my mother making the cold hard trip to take care of Rocky when she had her baby.

Some time later I was aware that Cissy was shaking me and saying over and over: 'Your father's here, Dan. You've got to get up.' It was like coming up out of a deep dark well. Finally I was on my feet, still groggy, until the thought hit me that my father had come to break up my marriage. I was fully awake then, and I looked at Cissy and saw that she was thoroughly frightened. The moment when she had to face my father beside me had worried her from the first.

I went into the front room. My father was sitting in front of the stove, his hands held out to it. He looked up when I came in. He said, 'Daniel, Frank told me what happened. I know you're tired, and I'm ashamed to wake you up, but...' He hesitated and began stroking his beard as he used to; but even as I watched him make the familiar gesture I realized that he wasn't posing or strutting. He simply didn't know quite how to say what he had to say.

I dropped into a chair and ran my hand through my disheveled hair. Cissy remained by the bedroom door, not sure, I suppose, whether she should stay or go into the kitchen. I said: 'Looks like it's afternoon. A man can't sleep all his life.'

My father's hand dropped to the arm of his chair. 'I might as well take the bull by the horns, Daniel. I need your help. I've got to do something tonight, and I'm afraid.' He looked at the stove.

'I didn't think I'd ever say that to you, but it's the truth. I guess you don't know what it is to be afraid, but—'

'I was afraid last night,' I said. 'So was Frank. What is it you want me to do?'

'Frank is getting word to the settlers that we're having a meeting tonight in the schoolhouse. I want you to come with me.'

I didn't know what he was calling a meeting for, and I didn't have the slightest idea why he was afraid. Now, looking at him, I had a startling thought. History would record him as a great man. Perhaps someday there would be

343

a statue of him in the courthouse square. And Perrin? There were a few who would revere his memory. Pedro and José and Ole and Alec Brown and others who had worked for him, but I was convinced that in the long run people would call him a greedy cattle baron, and the good things he had done would be lost in time.

If history made that judgment, I was not the one to question it. I had the reason before me. Somehow, some way, my father had learned humility; but Jim Perrin would not have admitted he was afraid of anything, not even of the storm that had taken his life.

'Of course I'll go,' I said. 'Cissy, will you fix us something to eat right quick? It's a long ride.'

As we ate, I had a strange feeling that my father didn't remember Cissy. She said nothing to him and he said nothing to her until we were done, then he rose and looked at her. 'Thank you for the food. Now I think we should go.'

He went outside as I put on my coat and hat and buckled my gun belt around me. I kissed Cissy and she clung to me, whispering: 'He doesn't hate me, does he, Dan? He *can't* go on hating me.'

'No,' I said. 'I'm sure he doesn't.'

I left, not sure at all. We didn't talk on the way to the schoolhouse. It was a long ride through the cold, and we had to keep pushing our horses to make it. When we reached the schoolhouse and went in, I saw that every man and boy along the lake was there.

'I want you to come up to the front with me,' my father said.

I followed him up the aisle to the front of the room. He stood behind the desk and looked at the men and boys who faced him, and they looked at him. I sat down in a chair facing the crowd. Their eyes were on my father, not on me. Then, suddenly, I realized how much their expressions were alike. Now that Jim Perrin was dead, things seemed different to them. Though the law could not touch them, they shared Lang's guilt and Ferguson's guilt. I think they had come in the hope that my father would lift the burden from them, perhaps even tell them that what had happened was the Lord's way of taking care of His people.

But my father wouldn't. He hadn't given me any idea as to what he was going to say, but it wouldn't be what they wanted to hear. He had come too far since the first Sunday he had preached in the schoolhouse.

I was aware that sweat was running down my face, that my hands were clenched at my sides, and that I was pressing against the back of my chair. The silence ribboned out, my father's gaze moving from row to row, and there was no sound, no sound at all. Then my father began to talk, and once more I thought of a fine organ, as I had so many times when I had heard him speak.

'I shall not preach a sermon tonight. I

345

suppose it would be more fitting to call what I have to say a swan song. First, I want to tell you that I think of you as my friends. Because I have been wonderfully happy here, doing the Lord's work with you, it is hard to say what I have to say, but I must.' He leaned forward, his hands gripping the edge of the desk.

'You all know a murder has been committed. Now, let's think back together. The first man I met when I came to the valley was Virgil Lang. He was thirsting for Jim Perrin's blood, and he never stopped thirsting until Perrin was dead. Hatred is a plague, and it is spread from him to all of us. Because we settled on land we knew might be Perrin's, we hated him. He warned us that the work we did might go to him, but still we hated him because we lived in fear that he would take our homes, and fear and hatred are kinsmen. But if you think back, you will not recall a single evil thing Perrin did, a single act of violence.' My father swallowed, his grip tightening on the desk.

'We have worked, or so we have said, to bring law and order to this valley. We created a county, and you honored me by electing me to the legislature. But when the day came that the law did not please you, you disregarded it. You sat here and cheered Virgil Lang when he offered a thousand dollars to the man who shot and killed Jim Perrin. You drew lots to see who would pull the trigger. No, *you* didn't do it, but that makes no difference. We are responsible

346

for Jim Perrin's death, I because I could not prevent it, you because you wanted a man killed so that you could keep a piece of land. You destroyed the very thing we had all worked so hard to establish.'

My father paused again, his head bowed. Matt Cartwright jumped up to say something, but Longley yanked him back. Cartwright hit him on the side of the face, and Longley let go. Cartwright was on his feet again, shaking his fist at my father.

He shouted: 'Sounds like you love Perrin, now that he's dead. You know as well as I do what he'd have done if he'd lived.'

'I did not love Perrin alive,' my father said, 'and I do not love him dead. The Lord forgive me for that. As to what he would have done if he'd lived, I suppose he would have taken our land. I don't know, but I do know that murder is not the answer to anything. If I have given you so little of God's way of life that you would draw lots to kill a man, then I have failed and I must resign. The Lord have mercy on my soul.'

He raised his hands and tipped his head back. 'Lord God, watch over Thy people. Cleanse our hearts of hatred and bitterness. We know we cannot undo that which has been done, but we ask for forgiveness; and we ask for strength and wisdom to live and work for the high ideal of law and order, for courage to tame the violence of this land so that it will be safe for our children and our children's

347

children. Amen.'

He lowered his hands and looked at them. Without another word he walked down the aisle and out into the cold night. I followed him, and just as we stepped into our saddles Matt Cartwright came running toward us. I thought he was going to apologize, to ask my father to come in and say he would continue preaching for them. But he didn't.

He looked up at my father, his short legs set far apart in the snow, and said, 'Your resignation is accepted, Brother Nathan.'

'Goodbye, Matt,' my father said. 'God bless you.'

We rode away. I said: 'I think I was the last one to talk to Jim. I should have told you before, I guess. He said, "Tell your people not to worry about losing their homes."'

'"Your people,"' my father sighed. 'Who are your people, just your mother and me, or everyone on the lake? If he meant everyone, then his death was sheer, stark tragedy, unrelieved by any excuse whatever.'

I couldn't tell him who Perrin had meant when he had said, 'your people.' I thought I knew, but I wasn't sure, so I didn't try to answer his question. Instead I said: 'You didn't need me tonight. Why did you want me to come with you?'

My father did not answer for a time. Finally he said: 'I needed you, but not because I was afraid they would harm me physically. It was because I was afraid I would fail at the last moment to say what I had to say. With you in the room, I knew I wouldn't.' He was silent for a moment, then added: 'They hate me now. Perhaps they may never love me, but I believe great good may come of what I said tonight. They will never forget it. I'm sure of that.'

I had to speak of the one thing that bothered me. 'You acted today as if you had never seen Cissy before, but she isn't what you—'

'Daniel.' He reached out and put a hand on my arm. 'Forgive me. I was so upset by what I planned to do that I was hardly aware she was in the house. If you love her, then we will love her. Tell her that, will you, Daniel?' He hesitated, he said, 'Perhaps you and Cissy will join us for dinner on Sunday.'

'Yes,' I said, 'we'll be glad to.'

I felt then as if we had completed a long journey. I would never again feel toward my father as I had on the day we had come to the valley. I still did not fully understand what had happened to him, but somehow he had absorbed from the land courage and humility and a towering sense of duty. But who can explain any of the miracles of life, of which love is one?

I did not stop to see my mother. I hurried on to the Rafter R, to Cissy.

Wayne D. Overholser has won three Golden Spur awards from the Western Writers of America and has a long list of fine Western titles to his credit. He was born in Pomeroy, Washington, and attended the University of Montana, University of Oregon, and the University of Southern California before becoming a public school teacher and principal in various Oregon communities. He began writing for Western pulp magazines in 1936 and within a couple of years was a regular contributor to Street and Smith's WESTERN STORY and Fiction House's LARIAT STORY MAGAZINE. BUCKAROO'S CODE (1948) was his first Western novel and still one of his best. In the 1950s and 1960s, having retired from academic work to concentrate on writing, he would publish as many as four books a year under his own name or a pseudonym, most prominently as Joseph Wayne. THE BITTER NIGHT, THE LONE DEPUTY, and THE VIOLENT LAND are among the finest of his early Overholser titles. He was asked by William MacLeod Raine, that dean among Western writers, to complete his last novel after Raine's death. Some of Overholser's most rewarding novels were actually collaborations with other Western writers, COLORADO GOLD with Chad Merriman and SHOWDOWN AT STONY

CREEK with Lewis B. Patten. Overholser's Western novels, no matter under what name they have been published, are based on a solid knowledge of the history and customs of the American frontier West, particularly when set in his two favorite Western states, Oregon and Colorado. When it comes to his characters, he writes with skill, an uncommon sensitivity, and a consistently vivid and accurate vision of a way of life unique in human history.

We hope you have enjoyed this Large Print book. Other Chivers Press or G.K. Hall Large Print books are available at your library or directly from the publishers. For more information about current and forthcoming titles, please call or write, without obligation, to:

Chivers Press Limited
Windsor Bridge Road
Bath BA2 3AX
England
Tel. (01225) 335336

OR

G.K. Hall
P.O. Box 159
Thorndike, Maine 04986
USA
Tel. (800) 223–6121 (U.S. & Canada)
In Maine call collect: (207) 948–2962

All our Large Print titles are designed for easy reading, and all our books are made to last.